FORBIDDEN FRUIT

His voice was deep and resounded through her consciousness. "I have wanted this for so long." He untied the rope that held her trousers up and pushed them over her hips. "I want to feel all of you."

Her words came out in a breathless sigh. "Oh, Reese, I didn't think you even liked me."

"Like you?" he breathed, touching his lips to the shell of her ear, his hand moving between her legs. "I can't take a breath without thinking of you." He trembled, wanting her, and he realized what he was doing was wrong. "I know what it feels like to stand at the door of Eden knowing you can't enter."

Desire lingered and played along her nerve endings, and she ached from the touch of his hand. "If I am Eden, I will take you in, Reese."

He suddenly stiffened. What was he doing?

He grasped her arms and surged upward, taking her with him, pulling her shirt together and lifting her trousers. "Saber," he said in a voice devoid of feeling, "you will have to forgive me. I lost my head for a moment. That's no excuse, and it won't happen again."

"Reese, I—"

"You are very desirable, and you made me forget your bridegroom is my best friend."

RIDE THE WIND

CONSTANCE O'BANYON

LEISURE BOOKS NEW YORK CITY

A LEISURE BOOK®

October 2000

Published by

Dorchester Publishing Co., Inc.
276 Fifth Avenue
New York, NY 10001

ISBN 0-8439-4777-2

Printed in the United States of America.

To Margaret Alice, (Maggie),
who has the sweetness of her great-great-grandmother,
the first Margaret Alice in the family. Maggie girl,
you are so special to Nanna, and I love you.

For they have sown the wind,
and they shall reap the whirlwind.
—Hosea 8:7

Prologue

Fort Worth
March, 1868

Saber Vincente listened to Winna Mae's soft
breathing and pounded her pillow to flatten it,
envying the housekeeper's ability to fall asleep
so easily. The hotel bed was lumpy, and she
squirmed and turned onto her back, trying to
find a more comfortable position.

What was the matter with her? This was supposed to be the happiest time of her life. Why
did she feel this stirring of unease? She was doing the right thing in marrying Matthew, wasn't
she?

11

Tomorrow they would see each other for the first time in two years. He would be escorting her to Fort Griffin, where he was stationed. The wedding would take place there as soon as her brother, Noble, and his wife, Rachel, met them there in three weeks. There were a round of parties planned for the bride and groom. She should be happy. What was wrong with her? She felt such a heaviness in the depths of her heart.

But what if Matthew's devotion toward her had changed—what if he no longer loved her and was marrying her only out of duty? After all, two years was a long time when their only communication with each other had been through letters. But his letters had been filled with plans for their future, and he'd expressed his heartfelt affection for her. She pushed her foolish doubts aside, remembering the many tender sentiments Matthew had expressed in his letters. And he had written her faithfully. Sometimes she would receive two letters in one week. Even their wedding had been planned by mail. Because of his duties as an army officer, they had decided that they would be married at Fort Griffin. His family was coming all the way from Philadelphia to attend the ceremony and to meet her.

Saber tried to imagine what her reunion with Matthew would be like. She would be shy, and he would look so handsome in his blue uniform and behave with such gallantry toward her. Their hands would touch, and when they were alone, he would kiss her.

Matthew had kissed her only once, but the kiss had melted her heart and made her realize that she wanted to spend the rest of her life with him. There had been obstacles to overcome because he was a Yankee, and she was from the South. When she'd met him, the war had still been raging, but she knew she and her aunt would not have survived if it hadn't been for Matthew.

Saber had begged her father not to send her to Georgia. But he had insisted that she spend the duration of the war with her mother's family, where he had thought she'd be safe. She hadn't known it at the time, but her father had been dying. Her brother, Noble had been an officer serving on the side of the South. Looking back on that time, Saber realized her father hadn't wanted her to watch him die, and he hadn't wanted to leave her alone and unprotected.

She hated to remember that horrible time in Georgia when it had seemed to her that the whole world was on fire.

She had never thought that the Yankees would bring the war to her grandparents' plantation in Georgia—but they had. The house had been burned and all the livestock stolen. She was glad her beloved grandparents were not alive to see everything they had cherished go up in smoke.

Saber and her great-aunt, Ellen, had been forced to take up residence in the overseer's deserted cabin. After the Yankee army had burned Atlanta, soldiers scattered throughout the Georgia countryside, wreaking havoc. Each day it was a challenge just to stay alive. Enemy troops had bivouacked on Opossum Creek, which ran through her grandparents' land, and she had been terrified that they would discover the overseer's cabin. How frightened she was in those first days! She wanted so desperately to return to Texas to her father's ranch, Casa del Sol, but there was no way to get home with the war raging around her.

Aunt Ellen had cautioned her not to venture out in the daytime, but they had no food, and her aunt was ill and needed nourishment. Saber waited until almost sundown to sneak back to the burned-out plantation house, hoping to find some vegetables in the weed-choked garden behind the kitchen. Of course, there was nothing for her to find—the Yankees had taken even the last shriveled vegetables. Saber ducked her head and cried, knowing that her great-aunt would surely die if she didn't find something for her to eat.

14

That day was still so vivid in her memory. A low fog had swirled around her as she dropped to her knees, digging her hands into the dirt and crying bitter tears. She had been so lost in her own anguish that she hadn't heard the rider approaching until he was upon her. The rearing of his horse and the rattling bridle made her jump to her feet, ready to take flight. When she saw the blue uniform of the enemy, she backed away, wondering if she could make it to the woods before he ran her down.

The Union officer had been blond and boyishly handsome. She could tell he was tall by how high he sat in the saddle. His blue eyes held an earnestness that lessened her apprehension. He must have seen the uncertainty in her eyes, because he smiled and gallantly tipped his hat to her.

"Madam, I mean you no harm. Don't run away."

There had been something in his voice or perhaps his demeanor that calmed her, and she began to trust him. That was the day she'd met Maj. Matthew Halloway, and the day she fell in love with the enemy.

Matthew had dismounted and walked with her back to the cabin. When he saw how ill her Aunt Ellen was, he had food and medicine brought to them that same day.

15

Afterward, Matthew came by the cabin daily, bringing food and supplies. The two of them took long walks. She told him about growing up in Texas, and he told her about his family in Philadelphia. Of course, she never told him that her brother, Noble, was a Confederate officer, although she was sure he suspected it.

They had never touched hands, because she always wore gloves. But one day while they were walking in the woods, he paused and drew her hand to rest against his chest.

She could still hear the sound of his voice as he'd proclaimed his love for her. He had kissed her so sweetly that her heart had taken wing. He had explained to her that he'd been ordered to Savannah to meet General Sherman and asked her to wait for him until the war was over. They had both known that it was only a matter of time before the war would end, and they both knew that the South would lose.

After her aunt had recovered, she had insisted that she and Saber make their way to Saber's Great-Uncle John's home in Mobile. Saber had remained in her uncle's home for a considerable time, but she had never stopped yearning for Texas. When the war ended, she'd returned to Texas to be reunited with her brother, Noble, and to wait for Matthew.

She closed her eyes, holding them tightly together, wishing she could fall asleep. Her eyes popped open, and she glanced at the trunk that held her wedding gown and veil. Now the waiting was over. Soon she would be Matthew's wife.

Tomorrow—oh, tomorrow she would see her love!

Saber heard Winna Mae stirring, but she was merely shifting positions. The streets were quiet now, with only the occasional barking of a dog to break the stillness.

Saber's eyes drifted shut, and she fell asleep at last.

The room was dark and so still that Saber wondered what had awakened her. She glanced at the open window but it admitted little light, since it was a moonless night. She stiffened, feeling as if someone was in the room with her. Sitting up, she started to call out for Winna Mae when a cruel hand clamped on her mouth, and a harsh voice whispered against her ear, "Don't make a sound, or you die!"

She could smell the man's foul breath and knew he'd been drinking. She was gagging; her lungs begged for air.

Winna Mae? What had happened to Winna Mae? she wondered frantically.

The harsh voice spoke again. "Don't worry about your maid. She's only messed up a bit. We

17

need her alive to deliver a message."

Rough hands dragged Saber from her bed, and the same hateful voice grated on her ears. "We're going to take you for a little ride, Miss Vincente. If you do just like I tell you to, you won't get hurt."

Other hands, rough hands, lifted Saber, and something was thrown over her head. She struggled and fought to get free, but something hard came down on her head, and she went limp and slipped into total darkness.

Winna Mae regained consciousness in time to hear the men ride out of town. Weakly she rose to her feet, and then paused to listen as her keen hearing picked up the sound of the riders returning and riding in the opposite direction.

The sound of the riders faded into the darkness. Before Winna Mae could make her way downstairs to sound the alarm, the kidnappers were well away from Fort Worth.

Chapter One

Reese Starrett's eyes were steel gray and had
about as much warmth as the cold, wintery sky
above the deserted streets of Fort Worth. A late-
winter storm had hit with the force of a blizzard,
and a chilling wind whipped around the buildings, blowing the snow into a frenzy. The cold
penetrated Reese's skin like icy fingers; he
turned up the collar of his full-length fleece-
lined coat and stepped into the Frontier Hotel.

He glanced around the small entry and found
it deserted. No one was behind the front desk,
but then he hadn't expected anyone at this hour.
More than likely the hotel clerk had not expected
anyone to be out in this blizzard. Probably he

was the only fool who had braved the weather, Reese mused.

He spun the registration ledger toward him and ran his finger down the list of guests until he came to the name he wanted—Maj. Matthew Halloway—room twelve.

He moved leisurely up the stairs, wondering what was so urgent that Matthew would send for him in this storm. Reese didn't have many friends, but Major Halloway was one of the few. If Matthew needed him, he'd damn sure drop everything he was doing to help him.

Reese had first met Matthew last summer in Comanche country, where Reese had done some civilian scouting for the army. He'd quickly gained respect for the major, even though he was a Yankee. Matthew rejected the principles of some of his fellow officers, who wanted to see the South punished for war crimes. Matthew always insisted that anyone serving under his command treat Southerners with respect. He also showed compassion for the Indians, and that had won Reese's respect more than anything else he could have done.

Reese found room twelve and rapped on the door. He pushed the door open when he heard a deep voice bid him to enter. He was surprised to see Matthew propped up in bed with his leg bound, splinted, and elevated on several pillows.

Reese removed his coat and draped it across a chair, then swept off his hat and slapped it against his leg to dislodge the snow. He pulled up a chair and turned it toward him, straddling it before he spoke. "Well, if I can believe my eyes, it appears that you've broken your leg, Yankee."

"No, it's not broken, but badly sprained." Matthew's eyes snapped with hostility. "You sure took your time getting here!"

Reese grinned. "In case you haven't noticed, I had to ride through a blizzard to reach Fort Worth. And besides, usually when I come to town, it's to spend a few pleasurable days with a pretty woman under me. Now, if you were a pretty woman, I might have gotten here sooner."

Reese noticed Matthew was not amused. He shrugged and met his friend's eyes. "So what happened to you? You look like hell."

Matthew winced as he raised himself up on his elbow. He groaned and quickly let his head fall back against the pillow. "Damned flea-bitten nag threw me, and if that wasn't enough, she rolled over on top of my leg."

A slight smile curved Reese Starrett's lips. "Don't tell me an old cavalryman like you let a horse get the better of you? So the horse walked away, and you didn't."

"Something like that." Matthew quietly assessed the man many Texans called a legend.

21

Reese was wearing the buckskin shirt and trousers that he wore only when he scouted for the army. Reese owned a small spread outside Fort Worth, and he was mostly a loner, keeping away from people and keeping them away from him. He was tall, probably six-foot-four, and ruggedly handsome. His hair was too long, but Reese didn't adhere to the rules that other people lived by. His gray eyes were now flickering with humor, but Matthew had seen them when they could pierce through a man's defenses. It was common knowledge that Reese was the best tracker in the state, and Matthew was counting on his help.

"I need you to do something for me, Reese."

Reese's eyes narrowed. "I can see you're worried about something, and it doesn't appear to be your leg. Where's the woman you've been mooning over ever since I've known you? Did she write and tell you the wedding is off, Yankee?"

"Reese," Matthew said worriedly, "I hardly know where to start."

"I've always found that the beginning is a good place."

There was desperation in Matthew's blue eyes, and he tried to sit up again, only to fall back in pain. "I need your skills as a tracker, Reese. I'm willing to pay you handsomely for your time."

Reese's face froze into a stony expression. "Don't be insulting. When a friend needs help, money doesn't come into it."

"But—"

"Forget it. Just tell me what I can do for you, Yankee."

"What I want from you will probably put your life in grave danger, but I don't know where else to turn. You are the only one who can do this for me."

"Are you going to talk me to death or get to the point?"

"Saber was . . ." Matthew paused as if he couldn't go on. He swallowed hard and met Reese's eyes. "Saber has been kidnapped!"

"Aw, hell," Reese said. He didn't waste time on trivial questions, but went right to the heart of the matter. "Tell me what you know about her abduction."

"Not much. I am scared for her, Reese. If I could get my hands on the bastards who took her, I'd kill them without a hint of mercy." He closed his eyes for a moment before he could continue. "I can't help her. I can't even walk or sit a horse for at least a week. Will you go after her for me, Reese?"

Reese looked reflective, his silver eyes almost colorless in the faint light of the room. "What kind of men are we dealing with here, Matthew?"

"The kind of men who would take an innocent young woman in the middle of the night. They're cowards! Dregs of the earth—saddle bums!"

Reese had often listened to Matthew's praise of the woman who was to be his bride. He'd bore anyone who would listen to him with tributes to the beauty and accomplishments of Saber Vincente. Reese had scoffed at Matthew's assessment of his intended bride. No woman was that perfect! Reese had once acknowledged that Matthew had the right to perceive her as a paragon of virtue, but begged his friend to spare him anymore details about Miss Vincente.

"Can you help me, Reese?"

Reese believed in facing the truth in any situation, and it was up to him to point out the obvious to Matthew. "There is a good chance that she's already dead, you know. Of course, if she's a looker, she could suffer a far worse fate."

Matthew paled. "I have considered both those possibilities. But she has to be alive—she just has to!"

Reese saw the desperation in the major's eyes and wondered what it would feel like to love a woman that much. More females than he could count had lain beneath him during his life, but none whose loss would tear his guts out. Reese had a powerful drive to make love to women. But he always grew tired of them after a short time and moved on to the next one, never involving his heart with any of them.

There was torment in Matthew's eyes. "There is a chance that she's still alive, isn't there, Reese?"

Reese proceeded more gently. "There's always that chance. Now that I think about it, why would they go to the trouble of kidnapping her if they were going to kill her? If I remember correctly, your bride-to-be comes from a wealthy family, doesn't she?"

"Yes. You have heard of her brother, Noble Vincente."

Reese frowned in thoughtfulness. "I've heard of the Vincentes who own the Casa del Sol Ranch and half of west Texas. Is he the same one?"

"Yes. That would be her brother, Noble." Hope flamed within Major Halloway as he looked into Reese's pale eyes. "Don't you think it's possible that they took her for ransom?"

"It's been done before. It sounds like the most likely reason for abducting her."

Matthew gritted his teeth when he tried to shift his position. "Damn this leg! I want to go after her, but I'd never make it with this."

Reese nodded. "Tell me everything. How was

she captured, where was she when she was taken, and who brought the news to you? Tell me everything you know about it."

"She was traveling with a companion, Winna Mae—the housekeeper, more like part of the family. Saber has written about her many times. She's of Indian heritage." Matthew looked down at his balled fists and paused for a moment. "The plan was for me to meet Saber and Winna Mae here in Fort Worth and escort them to Fort Griffin, where the wedding would take place." He dropped his chin on his chest as if he couldn't go on. "My folks are on their way here from Philadelphia to attend the wedding." His voice became almost inaudible. "We were to be married in three weeks."

"Why did she come to Fort Worth?"

"Because I encouraged her to meet me here." He shook his head. "Her brother didn't want her to travel until he and his wife could make the trip with her. It's my fault she's missing."

"You shouldn't blame yourself. How could you guess such a thing would happen?"

"Her brother sent three outriders with her, and I thought she'd be safe. But apparently Saber sent them home once she got to town, thinking she wouldn't need them when I arrived."

"Where is this Winna Mae? I need to know everything she can tell me."

"She's down the hall in room fourteen. According to Winna Mae, the men crept through the window of the hotel room and carried Saber away."

Reese's eyes burned with suspicion. "They didn't harm Winna Mae or attempt to take her with them?"

"They knocked her around a bit; the doctor had to bandage broken ribs. I think she's all right, but I couldn't tell for sure. Like most Indians, she's proud and doesn't reveal her suffering."

"Why do you suppose they let her live? Is there a possibility that she's involved in some way?"

"No. Not her. She's loyal to the Vincente family. I believe they let her live so she could give me the message about Saber's kidnapping."

"Sometimes people can deceive us. Are you sure of her loyalty?"

"She'd die for Saber before she'd let any harm come to her. I'd stake my life on that."

"I take it that the kidnappers haven't made any demands yet?"

"That's what troubles me. They haven't asked for anything." Matthew stared up at the ceiling. "I'm certainly not wealthy and neither is my family, so they couldn't want ransom from me."

"Which brings us back to her brother," Reese speculated. "He's the one with the money."

27

"Noble Vincente is not only wealthy in his own right, but he married Rachel Rutledge, who owns the ranch adjoining Casa del Sol, so his fortune has greatly increased."

"And Miss Vincente—does she have money of her own?"

Matthew nodded. "I don't know how much, but I believe she inherited a large fortune." He glanced into his friend's eyes. "I would marry Saber if she were penniless and barefoot. I love her. Do you know what it feels like to love a woman so much that you can hardly keep your mind on your duties?"

"No, I don't," Reese said flatly. Then he turned the conversation back to the kidnapping. "How did she arrive in Fort Worth?"

"By private carriage. Winna Mae said that Noble Vincente wouldn't allow his sister to travel by public stage." His eyes were filled with fear. "If anything's happened to her—"

"Have you sent word to her brother?"

"No. I have been so worried about Saber that I haven't given her family a thought. I suppose I should do that right away."

"Yes, I should think so."

Matthew doubled his fist and pounded his good leg. "My accident happened just ten miles out of town around the same time she was kidnapped. I should have been here to protect her!"

"It sounds like the kidnapping was a well-thought-out plan to me. What made your horse spook?"

"There was a sudden rock slide, and my horse just went loco."

"That might not have been an accident. Besides, I don't think you could have stopped them if you had been here with a whole troop of cavalry."

Anger rushed through Matthew, and he trembled from the intensity of it. "But you think you could have saved her if you'd been here—is that what you are implying, Reese?"

"No, that's not what I'm saying, and you know it. Matthew, if your woman can be found, I'll bring her back to you."

Matthew's face whitened even more. "These men have no respect for women. Suppose they have . . ." He licked his lips. "What will I do if they have violated her?"

Reese looked long and hard at his friend. "Just how much do you love this woman?"

"More than my life. But if they've . . . touched her, I just don't know how I'd feel about marrying her."

Matthew's admission made Reese feel suddenly sick inside. If what he said was true, Matthew was the most selfish bastard he'd ever met. He jerked to his feet, anger tightening inside him like a noose. "If the worst has happened, she will need your love and understanding more than ever," he said coldly. He moved to the door, opened it, and glared back at Matthew. "I'm going to question the housekeeper, Winna Mae. I suggest you get word to Saber's brother about what has happened. We may need his help."

Matthew nodded. "I hate like hell to let him know. Noble Vincente will probably think it's my fault."

"Just do it," Reese said, going out the door and closing it firmly behind him.

Reese had half expected to find Winna Mae wringing her hands and hysterical, but that was not the case. Although she moved restlessly about the room, she held her back straight, and her steps were sure.

Her Indian heritage was apparent in her coloring and her high cheekbones. She was tall. Her gray hair had been braided and pulled away from her face. Her eyes were dark and intelligent. His gaze fell to her hands, which were scarred, as if she'd been badly burned in the past. He guessed there must be a tragic story behind those scars.

Winna Mae's voice betrayed her irritation when she spoke. "I suppose you are going to be as worthless as the sheriff and the witless men he called a posse. I told them which way the kidnappers went, but they didn't believe me, because late last night someone saw three strangers riding in the opposite direction."

Reese looked past the scorn in her eyes and saw the concern she felt for Miss Vincente. "Suppose you tell me everything you know. I even want to know your impressions, everything you suspect, and anything you can think of that might help me. When I've heard your story, then I'll decide which way to ride when I leave town."

"I'll tell you everything you need to know if you will take me with you."

Reese shook his head. "You know I can't do that, ma'am. You'd only slow me down. I have to move fast if I am going to find Miss Vincente."

At last she nodded and eased herself onto a chair, trying to hide her wince of pain. "I told the sheriff that the men made a big show of riding south. But moments later I heard horses galloping to the north, and I know it was the kidnappers."

"There can be no mistake?"

"I have good ears, Mr. Starrett. They rode north. If Saber's brother, Noble, were here, he would believe me and act accordingly." She lowered her head. "But I have to rely on you because too much time will be lost before Noble gets here, and the trail may grow cold."

31

"It looks like I'm all you've got. Er, what do I call you?"

"Winna Mae."

"Winna Mae, you will just have to trust me."

"Are you saying you can find her and bring her back?"

"I'm saying I'm sure as hell going to try." He drew in a deep breath. "Now, did you overhear anything that would help me?"

Winna Mae frowned. "They hit me, and I do not know how long I was out. But when I came to, I kept my eyes closed so they would think I was still unconscious. I overheard one of the men say they had to meet a man named Felton in Dallas."

Reese looked closely at her. "Are you sure that's the name they used?"

"Yes. I am sure. Does it mean anything to you?"

"Yeah. I've heard he's a bit crazed and that everyone fears him and stays clear of him." He shifted his weight and tried to remember everything he'd heard about Graham Felton. His gaze went back to Winna Mae. "Anything else you think I should know?"

"I heard one of the men brag that after the kidnapping, people would have more respect for the Miller brothers."

Reese's broad brow furrowed. "How many were there?"

"I saw only two. But I had a feeling that there was another waiting below with the horses." She looked into his eyes as if seeking the truth. "Do you know who the Miller brothers are, Mr. Starrett?"

Reese nodded, and he felt a knot tightening in his stomach. "I have a hunch it's Earl and Eugene Miller. They have a younger brother—they could have brought him in on this. He could be the third one."

Reese listened while Winna Mae talked. She had a keen memory for details. The sheriff had been a damned fool for not listening to her.

He stood up and walked to the door. "I'll do what I can, Winna Mae. Take care of those ribs."

"Which way do you ride?" she asked, her dark eyes staring into his.

He placed his hat on his head and gave her a grim smile. "I ride east to see if I can locate Graham Felton, and then north to find your lady."

There was respect in Winna Mae's gaze. This man was no one's fool. If anyone could find Saber, it was him. "Saber is not easily frightened, but she will be afraid of those men. Find her quickly."

Reese gave her a slight smile. "I'll do my best."

*   *   *

As Reese rode out of town, he tried to fit all the pieces together. He knew Graham Felton only by reputation, and it was all bad. He'd once heard that the man owned a saloon, but Reese didn't know where. He did know that the two of them were about to meet. Destiny would throw them together, and he intended to come out the winner. He had heard of the Miller brothers—they were little more than thieves and saddle tramps. They were not the danger that concerned him—the danger would come from Graham Felton.

Chapter Two

Saber awoke slowly, groaned, and rolled her head from side to side. A dull ache started at the back of her skull and ran all the way to her forehead. When she tried to raise her head, the ache became a sharp pain, making her feel sick to her stomach. The room was spinning and wouldn't come into focus, so she closed her eyes again, hoping it would right itself.

Puzzled, she blinked her eyes and studied her surroundings. This wasn't her hotel room. It did resemble a hotel lobby, but it was dusty, the few furnishings were shabby, and there were cobwebs in every corner.

Where was she?

Slowly the events of her kidnapping came back to her, and she sat up quickly, but blackness threatened to engulf her, and she eased her head back down. The only furniture was a stove that gave off little warmth, a cot, two benches, and a rickety table. There were steps leading up to the second floor, but they were rotted and splintered, and she wouldn't want to attempt to climb them.

A deep voice spoke up beside her. "We was 'fraid you'd never wake up, Miss Vincente. We feared Earl'd hit you too hard."

Saber closed her eyes as sickness churned in her stomach. She turned her head to see who was speaking, but it was so dark in the room that the man was just a blur. She licked her dry lips. "Everything is spinning."

"You'll have to stay put for a while until the dizziness passes," the man told her.

"Who are you? What do you want with me?"

"It don't matter who I am. Just see that you don't try to get up. I don't want a sick woman on my hands. And don't think of escaping—you'd never get past the door."

Saber wondered if she had a concussion. The inside of her mouth felt like cotton, and every time she moved her head the pain was unbearable. A horrible thought came to her, and she suppressed a sob: What if the men had violated her body while she was unconscious?

She shivered in revulsion and thought of Matthew. He would never want her now. Not if what she suspected was true.

She opened her eyes when she heard the man bend down to her. The look in his eyes terrified her. She cried out when he boldly put his hand on her breast, kneading and pinching until she shoved his hand away.

"What have you done to me?" she asked weakly.

He leaned closer and whispered in her ear, his foul breath making her gag. "What do you think ol' Eugene's done to you, sweet thing?"

"You wouldn't . . . you haven't . . ."

"Honey, you're a delicate flower that makes a man lose his head. You go ahead and picture anything you want, because it just might be true."

With considerable effort, she turned her head to the wall and rolled into a ball. She was ruined. "Why didn't you just kill me?" she whispered. "It would have been kinder."

His hand tangled in her hair, and he jerked her head around. "Killing you is the last thing on my mind, sweet thing."

"Leave her alone, Eugene," a hard voice commanded.

That was the last thing Saber heard. She was

once more submerged in darkness where there was no fear.

It wasn't until two days later that Saber felt well enough to sit up. She looked around at the dusty room, wondering where she was. As she carefully eased herself to a standing position, her head throbbed, and her stomach still felt unsettled, but she managed to stay erect.

She moved toward one of the windows, walking awkwardly because her ankles had been hobbled like a horse so she could take only small steps. Her hands were tied at the wrists, and the rope cut into her tender flesh.

Rubbing her palm against the dusty window, she stared despondently out upon the deserted, weed-covered streets. The wind caught dirt and debris and whipped it aimlessly through the forsaken town. She remembered the gentle winds that blew off the Brazos River in spring, and how they had sounded almost musical; but this wind whipped around corners and through broken windowpanes, sounding like the howling of a hundred banshees.

She realized that this was a deserted town—a ghost town. She glanced at the run-down buildings that gave evidence of a once-thriving community. From across the street, she tried to make out the faded lettering on a sign that swung back and forth on rusty hinges. The town had not been large, and there were only six or seven decayed structures still standing. The place seemed to have been erected in a haphazard manner, as if the builders had been in a hurry to construct it. The town must have been prosperous at one time, because she could see faint lettering identifying one building as a bank. She craned her neck and stood on tiptoe. She could see a cemetery at the edge of town with faded wooden crosses and crumbling gravestones.

Heavy sadness enveloped her—this had once been a place where people lived, laughed, raised families . . . and died. She read the faded lettering of Gregory's Saddlery on the third building across from her. She wondered whether Gregory had been buried on the hill, or had survived to find another town in which to set up his trade. What had caused the town to be abandoned? From the number of headstones she could see in the graveyard, she would not have been surprised if some kind of sickness had made it into a ghost town. Whatever had happened here, this town was the final legacy of the former inhabitants, and for many of them it had become their final resting place. The neglected tombstones and the weed-choked graves were almost all that remained.

Her small frame trembled, and she turned away and hobbled back to the cot. She sat down, trying not to think about the vermin that lived in the creases of the lumpy mattress. She had no hope that anyone would find her here. The only inhabitants of this town were the men who had abducted her, unless she counted the rattlesnakes and jackrabbits.

Saber wondered why the men had stolen her away under cover of night. Although she'd asked them repeatedly, she received only ominous silence in response. Just by listening to their conversation, she had learned that the three men were brothers, and their last name was Miller.

Earl Miller appeared to be the eldest. It was easy to see that he made all the decisions, and the other two deferred to him most of the time. She thought he must be in his late thirties. He had black hair and even blacker eyes. He was shorter than his two brothers and much more serious, seldom saying anything that wasn't an order to the others.

Eugene, the middle brother, had thick arms and a barrel chest. A wide scar ran the length of his thick, black beard and along his jawline. Saber was more afraid of him than of the other two. He seemed to have no redeeming qualities—he was spiteful and mean, and he was always watching her. Every time he was near her, he would manage to touch her or bump up against her. She still feared what he might have done to her while she was unconscious.

Sam was the youngest. He couldn't be much over sixteen, because he was too young to shave, and there was an air of innocence about him, as if he hadn't yet grown callous and mean like his two brothers. Sam attempted to emulate his brothers by swaggering around with two guns on his hips, bragging about how he was going to spend his share of the money they would get from someone called Graham Felton.

So far Saber hadn't been mistreated, unless she counted the lump on the back of her head or what might have happened to her while she'd been unconscious.

Sam had offered her one of his shirts and a pair of his trousers, since she had been abducted in her nightgown. She'd refused to wear them until she saw the way Eugene kept leering at her. Of course, the trousers had been too big for her, so Sam gave her a length of rope to tie around the waistband. One day Earl had ridden out, and when he returned he had a pair of slippers for her. She didn't even want to know whom they'd belonged to as she slid her feet into them and found that they were a comfortable fit.

Later she'd heard Eugene laughing as he told his brothers how he'd spent the night with a

41

whore at Digger's Saloon, and afterward how he'd stolen the woman's slippers. Saber swallowed the revulsion that threatened to choke her. She'd never even met a painted lady, and now she was wearing shoes that had belonged to one of them.

Reese rode up to the Miller place and looked about him cautiously. He didn't really believe that the brothers would be there, but he had to be sure. He could see inside the barn, and there was only a swaybacked plow horse inside.

He saw immediately that this wasn't much of a spread—a squatter's farm with a run-down log cabin, a small barn with two milk cows, and a rotting fence around the corral that was falling down. He noticed the curtains being parted, and a woman's face appeared at the window.

As Reese dismounted, the woman came outside, her gaunt face creased with worry; her eyes were wide and watchful. She was a woman in her later years, probably looking older than her actual age. He assumed she must be the Miller brothers' mother.

"What you want, mister?" she asked warily.

He gave her a smile. "I'm looking for your sons, ma'am."

"You a friend of their'n?"

"No, ma'am. I've never met them."

Sadness lingered in her eyes as she brushed a wisp of gray hair from her face. "Well, they ain't here, and I don't know where they are. I don't know as I'd tell you iffen I did."

He decided it was best to be honest with Mrs. Miller. "I'm Reese Starrett, ma'am. I believe that your sons have abducted a woman, and her family wants her back real bad. Your boys are in a lot of trouble, but the law might go easier on them if they turn the woman over unharmed."

Fear reflected in the woman's careworn eyes, and her work-worn hands trembled as she wiped away a tear that was trailing down her cheek. "God help them," she said softly. "I never thought they'd stoop to hurting a woman. Are you sure of what you're a-saying, mister?"

"Yes, ma'am. Otherwise I wouldn't be here bothering you now."

There was pride in her stance as she stared into his eyes. "I've heard tell of you, Mr. Starrett. The word is you're an honest, decent sort of man. If what you say is true, I'm deeply ashamed of my boys."

"It's true, all right. I need to find this woman before they hurt her, Mrs. Miller. If you can help me, I'd appreciate it."

"Who is the woman? It could be that she went with them 'cause she wanted to. Eugene has a way with women."

"I don't think so. Her name is Saber Vincente. You may have heard of her brother, Noble Vincente."

Mrs. Miller's eyes widened with naked fear, and she lowered her head. "Noble Vincente's sister would not have gone willingly with my boys—not a lady like her." She shook her head as tears choked her voice. "Lord have mercy, what've they done?"

"There is a witness who says Miss Vincente was kidnapped out of a hotel room by your sons, ma'am."

"Will you promise me that iffen you find them, you won't shoot my boys down? Iffen you'll give me your word, I'll tell you what I know, which ain't much. My boy Sam's young. He ain't mean; he just follows his brothers."

"Mrs. Miller, I can promise you that I won't draw on them first. But if they draw on me, I'll defend myself."

There was acceptance in her expression, and she seemed to age before Reese's eyes.

"I really don't know where they are, Mr. Starrett. They was here three weeks ago, and I heard them talking about meeting up with a Mr. Felton at some saloon in Dallas."

"Would that be Graham Felton, ma'am?"

"I don't know, Mr. Starrett. The man's a stranger to me, and I gathered he's not known to my boys either. I think they was going to work for him." Her voice trailed away. Then she glanced into his eyes. "I hope they haven't hurt the Vincente woman. I've heard enough about Noble Vincente to know he won't stop until my boys are dead."

"Then it might be better for them if I find her first." He touched his hand to the brim of his hat. "Thank you for your time, ma'am. I'll see if I can find them. Good day."

"Mr. Starrett, watch out for my Sam. Iffen he comes home to me, I'll tan his hide and see that he don't ever get in trouble again."

"I'll do my best, ma'am."

Reese felt pity for Mrs. Miller. She seemed an honest, hardworking woman who knew her sons were trouble. She probably had known for a long time that they would come to a bad end. He imagined he'd have to kill one or all of them, and she must have known that too.

His mind rushed ahead. He had to decide what his next move was going to be.

Chapter Three

It was early morning, and Saber had spent another sleepless night. Eugene came into the room, and she cringed at the way he stared at her. He walked slowly toward her and pulled her upward, pressing her body against his. She struggled and tried to get away, but he held her fast.

"You make me sick," she said, turning her face away when he attempted to kiss her.

"Do I, little fancy piece? We'll just see about that."

She fought and struggled as he pushed her down on the cot and covered her body with his. At that moment the door burst open, and Earl entered. When he saw what was happening, he leaped across the room and tore Eugene off Saber.

"If you touch her again, you won't ever see another sunset," Earl said angrily. "She's going to bring us money, but not if you don't keep your hands off her."

Sulkily, Eugene slammed out the door. All the rest of that day he kept his distance from Saber, although his eyes seemed to be on her all the time. He made her feel as if he knew what she looked like with her clothes off.

She curled up on the cot, wondering if she would ever be free of these men, or if she would ever feel warm and clean again.

Saber had decided that the youngest brother, Sam, was the least threatening of the three. She hoped to catch him alone so she could attempt to win his confidence and perhaps her freedom. It wasn't likely he would help her, but she was desperate, and he might be her only hope.

Her chance came sooner than she expected. Earl ordered Eugene to ride up the hill and watch the road because he had to leave to meet someone. Earl then mounted his horse and rode out of sight while Eugene grumbled, picked up his rifle, and left.

Saber waited until she was certain that the two older brothers had gone before she approached Sam. She would never have a better chance to talk to him alone. She eased herself off the cot and hobbled over to sit beside him on the rickety bench near the wood-burning stove.

Sam glanced at her suspiciously and said in a surly voice, "You best get back to the cot. Earl won't like it none if he finds me talking to you."

"Please don't send me away. I'm so lonely and frightened. Let me talk to you for a moment. If we hear your brothers returning, I promise I'll go back to the cot right away."

He leaned back and looked at her for a long moment. "You've got a right to be afraid."

She gazed purposefully into his eyes; her lips were trembling. "Are your brothers going to kill me?"

He shook his head. "It ain't us you have to fear. 'Course, you need to be watchful of Eugene. He's always been mean to women, and I've seen the way he looks at you. Just stay away from him."

Saber could not suppress the shiver that rushed through her body. Just the touch of Eugene's hand on her had made her feel sick inside. "Did he do anything to me before I woke up?"

Sam saw her fear and tried to calm her. "I don't know. He was alone with you for more than an hour after we brought you here. But you don't have to fear him any now because Earl won't let him hurt you none." He lowered his voice, although there were only the two of them in the room. "You just have to make sure you ain't alone with him." His eyes widened as he looked into her eyes, and a blush stained his rough cheeks. "You're 'bout the prettiest woman I've ever seen. I ain't never talked to no grand lady before. What's your front name?"

"My what?"

"Your front name—you know, your given name?"

"Saber. My name is Saber."

He grinned, looking boyish. "That sounds more like a weapon than a name, ma'am."

"It is a family name on my father's side." She could see that he was softening toward her, and she wanted to take advantage of that softness while she could. "May I call you Sam?"

He nodded, unable to look into her brilliant blue eyes. "I reckon there's no harm in it. But only when we're alone."

"I understand. Sam, I would like to think we would have been friends if we had met under other circumstances."

She saw him swallow hard as he raised his gaze to her. "You wouldn't even have spoken to me if we'd met on the street, ma'am. You'da sashayed past me in your fancy duds, never even noticing me. I ain't good enough to—"

"Don't think that," she said, reaching out her hand to him, and then letting it fall to her side when she saw a blush stain his face once more. "You have been kind to me. I believe in returning kindness with kindness."

He shot to his feet. "I can't help you none, so if you're working up to me, hoping I'll turn on my brothers, you can forget it."

Saber shook her head. "No, I don't expect you to do that. It's just that I am so afraid."

He turned back to her, his eyes filled with pity. "I don't know what's going to happen to you when we turn you over to Graham Felton. He's a mean one, and he never let us know what he wants with you."

Her heart was thudding. "Are you saying my kidnapping wasn't a random act—that someone hired you and your brothers to abduct me?"

He was shaking, and fear lit his eyes. She watched as he wiped his sweaty palms down his stained trousers. "You won't tell my brothers I told you about Mr. Felton, will you? I don't know what Earl'd do. My being his brother won't stop him."

"Of course not, Sam. I would never do anything to make trouble for you. Please tell me everything you know."

"Well, this Graham Felton hired us to capture you and bring you here. Earl's gone into town to let him know we have you, and he'll let us know where to take you."

"Who is Graham Felton? I've never heard of him."

"We ain't never met him neither. One of his men hunted us up and asked us to do the job for him. So we did, 'cause he offered us a lot of money for you."

"What could he want with me?"

Sam looked puzzled and shook his head. "Just know that Felton is supposed to be the meanest varmint who ever walked the earth. When he takes you away, you might want to do everything he says. I've heard he kills people for no reason."

"Sam, why would he want me?"

"Money, most probably. Your brother's rich, ain't he?"

"Yes, he is." Saber thought for a moment. "Sam, if you and your brothers would take me back, my brother would pay you more money than Mr. Felton is offering."

"No!" His face whitened. "We ain't going to do any such thing. You may think Earl is just a no-good, but when he makes a deal, he keeps it."

Saber's heart sank. "Can you tell me anything more about Mr. Felton?"

"I tol' you I ain't ever laid eyes on the man. I 'spect you'll be meeting him sooner than you want to."

Neither of them had heard Eugene ride up. He stood in the doorway, glaring at his brother.

"Sam, get yourself off and watch the road for a spell. I'll guard our prisoner."

"No, I ain't," Sam said defiantly. "Earl tol' me to stay with the woman, and that's just what I aim to do."

Eugene's face reddened in anger. "Boy, you'll do what I tell you to, and you'll do it now. I've got me an itch for this pretty lady. She won't be none the worse for my loving on her."

Sam surprised both Eugene and Saber when he moved to stand in front of her. "If you don't leave her alone, I'll tell Earl when he gets back. You know he won't like it none. Most probably he'll shoot you down like a dog."

Saber was trembling with fear when she saw the murderous look in Eugene's eyes. "You wouldn't tell, Sam, because iffen you do, you'll live just long enough to regret it," Eugene threatened.

The younger brother stood his ground between Saber and Eugene. "I won't let you get at her. I swear I'll shoot you down if you come near her."

Saber saw Eugene waver. His hand went to his gun, and she knew in that second that he wouldn't hesitate to shoot his own brother. "If Sam doesn't tell Earl, I will." She threw her head back and glared at him. "If you lay one hand on me or Sam, Earl will hear about it."

Eugene looked undecided. *Damn it!* She was tying him in knots, and he wanted her beneath him. But his good sense won out over his burning lust . . . for now, anyway.

"I wonder what Graham Felton would do if he knew you laid hands on this woman?" Sam asked in a cold voice. "We don't know what he wants with her. He may want her for his woman. Felton ain't a man to cross. He said he wanted this woman unharmed, and he meant it."

At the sound of Graham Felton's name, Eugene's face paled. He turned and stormed out the door, slamming it behind him.

Saber pressed her hand over her heart, more frightened than ever. But she tried to push her fear aside, knowing there was nothing to gain by giving in to it. If a man like Eugene was afraid of Mr. Felton, then what kind of monster must he be?

Sam moved to the window and watched his brother ride away. "I don't think he'll be bothering you no more. No sirree. He's no coward, but he don't want to rile Graham Felton any."

Saber lay down across the hard bench, unmindful of the splinters. Her body was shaking with fear. Turning her head to the wall, she closed her eyes and cried silently. There was no help for her. Not even her brother, Noble, could help her now. And Matthew had to know about her abduction by now—what must he be thinking?

"He won't bother you anymore," Sam said again, thinking she was crying because of his brother, Eugene.

"But what about Graham Felton?"

Sam turned back to the window, hating to think about this soft, beautiful woman in that mad dog's hands. He liked Saber Vincente—he hadn't wanted to, but she was nice. "Like as not, he's seen you somewhere and wants you for his woman."

His words brought no comfort to Saber, and she could not stop her tears from falling.

Chapter Four

Acting on a strong hunch, Reese had camped near the road south of Dallas for three days. He'd watched the people who came his way, but none of them were the Miller brothers. One of the men he spoke to was able to give him a good description of the two older brothers.

For all he knew, the Millers might already have turned Miss Vincente over to Graham Felton. But he was gambling that the meeting hadn't yet taken place. Felton would be cautious, knowing that the whole state of Texas would be searching for the Vincente woman. Reese expected him to meet with the brothers and then decide where the woman was to be exchanged.

He was also gambling that the Miller brothers would attempt to sneak into Dallas by swimming their horses across the Trinity River rather than taking the ferry, where people might recognize them.

Reese shaded his eyes and judged it to be the noon hour. If none of the Miller brothers had shown up by evening, he'd ride into Dallas and see if he could pick up their trail from there.

It was late afternoon when he saw the dust of a lone rider approaching. He urged his horse behind a thick cedar bush, waiting and watching.

As the rider drew near, Reese guided his horse into the man's path and aimed his rifle at his heart. "Stop where you are," he commanded in a harsh voice. "And don't move."

The stranger pulled back on the reins and looked at Reese, seemingly undaunted. "If it's money you're after, you won't get much from me, mister."

Reese shook his head. "Don't want your money—I'm after information." He could see a strong resemblance between the stranger and Mrs. Miller. They had the same shape face, the same color eyes. And this man fit the description of the older brother, Earl. Reese could tell a lot about a man just by looking into his eyes. While Mrs. Miller's eyes had been honest and heavy with sadness, her son's eyes held a mendacious expression, and there was something sly and deceitful in the dark depths.

"Unbuckle your gun belt and drop it to the ground," Reese ordered. "Then carefully ease that rifle out of the holster and drop it, too."

Earl Miller looked into the stranger's hard, cold eyes and knew he meant exactly what he said. Slowly he unbuckled his gun belt and let it drop. He then unholstered his rifle and pitched it to the ground.

Reese motioned with his rifle. "Dismount slowly, but keep your hands where I can see them at all times."

Earl did as he was told, although he had trouble removing his foot from the stirrup with his hands in the air. Reese encouraged him by cocking the rifle and leveling it right between his eyes.

"Damn it, what do you want from me?"

"Let's start with your name. Who are you?"

Earl's eyes narrowed. There was something going on that he didn't quite understand. If the man didn't want his money, what did he want? No one could know that he'd kidnapped the Vincente woman—he'd been too careful in covering his tracks. But what if he was wrong; what if this man was a lawman? What if he had found out about the kidnapping and tracked him?

"Keep those hands up," Reese ordered when Earl dropped one arm.

Earl stared directly into the stranger's eyes. He was no coward, but he read something in those silver depths that warned him the stranger wouldn't hesitate to shoot him dead.

"And if I don't feel like telling you my name?" Earl asked recklessly, testing the stranger.

Reese shrugged with indifference. "Then you'd only be hurting yourself." Without hesitation, he aimed his rifle and fired.

Earl let out a cry of pain, followed by outraged cursing. He grabbed his ear and blood poured through his fingers. "Damn it to hell! Why'd you go and shoot my ear, you bastard?"

"So you'd know I'm serious," Reese replied in a voice as hard as steel. "You might want to remember that I always hit what I aim at." The rifle moved to Earl's heart. "Now I'm only going to ask you one more time," Reese warned. "What's your name?"

Earl licked his dry lips, and in spite of the chilled air, sweat popped out on his upper lip. There was no doubt in his mind that the rifleman meant what he said. And he had a feeling that the man already knew who he was, so he didn't dare lie to him—not with that rifle aimed at his heart. "Name's Earl," he said hurriedly. "Earl Miller." His eyes hardened, and he wondered if he could reach the derringer that was hidden in his sleeve before the man could pull the trigger. "Who are you, and why d'you want to know my name?"

Reese leaned forward, cradling the rifle across his arm, and said softly, "Earl, I'm your worst fear."

Earl could no longer look into those cold, penetrating eyes. "I don't even know you. What've you got against me?"

With the creaking of saddle leather, Reese dismounted, keeping his rifle trained on Earl Miller. "Let's just say that you have something that belongs to a friend of mind, and he wants it back."

"I don't know what you're talking about." Earl could feel the metal of his hidden derringer against his bare flesh. If he could keep the man talking and distract him, he'd have a chance at a clear shot, but he'd better aim for the heart because if he didn't kill this man, he'd be the one to die. "What does your friend think I have that belongs to him?"

Reese moved a step closer, and Earl took a step back. "Let's not waste time on meaningless conversation, Earl. You have a woman who doesn't belong to you, and you're going to take me to her, right now." He took another step toward Earl. "But first I want you to tell me about your deal with Graham Felton and where in Dallas you are supposed to meet him."

Suddenly the color drained out of Earl's face. He looked almost comical with blood streaming from his ear and his teeth clenched in fear.

Earl knew in his gut that he had no choice but to tell the stranger everything. "Why didn't you just ask me what you wanted in the first place? You didn't have to go and shoot me."

Reese smiled, but it was not with humor; it was a smile that sent chills down Earl's spine. "It seemed the right thing to do at the time, Earl. I didn't think you'd talk until I proved to you that I am dead serious."

Earl glanced into the cold gray eyes and quickly looked down at the ground. "If you'll put that gun down, I'll tell you 'bout the woman."

"I have been called many names in my lifetime, Earl, but 'fool' was never one of them. Now answer me this—have you and Felton ever met before?"

"No. But you know so much already, I'm sure you know that, too."

"Where is Saber Vincente? Take me to her."

Earl paled even more and extended his arm at an angle so the hidden derringer slid into the palm of his hand. He was fast, but not fast enough. The rifle fired, knocking him backward and slamming him to the ground.

Earl tried to move when the stranger bent down to him, but he was paralyzed. "It's bad, ain't it?" he said with a gasped.

"Yep. You're gut-shot, Earl. You don't have long to live. Looks like I'll be meeting with Felton in your place. I would have preferred to go after the girl, but you forced me to do it the hard way. Care to tell me where you were going to meet Felton?"

Earl stared into the other man's clear silver eyes and shivered. "Go to hell."

"Not today, Earl—that's where you'll be going." He watched Earl's body twitch, and the man's last breath came out in a gurgled sigh.

Reese mounted and guided his horse toward Dallas.

Reese tried to put himself in Graham Felton's place and think as he would. What did Felton want with Miss Vincente? There was always ransom, but Felton didn't need money. Perhaps he had a grudge against the Vincente family? That was the most likely possibility. Noble Vincente had probably made many enemies over the years; men of wealth and power often did. It could be that Felton merely wanted the woman in his bed.

Reese's only knowledge about the Vincente family was what he'd heard from other people.

Noble Vincente was like a king, ruling a ranch that was larger than some countries in the world.

Reese's lip curled in scorn. He could imagine what Saber Vincente was like: soft, beautiful, lofty, and full of her own importance. She had probably always been surrounded by servants, and didn't have to put her foot forward without someone else's help. She was exactly the kind of woman Reese had always detested. He'd met them before, even bedded them on occasion, but they had always left him cold. He wanted a woman who would think and do for herself; not some decorative ornament who needed to be pampered and coddled. That kind of woman would be just right for Matthew; in fact, Matthew was the sort of man who needed a woman of pure bloodlines, a wife he could show off to his eastern friends and say, "I own her—look but don't touch."

No matter what kind of woman she was, Miss Vincente didn't deserve what had happened to her. And he would do all in his power to get her back for Matthew.

It was growing dark when Reese rode into Dallas. His gaze roamed lazily across the buildings as he speculated where the meeting was to take place. He knew it would be one of the saloons, but which one? There were three.

Dallas, unlike many of the towns in Texas, had prospered after the Civil War. There was a wagon and carriage factory, a bank, and a newspaper office. Dallas was the center of the buffalo trade, and there were rumors that the railroad would soon cut through the town, bringing even more prosperity.

Reese stopped before the Lucky Seven Saloon and stared at it for a moment—it was too crowded, too noisy. No, Felton would choose a less frequented saloon for his meeting with Earl. Now that he knew that the two men had never met face-to-face, he had the edge he needed to approach Graham Felton. If he played his part right, he just might get Matthew's woman back for him without getting himself and her killed in the bargain.

Reese bypassed another rowdy saloon, then dismounted before the Blue Dog. He tied his horse to the hitching post and shoved open the bat-wing doors, entering the darkened interior. It took his eyes a moment to adjust to the dimness. The man who was playing the tinny piano was singing off-key, and it grated on Reese's nerves. He smelled the stale tobacco smoke mixed with the unpleasant odor of unwashed flesh and the sickening aroma of cheap perfume. There were two cowboys bellied up to the bar, their arms draped around gaudily dressed

women, and three men sitting at a table playing
cards. He decided that none of them was Felton,
although they might be his men, since they
watched Reese's movements closely.

Reese's gaze fell on a man sitting alone at a
table at the back of the room, and he drew in a
cautious breath. That was probably Graham Felton. With his jaw clenched firmly, Reese moved
through the saloon to the solitary gentleman.

As Reese approached, the man didn't look up
or acknowledge his presence in any way, so
Reese slid into the chair across from him.

"I didn't hear anyone invite you to sit at my
table."

Reese picked up the whiskey bottle and took
a deep drink before answering. "I see they serve
you the good stuff."

"It's the best. And I don't take kindly to anyone
inviting himself to a drink of my private stock."

Reese shoved the bottle back toward the man.
"If you are who I think you are, you'll talk to me.
I have something you want."

Now the man did look up at him. "You'd be
Earl Miller."

Reese nodded, studying the man and looking
for any indication that he was suspicious. Either
Graham Felton believed him, or he was a damn
good actor. Felton was in his late thirties or early
forties—it was hard to tell for sure. He was of

medium height and had light brown hair with gray at the temples. His eyes were such a light shade of blue that in the dimness of the saloon, they seemed colorless. His face was pockmarked, and he had a hooked nose that looked as if it had been broken more than once.

Felton leaned back in his chair and eyed Reese with equal directness. At last he asked, "So you got the woman?"

Reese nodded.

"Where is she?"

"Now, I'd be a fool to tell you that until I got my money, wouldn't I?"

Graham's eyes flickered, then narrowed. "You'd be a fool to try and play games with me. You'll never get out of this saloon alive if you cross me. Every man you see in here, including the piano player, has been hired by me."

Reese smiled slightly. "Now why would I want to cross you, since I went to so much trouble to come here in the first place?"

"If you came to ask for more money, or to tell me that the woman's dead, or that either you or one of your brothers has sullied her, you are as good as dead."

"I want her unharmed as much as you do. But I don't know why you want her so bad. What's so special about her?"

"I don't make it a habit to explain myself to a

small-thinking thief like yourself." He stubbed out his cigarette and met Reese's gaze. "Where is she?"

"Where we agreed I'd take her."

Graham nodded. "Las Lomas."

Reese's brow furrowed as he mulled the name over in his mind. Las Lomas was a ghost town a hundred miles east of Fort Worth. He knew it well, since he'd once driven a herd of cattle right through the town streets.

Felton took a drink from his glass, then shoved it away. "It's a four-day ride from Las Lomas to the border. Cross the Rio Grande at El Paso and look for the first saloon you come to when you cross the border. I know how long it'll take you to get back there from here. I'll give you two weeks from today to deliver the woman, and not a day more. After that, you'll not be able to find me—I'll find you."

Reese stood up; he had the information he'd come for. He knew where the woman was being held. "Until our next meeting," he said, tipping his hat and walking away.

Before Reese could reach the door, Felton hurried after him, calling out in a harsh voice, "I don't want any harm to come to the woman. I must be the first to have her. Is that understood?"

Reese turned to watch Felton limp toward

him. He hadn't known the man limped; he'd almost missed an important detail, and that could have been disastrous. "I understand. Now, I have a condition for you. If you have any of your men follow me, you'll never see the woman alive. Is that understood?"

Felton nodded. "At the border in two weeks. You'd better not waste time hanging around here if you're going to make it."

Reese stepped out into the night, drawing in a cleansing breath. "Damn," he muttered as he swung into the saddle. He'd be very surprised if he found the woman unharmed. The Miller brothers probably weren't known for their gallantry toward women. He wondered if Matthew would still marry Miss Vincente if the brothers had raped her. Matthew always strove for perfection in himself and insisted on it in those around him. He'd want his wife to be perfect in every way. Reese hoped Matthew loved the woman enough to overlook her imperfections if she were less than pure when he got her back.

Hell, if he loved a woman, and she'd been sullied by those bastards, he'd only love her more for what she had endured. But of course, he wasn't Matthew Halloway of the Halloways of Philadelphia.

Reese's mother had left his father the year Reese turned five, and to make it worse, she'd run away with his father's best friend. Reese had watched his father try to eke out a living and keep the bank from taking the ranch. Frank Starrett had grown more bitter with each passing day and had finally died a broken man, leaving Reese to make it on his own since the age of fourteen.

Reese had always sworn that no woman would do to him what his mother had done to his father. And he would never betray a friend the way his father's best friend had betrayed him.

A grim expression glowed in his eyes. There was little chance the woman would come out of this as pure as she'd been when they'd kidnapped her. His heart swelled with pity for her. She didn't deserve what had happened to her, and he would rescue her or die trying!

Chapter Five

The weather had turned colder, and Saber lay huddled beneath the thin blanket that she'd been wrapped in when the men had kidnapped her. Although she was cold, she refused to use the wool blanket Sam had offered her because it was smelly and filthy.

She listened to the howling wind that seeped through the cracks of the old building, rattling the windows and shaking the door, making it sound as if someone were trying to get in.

She had lost count of the days since her abduction and had long ago given up hope of ever being rescued. She dared not think about what the future held for her. Although she continued to question Sam, he refused to tell her why she'd been kidnapped or who Graham Felton was.

Sam appeared at her side, untying the ropes at her wrists and ankles before handing her a cup of steaming coffee. He had recently started untying her when she ate because there wasn't anyplace for her to run. "The coffee's right strong, but it's hot. It'll help warm you a bit, Miss Vincente."

She gladly accepted the steaming offering and took a sip of the bitter brew. "What's going to happen to me, Sam?"

He hesitated and avoided meeting her gaze. In the short time he'd known Saber Vincente, he'd grown to respect and care for her. He'd never met a woman who could touch her in looks and manners, and she was brave, too, although he knew she was scared most of the time. For the last two days he'd battled with the notion of taking her back to Fort Worth to her people. But of course, he didn't dare give in to that impulse. He'd be a dead man before he even reached the edge of Las Lomas—Eugene would see to that.

The most he was able to do was to keep Eugene away from her. At night when he bedded down, he'd position his blanket beside her bed, and so far Eugene had left her alone. But he wished Earl would get back, because he couldn't handle Eugene much longer. Every day his brother grew bolder, and his gaze never left their prisoner.

Sam lifted the water bucket. "I'm just going to the well for fresh water. Stay put, 'cause I wouldn't want Eugene to find you wandering the streets."

"Don't leave me alone," Saber begged, her stomach tensing into a tight knot. "What if he comes back, and I'm here alone?"

"I'll be right close by, and I'll hear you if you call out."

She watched Sam leave, feeling desperate and helpless. There had never been a time in her life when she had not been able to do something about her situation. Not even during the war, when the Yankees had burned her grandmother's plantation, had she been as frightened as she was now.

Saber caught her breath when she heard the front door open. A scream formed in her throat when she saw Eugene, but she couldn't make a sound. Sam hadn't tied her up, and she wondered if she dared run for it. Could she make it to the door before he caught her?

Eugene walked toward her, his eyes going to her breasts, which strained against her shirt. "So I have you alone at last. You gave me a lot of sleepless nights, fancy piece. But I bet I'll sleep good tonight."

71

She pressed her back against the wall. "Sam will be back any minute," she said hurriedly. "He just went to the well for water."

Eugene unfastened his gun belt and dropped it onto the table. "No. My brother won't be bothering us anytime soon. When he comes to, it'll be too late for you. You see, I kinda put him to sleep with the butt of my gun."

"No!" she cried, looking at the door as if Sam might come through it at any moment. "I'll scream if you touch me."

He laughed and stepped closer. "No one will hear you. Go ahead—scream all you want to."

With a quick motion, Saber's hand tightened on the coffee cup, and she dashed the hot brew into Eugene's face. Hurling herself forward, she darted for the door while Eugene covered his eyes and screamed out in pain. She threw the door open and ran into the growing darkness. She had hoped to find Eugene's horse tied out front, but luck was against her—there was no horse. He must have left it at the edge of town.

She could hear Eugene cursing and calling to her. Fear gave wings to her feet, and she started running with no particular direction in mind. She just knew she couldn't let him catch her. Her only hope was to lose him in the dark.

Saber had almost reached the graveyard when a man stepped in front of her. She screamed out as he grabbed her shoulders and held her in a tight grip. Saber, thinking it was Eugene and that he'd managed to work his way in front of her, swung at him with her fist. She heard a muffled sound of pain just before she drew back her leg and kicked him in a place that made him release his hold on her and double over in agony.

She turned away and came face-to-face with Eugene! If Eugene was in front of her, then who was the man she'd just attacked?

Eugene grabbed her arm and yanked her forward. "I'll have you, and I won't be too particular about how rough I am. I got me a score to settle with you for dousing me with that coffee."

A deep voice spoke up from behind her. "Let her go."

Eugene strained his eyes in the darkness. "Who in the hell are you?" he asked, reaching for his gun and realizing he'd left it back on the table.

The stranger's hand came down heavily on Saber's shoulder, and he moved her behind him. "I'm the man who is going to kill you if you've harmed Saber Vincente in any way."

"Who are you?" Eugene asked again.

The man was a stranger to Saber. But if he knew who she was, perhaps he'd been sent by her brother! However, his next words dashed her hopes and made her tremble with renewed fear.

"My name is Graham Felton. I assume you've heard of me?"

Saber strained her eyes to see in the near darkness. She was overwhelmed by his size. He was taller even than her brother, and Noble was over six feet tall. His shoulders were broad, and his voice was deep, almost raspy. He wore a long coat, but it was pushed open so he could easily reach the holster that was strapped to his thigh. Her gaze fell on the gun, and she felt more afraid than ever. Most men in Texas wore guns, but she had a feeling this man knew how to use his better than most. She was well aware that Eugene had stepped back several paces—even he was afraid of Graham Felton.

"I didn't hurt her none. I was just having a little fun with her," Eugene said in a shaky voice.

Although the stranger was a strongly built man, his grasp was gentle where he gripped Saber's wrists. He didn't have a tight hold on her, but it was secure enough that she could not pull free. She wondered if he would make her sorry that she had attacked him.

Reese glanced down at Eugene, and his lips thinned into a hard line. It was all he could do to keep from drawing on the bastard. "Let's get her out of this cold." he said in a strained voice. "Then we'll talk."

Eugene was suddenly contrite, trying to placate the man whose name shook him to the core. "We got a fire going back where we're holed up. It's nice and warm there."

"Lead me to it. If you'll accompany us, Miss Vincente."

He urged Sable along, supporting her when she stumbled. She tried to stay upright without his help, but her legs were almost useless. Any small hope she might have had of being rescued was gone. She felt the man's hand move from her wrist to her shoulder as he kept urging her forward. His touch was surprisingly gentle, but that fact brought her no comfort. This was the man who had hired the Miller brothers to kidnap her in the first place.

She could feel in the very depths of her being that this man was to be feared much more than all three of the Miller brothers. She couldn't run; she couldn't hide. He'd come for her, and she would be forced to go with him.

His voice was strangely gentle. "Are you all right, Miss Vincente?"

She shoved his hand away and walked a pace in front of him. His searing touch still lingered on her bare skin, and she was disturbed by her strange reaction to him; it wasn't revulsion, like what she felt for Eugene—it was a feeling that she couldn't put a name to because she'd never experienced such a sensation.

By the time they'd reached the hotel, Sam was there, rubbing his head where Eugene had hit him. There was relief in his eyes when he saw Saber, but it was quickly replaced by caution and distrust when the stranger entered behind her.

Saber moved to the woodstove and held her hands out to the warmth, her eyes going to Felton. Something frightening lurked in the depths of those silver eyes, and she knew instantly that he was not a man to cross. There was a dangerous quality about the way he stood and moved, and it was reflected in the rough planes of his face. He was appraising her, and his gaze struck her like an earthquake and left her quivering with aftershocks. He was the most magnificently frightening man she'd ever seen. She knew he would be unyielding and uncompromising, and the others felt it, too. He was hard and muscled, his broad shoulders straining against his buckskin shirt as if he might burst the seams at any moment. Fear erupted into full-blown terror when he stared into her eyes.

What did he want with her? She had the fleeting thought that she might be safer if she remained with the outlaws rather than leaving with this man. Her gaze went to Sam, but she knew he couldn't help her—no one could.

"How do we know you're Graham Felton?" Eugene asked cautiously.

Reese advanced into the room with a dangerous expression in his eyes. For the first time Saber noticed that he limped.

"You'd be him, all right," Eugene said, his eyes going to Saber. "You got the limp, and you knew where to find us. But why wasn't I told when the plan changed?"

Sam fixed the man with a doubtful expression. "Earl said we was to bring the woman to you."

Reese's gaze settled on the youngest Miller brother. "You had better ask why your brother changed the plan. He asked me for the money and told me you had the woman here."

Eugene's eyes clouded with suspicion. "Now, why'd he do that and not tell us?"

Reese smiled the merest bit. "You know your brother better than I do. I gave him the sum of money we agreed on, and he left ahead of me. I half expected to find him here." He shrugged. "As I see it, one of two things could have happened to him—he could have been ambushed by someone who knew he was carrying a large amount of cash. . . ."

Eugene's voice held a sarcastic tone. "And the second thing?"

"Well," Reese said softly. "Is there a chance he didn't want to share the money with the two of you?" Reese shrugged as if it made very little difference to him. "As I said, you know your brother better than I do."

Eugene swore loudly. "Damn it to hell! I should have been suspicious when Earl went riding off on his own and wouldn't let me go with him! He done went and crossed us." His murderous gaze turned to Reese. "If I find you've played us false, I'll come after you."

Reese countered Eugene's threat with one of his own. "If I find you've harmed this woman, I'll come after you."

Sam spoke up. "Earl wouldn't have done us wrong. If he's not here, it's because he's in trouble somewhere."

"And night ain't night," Eugene said in a hard tone. "I thought Earl was acting funny." He glared at his younger brother. "We're going to find that bastard and get our share of the money." He jerked up his gun belt and fastened it about his waist. "I'll kill him for this!"

Both brothers began shoving supplies into a canvas pack and moved to the door. Eugene turned to glance back at Saber. "I think our paths may cross again, Miss Vincente."

Saber cringed inside at the lustful look he gave her and turned her face away from him.

Pausing in the doorway, Sam spoke to Reese. "Be good to her, Mr. Felton. She's not used to rough treatment."

"You'd just better hope you or your brothers haven't harmed her," Reese told him in a deep voice that reverberated through the room.

Sam looked at Saber for a moment. "I'm sorry I wasn't able to protect you from Eugene." Then he left abruptly, closing the door behind him.

The room was silent for a long moment, and then Reese turned his attention to the woman. She was dressed in filthy trousers and a shirt that were both too big for her. Her golden hair was tangled and dirty. Her face was smudged with dirt. He saw nothing about her that would make a man like Major Halloway want her for his wife. She looked more like a pitiful waif than a legendary beauty.

Saber tried to meet the man's gaze bravely, but his eyes were too intense, and he was too powerful. "What are you going to do with me, sir?"

He wondered if he should tell her that Matthew had sent him to rescue her. But there was a chance the Miller brothers might follow them, so it was best to tell her later on. His first duty was to get her to safety. "That, Miss Vincente, remains to be seen. But you don't have anything to worry about." He glanced about him. "I suppose you have nothing here to take. Let's be on our way."

She shivered at the coldness in his voice. Still, her pride came to her rescue. "I want you to be aware that I will escape the first chance I get."

He smiled, showing strong, white teeth. "Be advised, Miss Vincente, that you will be far safer with me than left to the mercy of the elements, or with those two blunderers who just left here. You will welcome my protection If they decide to come back for you—and they will come back for you, make no mistake about that."

"What are you talking about?" she insisted.

"Are you ready to go?"

"Not until you tell me what you are going to do with me."

When he didn't answer, she flew at him, her hands reaching for his face, trying to claw at his eyes. With ease, he subdued her, locking both her hands in a firm grip.

"Stop it. You'll only hurt yourself." He pulled her against his hip and held her there. "You can't win against me, so save yourself the trouble."

She struggled and kicked out at him, but she soon recognized his superior strength. Thoroughly exhausted, she subsided stiffly against him. But her blue eyes burned with contempt, and he knew she would try to escape if he didn't watch her. That was certainly what she had been trying to do when he'd found her.

He admired her spirit, but it would probably get them both killed if he didn't curb it. "For now, all you need to know is that we are leaving. Grab that extra blanket. You'll need it for warmth."

She blinked her eyes in revolt. "No, I won't!" she declared, glaring at him. "It's filthy. I didn't use it when it was offered to me by Sam, and I won't use it now."

His voice had an edge to it, and he cast her an intolerant gaze. "That blanket is probably cleaner than you are. You could do with a bath."

She opened her mouth to protest and then glanced down at the stained trousers; it was difficult to tell what color the shirt was. At the time Sam had given them to her, her only concern had been to discourage Eugene's attention. "When they took me away, I wore only my nightgown. Sam let me have these."

Seeing the fear in her eyes caused a painful twist inside Reese. He had the strongest urge to hold her until she lost the forlorn expression—to protect her with his last breath if he had to. He wanted to assure her that everything was all right, but he didn't dare—not yet. He moved to the door and turned to her. "Grab that second blanket. You're going to need it. We have to leave now because I want to put miles behind us before sunup."

Having no other choice in the matter, Saber took the blanket and flung it over the one she'd been wrapped in when the millers had kidnapped her. She followed the man out the door and across the street, where he led her through a narrow alley. Behind the old bank building were two horses and a pack mule. Apparently they had a long journey ahead of them if they needed enough supplies for a pack mule.

When the man came forward to help her mount, Saber shoved him away and slid her foot into the stirrup, hoisting herself into the saddle. It gave her some small satisfaction that she could make at least one decision for herself, even if it was only a small one.

As they rode away from the deserted town, past the neglected graveyard, Saber shivered. She had a feeling her destiny was tied to this man's, although she didn't know why. She weighed her chances of getting away from him, but she remembered the six-gun he wore about his waist, and the rifle he'd placed in his saddle-bag within easy reach. He'd probably kill her before he'd let her escape.

She huddled beneath the blankets while the icy wind chilled her to the bone. She was more frightened than ever. Closing her eyes, she wished her brother would find her. It didn't occur to Saber until later that she hadn't thought of Matthew at all. Always in the past, when she had been frightened, her mind reached out to her brother, just like now.

"Oh, Noble, come for me soon," she whispered. "I am so afraid."

Chapter Six

Saber had no way to gauge how long they had been riding. She had never been so cold and exhausted, and she could hardly stay upright in the saddle. When the man finally stopped to rest the horses, she wearily slid to the ground and almost stumbled. Bracing her hand against the sturdy bay, she drew from the animal's warmth and strength. She wondered if she could jump back on the horse and ride away. After all, she was a good horsewoman, and his horse was as tired as hers.

The man who had caused her fear and weariness sat mounted on his great black horse, his demeanor placid. It appeared that he was un-

aware of anything that went on around him—
but she knew better. She knew he was aware of
everything and would spring to life if she made
an attempt to escape.

Too afraid to let him see she had been contem-
plating escaping, she fixed her gaze on the rugged country ahead of them, wondering what
would happen to her at the end of this journey.

It was sometime later that they stopped to
make camp. When he'd built a fire, she gravi-
tated toward it. Going down on her knees, she
held her frozen hands to the flames. He'd been
right about the second blanket; she would have
frozen to death without it, but she'd never admit
it to him.

He moved with such catlike quiet that she
hadn't heard him come up behind her, and
jumped when he spoke.

"Are you hungry, Miss Vincente?"

She shook her head, staring into his eyes with
amazement. He was a man of the land, and the
sky was reflected in those unusual silver eyes.
How could such a man be evil? Why did she
sense something strong and comforting and
protective about him?

"If you aren't hungry, I suggest you get some
sleep. We'll be breaking camp before daylight.
We'll have a long day ahead of us tomorrow."

She braced her back against a wide boulder

and tightened the blanket about her, watching him unsaddle the horses and lead them away to be hobbled and fed. He was not at all what she'd expected. He was strong, such a commanding presence. Why would he hire others to kidnap a woman if he wanted her. Something just didn't fit. If he was of a mind to, he could crush her with one hand, and yet so far he hadn't harmed her at all. But neither had he been overly concerned about her comfort.

Saber doubted she'd be able to close her eyes for fear the man might pounce on her during the night. But her eyelids were so heavy, and weariness took over. Her head fell to the side, and she was instantly asleep. She did not know when Reese covered her with his long coat, and she was unaware that he slept lightly so he would hear if anyone came up during the night.

It seemed Saber had just closed her eyes when the man nudged her awake with the tip of his boot. "Time to ride, Miss Vincente. You have ten minutes to do whatever women do to get ready."

She came fully awake, scrambling to her feet. "Where are you taking me?" With the dawning of the new day, her fear had returned. Her breasts were heaving, and she tightened her hands into fists. "Tell me now, or you'll be sorry!"

He startled her when he chuckled and rubbed

his cheek where she'd hit him when they'd first met. "You pack quite a wallop, Miss Vincente, but I wouldn't advise trying anything again. Next time I might not be so forgiving."

She folded her arms stubbornly across her chest. "I'm not budging an inch until you tell me what you are going to do with me. You can force me to go with you because you are stronger than I am, but I will never go willingly." Her eyes snapped with anger, and her chin jutted out obstinately. "I am tired of men telling me what to do."

His head swiveled in her direction, and there was a scowl on his face. "You will do as I say, and maybe—just maybe—I can keep you alive. As for not budging, you have little choice in the matter. And as far as explaining my intentions to you, that'll come when I think the time's right."

She felt suddenly deflated. "Can't you just let me go?"

Without ceremony he reached for her, lifting her over his shoulder and plopping her none too gently onto the saddle. Then, wordlessly, he mounted his horse, took up her reins, and started out at a gallop.

Saber was a good rider, but the rough terrain made the going hard, and she was forced to hold onto the saddle horn to keep from being unseated. She glared at the broad back of the man in front of her. He was arrogant and so sure of himself, and she wanted to fly off her horse and scratch his eyes out. But she didn't dare. He was a man to be feared, and she was certainly afraid him.

He chose that moment to turn around and motion her forward. "I want you next to me so I can keep an eye on you."

She opened her mouth to make an angry response, but the look he gave her silenced her, and she did as he asked.

After they had ridden awhile longer, Saber took her courage in hand and said, "My brother will hunt you down no matter where you go. You'll be sorry you ever heard the Vincente name."

"I'm already sorry." He gave her a dark look. "As for your brother, should I be trembling in my boots?"

"My brother is a man to be reckoned with. You had better fear him."

His lip curled. "I've heard of Noble Vincente. Like many of the wealthy landowners, he's probably grown soft letting others do his work for him. I believe he's a Spanish don or grandee or some such."

Saber bit her lip in vexation. There was no

talking to this man; she wasn't even going to waste her time trying.

As the day progressed, it warmed up a bit. But by late afternoon, dark clouds were gathering in the west. Red and gold streamed through a break in the clouds, and it looked to Saber as if an artist had splashed color across the horizon.

She glanced at Graham Felton and was about to comment on the beauty of the sky, then clamped her lips together. She didn't want to share her thoughts with the likes of him. Absently her gaze fell on his strong hands, which held his reins in a loose grip. She'd already felt the strength of those hands, and she shivered, thinking he could break her bones without even trying. She wondered what it would be like to feel those hands run over her body caressingly.

With a start, she blinked her eyes and blushed at the impure thoughts she was having about such an unworthy man. What was the matter with her? He was the enemy—the man who had paid to have her abducted—and she should be thinking only of Matthew. Her thoughts turned to her fiancé. Matthew must be out of his mind with worry by now. Would she ever see him again?

The sun was setting by the time Reese called a halt. Saber dismounted, wishing she had gloves to protect her hands from the raw cold, which had intensified with the setting of the sun.

"Why are we stopping here?" she asked, eyeing him warily. "There is no protection from the wind."

"Shh," he cautioned, grabbing up the reins of both horses and gripping her shoulder, shoving her against a cliff wall and pressing his hard body against hers. He removed his gun and cocked the hammer.

"What—"

His head swiveled in her direction, and he glared at her. Should she scream? she wondered. If someone was out there, they might help her. His eyes were frosty, and he had the look of a predatory cat. She decided against calling out, because she could feel the strength in the body pressed against hers. She was once more reminded that he could crush her with his bare hands if he wanted to.

He was watchful, motionless, as though listening for any sound that might alert him to danger. When he turned his attention to Saber, his silver eyes bored into her, and she became aware of the hard body pressed against her. He was so near she could see the pores in his skin and the dark stubble of his beard where he hadn't shaved for several days. She could smell the muskiness of him, and something twisted inside her; then something unexplainable ran hotly through her whole body. It was as if her blood were on fire. He moved slightly, and she felt his erection swell against her as they became aware of each other in a new way. For a breathless moment, she thought he was going to kiss her. His mouth was so close to hers that her lips parted invitingly.

In a sudden motion he moved away from her, and she felt the tension ease. He turned his head to listen and then holstered his gun.

She had to swallow several times to take a gulp of air before she could speak. Her throat went dry, and her nerves tightened. "Who was it?" she asked, trying to gather her thoughts and not think about what had just happened to her while his body had been pressed against hers.

"Comanche," he said, turning his head as if he heard something she couldn't.

Her eyes widened with fear—she was glad that she hadn't cried out. The Comanche were considered the fiercest Indians of all, and the mere mention of their name struck fear in Texans' hearts. "What would have happened if they had seen us?" she inquired in a shaky voice.

"You are fortunate you didn't have to find out. We are trespassing on their land, and intruders don't make them any too happy."

"I don't care if this is Comanche land. I'm tired," Saber said, dropping down on the ground.

Reese drew an intolerant breath, his gaze sweeping the rise. At that moment, several Indians appeared at the top of the canyon, and for a long, tense moment, Saber was frozen with fear. At last the Indian raised his arm, and Reese returned his salute.

"A-are they coming after us?" she asked, her voice once again trembling.

"I'm not sure of anything where the Comanche are concerned. Stand close to me and don't utter a word."

"Who is that tall Indian?"

"Miss Vincente, you are looking at Quanah Parker, chief of the Comanche."

"Do you know him?"

"If anyone outside his tribe knows him, yes, I know him enough to respect him—and to fear him."

"Wasn't his mother the one who was captured by the Indians when she was just a girl?"

He frowned, his gaze still on the mesa above them. "Yes."

"And he chose to stay with the Comanche, though he could have lived in the white world."

Reese looked at her with sudden humor dancing in his eyes. "Quanah would scoff at your reasoning. Why would he want to live with white people, who would only despise him, when he is a great and respected chief among the Comanche?"

Saber licked her dry lips, and her throat grew tight with fear. "Are you sure he isn't going to attack us?"

"Put your mind at rest. He just gave me the peace sign. But do as I warned and don't move or speak. He's riding in."

Saber felt her body quaking with fear as the tall Indian broke away from the others and rode down the hill toward them.

When he had reached them, he dismounted in a smooth motion and clasped hands with Reese while his dark eyes moved over Saber. She cringed with fear and stepped behind Reese.

Reese and Quanah spoke in the Comanche language. Then Reese nodded and gathered up the reins of Saber's horse and handed them to the Indian. Quanah then pointed to the pack mule, and Reese nodded his agreement.

Saber watched with amazement as the Indian mounted and led her horse and the pack mule away. That left them only one horse! She watched the Indian ride out of sight, still unsure whether he would gather his tribe and come storming down on them.

She gripped Reese's arm. "Will he come back?"

"I don't think so. He has what he came for.

Just be glad horses were all he wanted."

"What will we do with only the one horse?"

"We thank God we're still alive, and we ride double. We're lucky that he left us my horse."

She turned toward him, and his gaze moved over her features. Her face was so smudged with dirt he could hardly tell what she looked like, but she appeared to be none too pretty. But what did it matter? She had the Vincente money behind her, and Matthew loved her.

Again, he felt the unwelcome tightening of his loins, and the swelling of his desire, which had momentarily distracted him. "Ma'am," he called, stopping Saber in her tracks. "If you'll get your business over with, we need to ride on."

"Is it safe now?"

"Yes, ma'am. As I said, Quanah gave me the peace sign, and he would never go back on his word."

"What I don't understand is, if you knew this was Comanche land, why did you choose to ride this way?" she said, turning and stalking away.

Reese stared after her. Even with her ill-fitting trousers, he could see that her hips were softly rounded and she had long, shapely legs. Her slow, easy steps were provocative and enticing. She had a good shape to her, all right. And he'd reacted to her body moments ago, until he reminded himself that she belonged to Matthew.

94

He glanced at the rise where Quanah had just appeared and waved to him. He heard the sound of the Indians riding away and relaxed.

When Saber rejoined Reese, he wasn't in a very good mood. "Ma'am."

"Yes."

"To answer your earlier question, I rode this way because it's unlikely that anyone will follow us into Comanche territory."

She was startled by his reasoning. "So this way, all we had to worry about was the whole Comanche nation."

"I'd hoped if we ran into Quanah, he'd remember me. Apparently he did." He mounted his horse and reached for her hand. "Let's ride. I want to put some miles between us and the Comanche."

She took his hand and he pulled her up, placing her behind him. When they started off at a trot, she had to put her arms around him to keep from falling off. After they had ridden for some time, her head fell against his strong back, and she was somehow comforted by the steady beating of his heart. She could feel the strength that radiated from him. She closed her eyes, feeling as if nothing in the world could harm her when she was with him.

Her eyes flew open. He was the reason she had been ripped from her family and Matthew! She

95

should fear him more than she did the Comanche!

Reese was setting up camp when Saber walked down to the small creek. She was eager to wash her face and hands. Walking around the thornbush and down a slight incline, she found a shallow creek. Going down on her knees, she broke the ice, cupped her hands, and drank thirstily of the cold water. She shivered as she washed her face and hands; then she tried to work the worst of the tangles out of her hair and braided it into one long braid. Tearing a strip of cloth from her shirt, she secured the end of the braid and felt somewhat better.

When Saber returned to camp, Reese had unsaddled the horse and tossed the saddle on the ground. "I'm afraid we'll have to eat a cold meal," he told her. "I don't want to remind the Comanche that we're on their land and taking advantage of their hospitality."

"I'm starved," she said, going down beside him. "I don't care what I eat as long as it's filling."

He handed her a chunk of jerked buffalo meat. "This will have to do until we are well away from here."

She stood up, tearing a piece of dried meat with strong teeth. She was watching a flock of blackbirds flying in formation and didn't notice that Reese was watching her.

Like a man caught in a dream, he couldn't drag his gaze away from the fragile beauty of Saber's face. Her skin was like satin, her lips full and rosy, and her long, thick lashes curled against her cheek. Her head was thrown back while she observed the birds, and it revealed her long, slender neck. He was speechless in the face of such beauty, and he wondered what had ever made him think she was homely. Hell, no wonder Graham Felton had wanted to kidnap her, and Matthew was so anxious to get her back. Saber Vincente was probably the most stunningly beautiful woman he'd ever seen.

She glanced questioningly at him, and he was struck by her sapphire blue eyes. "How do you suppose they do that?"

"How who does what?" he asked in a thick voice.

"Birds fly in such a perfect formation. They seem to sense just when to turn, weave, or dip. They must communicate in some way, don't you think?"

He tore his gaze away from her and glanced upward, his heart beating like a drum. "I've never thought much about it. I suppose every species communicates in one way or another." He was thinking that his body was communicating with hers, and he wanted to reach out and touch her, to pull her into his arms, to protect her and never allow anyone to hurt her again.

She glanced at him forlornly. "I envy them because they are free, and I'm not."

He saw the suffering in her eyes and knew that it was time he told her who he was. "Sit down, Miss Vincente. I want to explain some things to you."

She nodded and sat down, curling her legs beneath her. "I hope you are going to tell me why you had me kidnapped, Mr. Felton."

"I didn't have you kidnapped."

"Then why—"

"I couldn't tell you who I was until I was certain that the Miller brothers weren't following us. My name is Reese Starrett, Miss Vincente. I'm a friend of Matthew's. I only pretended to be Felton to get you away from them."

He watched several different emotions play across her face: disbelief, hope, doubt, and then joy. "Is it really you? I have heard so much about you from Matthew. Where is he?"

"He's laid up with a sprained leg or else he'd be here himself. His horse fell on him when he was on the way to Fort Worth to meet you."

Before Reese knew what happening, Saber lunged forward, throwing her body against his.

Her arms went around his neck, and a sob broke from her throat.

"Matthew has often written of you. I'm so happy it was you who found me!" She was shaking and trembling, and his arms went around her protectively.

"There's nothing to cry about. You're safe now."

She pressed her wet cheek against his rough one. "Thank you for what you did." Her head moved to his shoulder. "I don't know how I could ever have mistaken you for that awful Felton person. I knew from the moment I saw you that you were different from other men."

His chest expanded, and he hadn't realized that he'd been holding his breath. "In what way?"

Her head still nestled against his shoulder, and he found he liked it there. "You are everything Matthew said you were." She raised her head and smiled at him, feeling joy in her heart. "He thinks you are something of a hero, you know. And I'm inclined to agree with him." Tears sparkled in her eyes, and it took her a moment to go on. "I don't know how you found me, but I am so glad you did."

He'd never been good at dealing with women's tears, and Saber's were tearing his heart out. She hadn't cried when she'd thought he was her kidnapper, but now that she was safe it seemed she couldn't stop crying. His eyebrows came together in a frown, and he thought he knew why she was crying. Maybe one or all of the Miller brothers had raped her. His arms tightened about her even more, and he cradled her body against his.

"Nothing can be that bad, Miss Vincente. Please don't cry; everything will be all right now."

She buried her face against his neck, and he felt his flesh come alive. His hands ran up and down her back, and the pleasure of touching her was so intense it alarmed him. When she drew in a deep breath and her breasts pressed against his chest, he could hardly breathe.

Reese gloried in the female smell of her, and he envisioned what she'd look like lying naked beneath him. He'd never been dazzled by a woman before, but there was no other word for how he felt about her—he was definitely dazzled by Saber! Heat shot through him and settled in his loins. He had to stop thinking about her in that way. She wasn't his—she belonged to his friend!

He stood up and put her away from him. Desire for her made his voice harsher than he'd intended. "You'd better get some sleep. We'll be riding on as soon as it's dark."

"Why at night?"

"Because we'll be harder to track if anyone is following us, and we'll be out of Comanche territory by dawn."

"You wouldn't be worried if I weren't with you, would you?"

"Not as much," he admitted. "Now get some sleep."

Saber was too weary to argue, and lay back on her blanket. She dreaded the thought of riding all night, but she was more afraid of meeting up with a Comanche war party. She closed her eyes and felt Reese place a warm blanket over her. She was safe now that Reese Starrett was looking after her!

Chapter Seven

It was a bitterly cold morning, but the air was sharp and clean. Saber loved riding and always had, but being in the open and exposed to the cold took the enjoyment out of it. She felt guilty again because her thoughts were not often of Matthew, but of Reese. Her arms were clasped about his waist, and she pressed her face against him. She could feel his taut stomach muscles and each intake of his breath.

When they began backtracking she knew he was worried that they might have been followed. Suddenly he rode behind a thicket, cautioning her to be quiet. His hand rested on his gun, and she knew he could have it in his hand in an instant.

Saber laughed when a herd of deer moved past their hiding place. "Don't worry, Mr. Starrett. I'll protect you from them," she said, laughing so hard she could hardly catch her breath.

He glanced back at her, his eyes glinting with amusement. "I feel comforted by that, Miss Vincente. Let's ride on."

They rode in companionable silence for most of the day, stopping often to rest the horse, since the animal had to carry them both. Late in the afternoon they ate a quick meal of dried meat before mounting up and riding on once more.

As evening advanced, a serene quietness settled over the land. Reese halted the horse and spoke softly, as if any noise were an intrusion on the tranquillity. "It's going to be colder tonight, so I have to find shelter or we risk freezing."

"If you hadn't let Quanah take our pack mule with the blankets, we'd have something to keep us warm."

He gritted his teeth. "At the time it seemed the right thing to do." He shifted in the saddle and glared at her. "Do you see those dark clouds?" He rushed on without giving her a chance to answer. "A blizzard is heading our way."

Even as he spoke, snow began to fall. In no

time at all they couldn't see beyond the horse's head.

"Are you always right?" she said with a pout on her lips.

"Almost never since I met you," he mumbled.

"I'm cold."

He rubbed the back of his neck while he pondered the best thing to do to save her life. "I know of a place that might offer us some protection. It's only the remains of a burned-out squatter's cabin, but it's the closest place to us."

He guided his tired mount down a small hill, hoping he could find the ruins in the blinding snow. After they had been riding for over an hour, he halted the horse.

"There," he said, pointing to the dark ruins that seemed to have emerged out of nowhere. "I was afraid I would miss it in the snow. We can hole up there until the worst of the storm is over."

He lifted Saber to the ground and led her toward the shelter. As luck would have it, one whole wall, part of the roof, and the stone fireplace were still standing. Reese seated Saber and draped his coat about her. "There's certainly lots of wood to start a fire," he said, beginning to pick up charred logs.

Saber knew she should help him, but her teeth

were chattering, and she was shaking from the cold.

In no time a small fire was burning, but it seemed to Saber that it gave off little warmth.

"Should we be afraid of the Indians or the Millers?"

"The Indians already know we're here, and they seem to have granted us the right to pass through their land. As for the Millers, they hardly seem the sort who would go after anything in this kind of weather."

"No," she said, holding her shaking hands to the flames. "We're the only fools out tonight."

He staked the horse behind the shelter of the wall and left the horse blanket on the animal to keep it warm. "If we lose him, we walk. And when you're forced to walk out here, you're dead."

"What will we do for cover?" she asked.

"I'll try to keep the fire going, and we'll just have to share the one blanket and my coat."

She nodded when he took the blanket from her. She shook with cold as he held the blanket to the fire to warm it. He then placed it about her shoulders, and blissful heat worked its way through her body. She sighed with contentment, but then she saw that Reese was in his shirt-sleeves.

She held out the blanket. "You said we'd share."

"Not until I have stacked plenty of wood up to last through the night." He proceeded to gather logs that had survived the fire. At last he sat down beside Saber, and she drew the blanket about him.

"What happened to the house, do you know?"

"Yeah. The Dickersons lived here until they got burned out by the Comanche."

Saber shivered. "Were they killed?"

"They weren't at home at the time. But if they had been, they would have been killed."

"That's monstrous!"

"If you build on Comanche land, you can expect retribution. It would be no different if some squatter built on your brother's land."

"I'd like to think he'd be more understanding."

"No, he wouldn't. A man's land is his life out here. No squatter, homesteader, or whatever they want to call themselves has a right to take it over."

"I suppose, if you put it that way." She yawned and laid her head on his shoulder.

"Here," he said, spreading his coat on the hard ground and laying her down close to the fire. Then he warmed the blanket again and placed it over her.

She was still shaking so badly that he lay down

beside her, drawing her into his arms. She snuggled against him, sliding one arm around his waist. He began rubbing his hand firmly up and down her back, trying to warm her. After a while he heard her sigh, and she fell asleep.

Reese watched the snow sifting through the cracks, glad that the roof nearest the fireplace had been strong enough to withstand the fire. Saber snuggled her head against his neck, and he caught his breath, willing himself to think of her only as a warm body and not as a desirable woman.

He carefully removed his gun from the holster and laid it within easy reach. His horse stomped and whinnied; then, after a while, all was quiet except for the crackling of the fire.

It was a long time before Reese fell asleep.

He jerked awake, his senses alert. Something had brushed against his face. He automatically reached for his gun, then realized it was only Saber's hair. He stiffened when he realized that she had crawled on top of him and was snuggled there.

He groaned as she cuddled closer to his warmth, grinding her breasts against his chest. He swallowed deeply when she shifted again and his painfully swollen erection fit snugly between her legs. He dared not move, and he hoped she didn't either, because every movement only heated his blood more and made him want to slide inside her to find relief. He tried to think of anyone but the woman who was driving him slowly out of his mind.

He reached up to brush her hair out of his face, but instead, when he touched the silky texture, his fingers moved through it. Her mouth was so near his that if he turned the slightest bit, his lips would touch hers. And he wanted to—he ached and throbbed to kiss her until her lips parted for him. He wanted to unfasten his trousers, rip hers off and—

Oh, hell, he thought when she moved again, this time sighing against his ear.

He remembered Matthew, his friend, and attempted to beat down the desire that threatened to dishonor him and the woman he had sworn to protect.

He eased her off him, wrapped the blanket about her, and stacked more wood on the fire. While she slept, he watched the flames play across her face, and he felt a deep, burning need start in his loins and move to his heart. She had awakened something in him that went beyond desire.

Saber Vincente had touched his heart.

No matter how hard he tried, he couldn't suppress the desire that coiled inside him, and he

tightened the corded muscles that made his
trousers damned tight and uncomfortable.

Saber slept blissfully, not knowing that she was
affecting Reese in any way. It was hours later
when she heard the horse stomping and opened
her eyes. Reese had already saddled the animal
and was loading their meager supplies.

She stretched her arms over her head and
yawned. "I slept the whole night through. I
wasn't a bit uncomfortable, were you?"

He glanced at her and turned away. "Put my
coat on and wrap the blanket around your
shoulders."

"But you'll be cold. You keep your own coat.
I'll be just fine with the blanket."

"Miss Vincente, do as I said."

She angrily shoved her hands into the sleeves
and held out her arms so he could see that the
sleeves were far too long. "Are you satisfied?"

"I have never been less satisfied in my life," he
mumbled under his breath. "It's easy to see that
you are accustomed to getting your own way,"
he said so she could hear.

"Really." Her hands went on her hips, and her
eyes sparkled with blue fire. "What part in all
this is my design? If I had my way I'd still have
my horse and the blankets."

Reese smiled to himself, not daring to let her

see his mirth. She was ungracious in defeat. After last night he'd never think of her in the same way again. Not only did he desire her; he was beginning to like her more and more. She was quite a woman and would make a fine wife. Matthew would never know a dull day with her beside him.

But Reese knew that he wanted her for himself, and that that would never happen. Being denied what his body craved suddenly made him cross, and he nodded toward the horse. "It's time to go."

"I'm ready," she said in an irritated voice. "You don't have to speak to me like I am a child."

His annoyance grew until it was full-blown anger—not with her, but with the situation he found himself in. He turned away from her, but not before she saw the corded muscles in his neck, and his clenched teeth.

Why was he acting so strangely? she wondered, watching him walk away. She felt as if a moment of understanding had been lost, a moment when he would have confided in her—but the moment had slipped away.

Chapter Eight

The half-moon shed enough light so that Reese could see ahead to avoid hazards that might cause their horse to stumble. He felt Saber's head slump against his back. "You need to stay awake, Miss Vincente."

She nodded and raised her head, feeling so weary.

"My brother told me that horses don't have the best eyesight at night. This fellow could step in a hole, and then where would we be?"

"That's why I need you to help me watch."

She straightened her spine. If Reese could go on, then so could she. The night seemed endless, and riding astride was causing her to ache in places that had never ached before. There were times when she thought she couldn't stay on the horse, and twice she nodded off. But a harsh word from Reese brought her back to consciousness.

"Can't we stop?" she asked.

"We don't have the protection of being on Comanche land now, so if you want to put miles between us and the Millers, we have to keep moving, Miss Vincente. You can sleep tomorrow—at least half a day."

Wordlessly she watched the trail ahead of them, wondering what power and strength pushed Reese. She guessed he'd stayed awake most of the time while she slept in the squatter's shack. How could he keep going like this without sleep when she was so utterly exhausted?

She tried to think of Matthew, but instead her mind wandered to the letters he'd written to her about Reese Starrett. Suddenly something startling and overwhelming expanded in her chest. Every time Matthew had mentioned Reese in his letters, she had been fascinated by his description of his friend. Reese owned a small ranch past Fort Worth on the Trinity River. He had fought for the South during the war, just as Saber's brother had. Matthew had come to Texas to oversee the location and construction of several army forts that were meant to help control

the Indians and make the area safe for the white
population.

She thought of their encounter with the Comanche. Apparently Reese had no trouble with
the Indians. She imagined that Quanah Parker
had let them pass through his land because he
liked and respected Reese.

Her mind went back to the first time Matthew
had mentioned Reese in one of his letters. Matthew had been overseeing the building of a fort
somewhere in the panhandle of Texas when the
Comanche had attacked, forcing Matthew and
his soldiers to seek protection behind the incom-
plete walls of the fort. According to Matthew's
letter, Reese Starrett had appeared from out of
nowhere that day. He told Matthew to cease fire,
and Reese had gone to talk to the Comanche
chief. After long negations with the Indians on
the army's behalf, Reese had bidden good-bye to
the chief, who had ridden away with his warri-
ors. Perhaps the chief had been Quanah Parker.
Matthew had praised Reese's valor, and wrote
that many lives had been saved that day. After
that, Matthew always seemed to mention Reese
in his letters. But even Saber's imaginings of
Reese could not have made him more perfect
than the real man.

She slumped against his back, then drew herself up straight. "Please, can't we stop and camp soon?"

He felt her limp hands clasped about his waist and nodded. "Yes, I believe we can. If you can make it for another mile, I know a place we can camp and light a fire."

She only hoped she would be able to make it that extra mile without falling asleep.

Reese had found a campsite on a plateau, where they could see the countryside in every direction. For shelter, there was a rock formation with a wide overhang and walls that would protect them from the wind. Bone-chilling wind rippled through the buffalo grass, which was as high as a horse's haunches.

Saber slid to the ground and blew on her fingers to warm them while Reese unsaddled their horse. By the time he'd joined her, she was having trouble keeping her eyes open. He laid a fire and then placed the warmed blanket about her. A contented sigh slipped through her lips.

When he returned to camp after hobbling the horse, he sat down with his rifle resting across his lap. Saber was asleep, and he watched how the dancing flames from the campfire flickered across her pale skin. He allowed himself to feast on her beauty. She was like the brightness of the sun, and as far above him as the sun was from the earth. She was pure Texas aristocrat, and he was just a broken-down cowboy with a small ranch and a few hundred head of cattle.

A strange, piercing ache filled his heart, fanning out through his chest. He could never have her, or even touch her, as he wanted to. She was silk, and he was leather. She was a lady, and she belonged to his friend Matthew, and he would never betray a friend.

His body tensed when he thought of her lying in Matthew's arms, Matthew touching her and kissing those inviting lips—yes, she belonged to Matthew. He felt desire run wild through his body as he considered what it would feel like to have her beneath him.

"Damn," he ground out, and shot to his feet. He walked in the direction of the horse and stood for a long time staring up at the moon. He had to make a decision about what to do with Miss Vincente. His first concern had to be her safety. He didn't think it would be wise to take her back to Fort Worth. Felton would be in Mexico now, waiting for the Miller brothers to deliver Saber to him. When he realized that he'd been tricked, he would send someone else to find her. Neither Felton nor the Millers knew Reese's true identity, so she would be safe with him for a while. There was no use sending the law to Mexico after Felton; he would be gone before they could get there. There were the Miller brothers to worry about, also. They would soon find out that their brother, Earl, was dead, and in their bungling way they would be a problem. He could keep her at his ranch until either Matthew or her brother could come after her.

He turned his face up to the night sky. There was a storm coming—he could feel it in his bones. He had to get her out of this weather as soon as possible.

Was he taking her to his ranch because he wanted to keep her with him longer, or for her own protection? Hell, he didn't know anymore.

Saber woke to the aroma of frying bacon. She blinked her eyes and found Reese kneeling beside her, offering her a cup of coffee.

"Careful, the tin cup is hot," he cautioned.

"Where did you get that?" she asked in amazement.

"It was in my saddlebag."

She gave him a smile and handed him back his coat. "Thank you for this. Thank you for everything. I know you risked your life to rescue me."

Then she looked into his eyes, and he almost melted. "No thanks are necessary."

She snuggled closer to the fire. "That's not the way I see it."

He shot to his feet, and his gaze went to the western horizon. "I was just doing my job, ma'am. Your major is paying me to bring you back, so don't go making me out to be a hero."

She nodded, feeling crushing disappointment at his words. "I thank you all the same. You did put yourself in danger for me."

When she stood and moved closer to him, Reese noticed that the top of her head came just above his shoulder. She was tall for a woman, but small-boned and fragile. How had she survived the rough handling of the Miller brothers? His voice was gruff when he spoke. "You'll have to wash from the canteen, since there's no creek nearby."

She glanced at the bacon sizzling in the iron skillet. "I'll make do. Now why don't you tend to the horse, and I'll see to the cooking."

He arched a dark brow. "You can cook?"

Laughter sparkled in her eyes. "Mr. Starrett, you might be interested to know I'm a very good cook."

His mouth eased into a grin. "I'll trust you on that, ma'am. I'll just get more wood for the fire."

Saber hummed to herself while she went through his saddlebag and found flour, then mixed the ingredients for pan biscuits. By the time Reese had returned, she was turning golden biscuits onto a tin plate.

Saber ate one biscuit and half a slice of bacon, while Reese hungrily devoured four biscuits and most of the bacon.

"Well?" she asked, watching him bite into the last biscuit with relish. "Can I cook?"

He gave her a slow grin. "Yes, ma'am, you can cook. But can you cook real food?"

"Real food?"

"In a kitchen."

"Of course I can. Why would you doubt it?"

"You are a Vincente. Somehow I can't imagine you in an apron—silks and satins maybe, but not an apron."

Saber's usual good nature plummeted. How could he have such an unflattering opinion of her? Dark lashes fell across her eyes to hide her hurt. "I don't see what the one has to do with the other."

"Ma'am, this isn't a gentle land, and most of the women out here work hard and are old before their time. That will never happen to you. You were born a lady to adorn the arm of a gentleman. Probably most men wilt when you bless them with your smile. But when they look at you, most of them will have one thing on their minds and one thing only."

She was incensed. "Perhaps you have just described yourself, Mr. Starrett, but I doubt there are many more like you." She dipped her head, thinking of the Miller brothers. She still didn't know what had happened to her while she'd been unconscious.

He looked at her lazily while shoving bullets into the chamber of his six-gun. "I described myself right enough, Miss Vincente. I appreciate a beautiful woman as much as any man, and I appreciate your looks. I don't care if I have your good opinion, but I'd not object to having you in my bed. Of course, that will never happen, but I have my fantasies."

Her cheeks flamed, and she glared at him, wondering why he was speaking so coarsely when he never had before. Then she noticed that his attention wasn't on her at all. He appeared to be looking over her right shoulder. "You are right about that, sir. I would never lie in your bed, and I don't care to be part of your fantasies."

His eyes were sharp, compelling, intense, sending an unspoken message that she didn't understand. He took her arm, and she tried to jerk away, but he was too strong for her. He held her steady.

Saber watched him ease his thumb toward the trigger. "Maybe not, but you sure as hell need my protection." He raised his gun, and she screamed, thinking he was going to shoot her. But in a quick motion he knocked her to the ground and fired into the bushes just behind her.

Reese stood over her. She couldn't move because the fall had knocked the wind out of her, and she was having trouble catching her breath.

When he spoke, Reese's voice took on a hard, commanding tone. "I know you're there. The next bullet won't be over your head. Come out slowly with your hands over your head."

Saber rubbed her shoulder and got shakily to her feet just as a man called out in a heavy Spanish accent, "Don't shoot, señor. I am coming out now."

"Tell your amigo to join us," Reese said in a steely voice. "Tell him to throw his gun out first."

Saber let out a surprised cry and rushed past Reese to throw her arms around her brother's *gran vaquero*. "Alejandro, I am so glad to see you!" She turned to Reese with anger in her eyes. "You could have killed him! Why didn't you ask who it was instead of talking crazy and shooting wild?"

"If I had wanted to put a hole in him, I would have." Reese still held his gun pointed at Alejandro. "I don't know this man. And there is still his friend lurking in the bushes. Tell him to come out—*now!*"

A white-haired man poked his head around the bush and grinned when he saw Saber. "Your brother's tearing up the countryside looking for you, Miss Saber. Is this man friend or foe?"

She glared at Reese. "I'm not sure at the moment, Zeb. How did you find us?"

The old man let out a spew of tobacco juice and scratched his white hair. "Well, sir, Noble sent men in every direction a-looking for you. Me and Alejandro came upon your tracks last night. Didn't know iffen it was you or not, but we followed anyway."

Saber smiled at Zeb, who was so dear to her. He ambled toward her, seemingly unafraid of the man with the gun pointed at him. "He hasn't hurt you none, has he, Miss Saber?"

"No. He hasn't hurt me. Zeb, Alejandro, meet Reese Starrett. He rescued me from the kidnappers."

Alejandro still looked suspicious and kept a protective arm around Saber, while Zeb planted his body between them. "We're much obliged to you for your help. But we'll just be taking Miss Saber off your hands now."

Reese shook his head. "No, I don't think so. Miss Vincente stays with me!"

Saber and the two men turned to look at Reese in surprise. Zeb was the first to speak. "Now, just what makes you suppose that we'll leave her with you?"

"Because when you think about it, you'll realize that it's the best and only way to protect her. The Miller brothers and Graham Felton will all be combing the countryside searching for her, and they want her real bad. I'm taking her to my spread, where she'll be protected. The two of you find her brother, tell him what happened, and inform him that his sister's under my protection. You will also want to get word to Major Halloway and let him know she's come to no harm."

"I'm supposing this Graham Felton is the one what took her out of the hotel," Zeb stated.

Reese shook his head. "Graham Felton paid the Miller brothers to kidnap her. You might want to tell her brother that."

"Well, now, I'll just do that very thing," Zeb said. "But I'll be taking Miss Saber with me all the same. Her brother wouldn't want us leaving her with you," Zeb said, inching closer to Saber. "You see, we don't really know you. And we don't know that you're who you say you are."

Reese gazed eastward. "You don't really have any choice in the matter. A storm is coming our way. It'll hit by tomorrow. We need to get her out of this cold, and my ranch is the closest place to do that."

The *gran vaquero* nodded in agreement. "There is a storm coming, amigo." His gaze went to his *patron's* sister. "Is this what you want to do, Señorita Saber—stay with this man? Do you trust him?"

She smiled at Alejandro's concern for her. "I believe it will be best to stay with him. I know my brother won't rest until the Millers and Mr. Felton are behind bars, and I would only be in his way." She looked at Reese. Although she was still angry with him, she knew it would be wise to go with him. "Are you sure you don't mind taking me with you?"

He was surprised she'd agreed to accompany him without an argument. "It's the only way I can keep you safe."

Saber realized in that moment that she had become entangled in Reese's life, and she didn't want to leave him. She turned her gaze on the *gran vaquero*. "You and Zeb will sleep here tonight, and tomorrow morning head out to find Noble to assure him that I have come to no harm."

Zeb nodded reluctantly. "If that's the way you want it."

"It is," she assured him.

Zeb took her arm and led her a little away from the others so he could speak privately with her. "You sure you're all right, Miss Saber?"

She laughed and hugged him. "Yes, I am sure."

He scratched his beard. "I almost didn't know

you all dressed like a boy, and none too clean at that."

She glanced down at her filthy trousers. "I know. I can't imagine what Noble would say if he could see me wearing these. I am tired, dirty, and I long for a bath—but thanks to Reese Starrett, I am unharmed."

"If you want to leave with us, just say so."

"Reese wouldn't hurt me, Zeb. And if I went with you, I'd only slow you down." She glanced down at her trousers again. "As you see, I'm not properly dressed to ride about the country."

He was still reluctant. "If you're sure . . ."

Saber studied the crusty old cowhand who had come to live at Casa del Sol when her brother had married Rachel. In a short time Saber had grown fond of the old man who was her sister-in-law's watchdog. "What do you know about Reese Starrett, Zeb?"

"I heard he's one tough son-of a—er, a tough 'un. But I never heard anything bad said 'bout him. Got himself a spread not far from here. They say he's a loner. No one knows much about his past. I reckon it don't matter none, though. It's more important that he's respected and feared. Make no mistake about it, Miss Saber; he's deadly with a gun and meaner than hell— eh, begging your pardon, Miss Saber—eh, he's as mean as they come."

She placed her small hand on Zeb's rough one. "He won't hurt me, Zeb. He's Matthew's friend."

"Yeah. Like I said, he's a man of honor. I've heard that 'bout him."

"Tell Noble not to worry about me. Tell him to be careful when he catches up with the Miller brothers. The two older ones are ruthless, but the younger one, Sam, is only a boy. He was good to me, and kept Eugene Miller from . . . from harming me."

Zeb nodded. "I'll tell Noble, but I 'spect it won't make no matter to him. He'll want to see them all dead."

Reese appeared beside them. "Tell your boss that there are only two Miller brothers now. I had to kill Earl."

Saber recoiled from Reese, feeling fear crawl up her spine. He could be ruthless, and he could kill a man. Still, she could not find it in her to be sorry that Earl Miller was dead.

The campfire had almost gone out, and Saber slept peacefully on the clean blanket Alejandro had given her. The three men talked in low voices so they wouldn't disturb her. She sighed in her sleep, not knowing that Reese was staring at her.

Reese's heart was light because Saber had agreed to go with him. He'd insisted partly because he wanted to protect her, but he was honest enough with himself to admit that he didn't want to give her up—not just yet. He leaned back against his saddle, wondering why he wanted to hold onto her. She didn't belong to him, and she never would.

"Hell," he muttered, turning his back to her and closing his eyes. She was getting past the barrier he'd built around his heart, and a woman was the last thing he wanted in his life—especially Matthew's intended bride!

Chapter Nine

The next morning Zeb and Alejandro had saddled their horses and were ready to ride out before the first light of dawn touched the eastern horizon.

Saber stood looking up at Zeb. "Tell my brother not to worry about me. I will be safe. And don't let him go out on his own looking for the Millers or Mr. Felton. You know how he is."

Zeb switched a hunk of tobacco from one side of his jaw to the other, looking doubtful. "Now, Miss Saber, you know iffen Noble takes it into his head to do something, no one's gonna talk him from it, 'cepting maybe Rachel."

Saber nodded. Her sister-in-law was the only

one who could tame Noble's impulsive spirit. "The trouble is, Rachel is at Casa del Sol, and Noble is probably in a temper. Alejandro, you try to talk some sense into him. Have him tell the marshal or the sheriff what has happened. Don't let him act impulsively."

"I will try, Señorita Saber. It could be that he will want to first see for himself that you have not suffered at the hands of the Millers."

"I know. And you must convince him that I have come to no harm." She laid her hand on Alejandro's. "Tell him where I am. He can come and see for himself if he wants to."

The *gran vaquero* nodded. "The Starrett Ranch is known to me—I will tell him you are there." Then Alejandro's gaze went to Reese. "Keep her safe, señor." It sounded like a warning. "I want no harm to come to her. Her brother would not like it if it did, and neither would I."

Reese gave a quick nod. "We are all of the same mind."

Saber stepped back and watched Zeb and Alejandro ride away. Lost in thought, she didn't hear Reese when he came up beside her.

"We'd better ride, Miss Vincente."

Saber nodded. She was worried about Noble. "Perhaps I should have gone with them. Or maybe I should go to Casa del Sol and tell Rachel what has happened."

"I don't think so." He steered her toward the horse. "We are only a day's ride from my place. It's a seven-day ride to Casa del Sol."

Saber knew he was right. "I worry so about Noble's impulsive nature."

"It must run in the family," Reese observed.

"It does. That's why I'm worried. I am very like my brother in that way. You can see why I'm concerned. I know what he'll do." She mounted and turned to watch Zeb and Alejandro ride over a rise and out of sight. "If you knew my brother, you would realize that he's a force to be reckoned with."

"That's as it should be. Let him handle this in his own way. A man has the right to defend his sister."

"He might get himself killed."

"Of all the things I have heard of your brother, I have never heard him called a fool. He will want to know why Graham Felton had you kidnapped in the first place. I would expect no less of him. And until we can find out that reason, you will never be completely safe."

"You are right, of course."

Reese mounted and pulled her up behind him. The brown, muscled horse galloped down the mesa with ease. They rode silently and steadily all morning. But Saber could not banish the dark uneasiness that clouded her mind.

129

*   *   *

The last dying rays of the sun fell softly, bathing the countryside in its golden light. Reese made camp in a grove of oak and sycamore trees that helped protect them from the continuous wind.

Saber shaded her eyes and gazed out on the land, which seemed almost magical in the dying light. She had never been in this part of Texas and had not known it was so wooded.

Reese came up beside her, reading her thoughts. "You should see it in the spring and summer. It's green and lush with cottonwood and hickory trees in foliage. There are bramble bushes and dense thickets for as far as the eye can see."

Her gaze followed the brown water that snaked and circled between the trees to be lost beyond the cliffs.

"I love it here now. I can only imagine what it would look like in the spring," she said softly. "It's breathtaking."

Reese stood beside her, and for a long moment they both stared at the countryside, sharing the beautiful sunset. "We are on my land, Saber. I'm glad you like it."

She turned to him, pleased that he had called her by her first name. "I thought you had only a small spread?"

"I did. I just bought this land two months

130

ago." Of course, he didn't tell her that he'd saved every dollar he could get to buy the land, and that it left him very little to live on.

Reese turned away. "I'll set up camp. There's firewood and fresh water aplenty here."

"How far is it to your ranch house?"

"We will be there before noon tomorrow. I wish I could have gotten you out of the weather today, but the horse is just too tired to push any farther."

"Will this storm be as bad as the one two nights ago?" She glanced at the dark clouds in the distance. "They don't look too menacing."

"One can never tell in this part of Texas. It will hit later this evening."

He looked worried, and she knew his concern was for her. Wanting to reassure him, she touched his hand. "I have the second blanket Alejandro gave me."

He looked at her for a moment and then said, "Let's eat."

Later, they sat around the campfire, having eaten and tended the horse. The storm still hadn't struck, and it wasn't so cold near the fire.

"Reese, I'm trying to picture you in a domestic setting. Is there a woman in your life?"

"I'm not married, if that's what you're asking."

She made a wide sweep with her hand. "There

must be someone you want to share all this with."

When he glanced down at her, there was smoldering fire in his eyes. Saber was caught by the moment and could not look away. Reese didn't have the chiseled, aristocratic looks of her brother or the boyish good looks of Matthew. His features were harsher, his eyes disturbing, as if he'd lived hard and cared about nothing—and no one.

"There is no woman I want to share my life with." He turned away so she wouldn't see the pain in his eyes. He'd share it with her, he thought, chastising himself for coveting Matthew's bride-to-be.

Saber felt sad because he seemed so alone. "The wind has intensified," she remarked, turning her thoughts to the weather.

"Yes, I know. Don't wander far from camp. I've heard of people freezing to death just steps away from their houses."

"I know about northers. I'm from west Texas, remember?" She shivered with a sudden chill. "It already feels like the temperature is dropping."

"I'm going to shelter the horse. You'd better get under the blanket. We can't have a fire in this wind."

Saber rushed about, gathering supplies and

shoving them into his saddlebag. Then she took her blanket and moved against the wide trunk of a cottonwood tree to find protection from the bitter cold. In just a few minutes, the temperature had dropped drastically.

Moments later, Reese joined her. Sitting beside her, he draped all the blankets around both of them and pulled her into his arms.

"It'll be warmer this way," he said, smiling when she looked at him questioningly.

That was all the encouragement Saber needed. She curled against him, melting into his arms. She laid her head against his shoulder, feeling the deep intake of his breath. In that moment, something poignant and alarming happened to her. She felt as if she'd been born to be with Reese. She knew in a rush of feelings that this was love—deep, lasting love. She wanted to live with him, bear his children, grow old with him.

She loved Reese! Oh, how could this have happened? She had thought she loved Matthew, but that hadn't been love, not like this. The powerful feelings she had for Reese were nothing like the young girl's affection she'd felt for Matthew. She turned her head and rested her cheek against his neck, allowing warmth and love to flood through her body.

What would Reese do if he knew what she was

feeling? Would he despise her for betraying his friend? She despised herself for being faithless. She was going to marry Matthew—why had this happened to her now?

Her hand moved up his hard chest to rest there. If this was love, it was the most painful feeling she had yet experienced.

His voice was deep as he pulled her tighter against him. "You'd better get some sleep. I'll keep you warm."

She sighed, touching her lips to his throat and feeling him stiffen. She turned her face away, wanting to stay awake all night so she could savor this time. This was the last time she would feel his arms about her. And maybe the last time they would be alone together.

At last she fell asleep, feeling safe and warm, although the cold wind struck with a punishing force. Reese held her to him, wishing this night would never end.

It was after midnight when the wind died down. Reese's body was cramped from remaining in one position for so long, and his arm had no feeling in it. Yet he wouldn't move for any reason, because he held his sleeping love close to his heart. Tomorrow he would have to let her go, but tonight she belonged to him.

He glanced down at her. She looked so innocent curled up in his arms, so trusting. She had been protected all her life, and she trusted too easily. Hell, if she knew what was on his mind, she'd come awake fast enough. She wasn't aware of the swell of his erection as he thought about her sleeping naked in his arms. He wanted her more than he'd ever wanted a woman before. He reminded himself again that she was the one woman in the world he could never have.

She stirred, opened her eyes, and smiled at him. It had begun to drizzle, and a cold wind whipped through the valley, but to Reese it seemed that the sun was captured in her smile.

Saber nestled her head against his shoulder, reluctant to move. "How long have you been awake?" she asked sleepily.

His voice was low, his tone strained. "Quite a while." He could have told her that he hadn't been to sleep because her soft body was driving him out of his mind. He gazed down at her and admitted, "I have been watching you sleep."

Her hand went to his shoulder, and she sank further into him, seeking his warmth. "Why?"

"You remind me of a kitten curled up by the fire."

"I'm not sure that's a flattering comparison."

"Mm-hm. Yes, it is."

She smiled again. "That's not fair. Watching

135

someone sleep is a little like eavesdropping, don't you think?"

"Maybe. But you are so pretty when you sleep."

She was accustomed to being complimented, and she had no false modesty and was too honest to play coy. "Thank you, sir. I was beginning to think you didn't know I was a woman."

He wanted to let his hand slide down and touch one of the breasts that were so enchantingly pressed against his chest. "I am all too aware that you're a woman," he said gruffly, knowing they should get ready to leave now. But he was still reluctant to break contact with her.

She moved forward, stretched her arms over her head, and stood in a motion that was so provocative he had to look away or risk throwing her on the ground and ripping her clothing off.

What in the hell was wrong with him? He'd never been on the verge of losing control with a woman before now. He rolled to his feet and shook out the blankets. "If you think you can hold off eating, we'll be at my ranch in time for the noon meal." He gazed up at the darkened sky, and it looked like it might snow. "It would be best if we hurried."

She took the blankets from him and went about rolling them in a bundle. "I am ready to ride when you are. I confess it will be nice to be under a roof." She laughed out loud. "Of course, you kept me warm last night."

He let out a slow breath. Being with her was sweet torture, and she didn't even know that he wanted her so damned badly that he could think of nothing else. "I'll get the horse," he said, stalking off down the hill.

It had grown colder and had begun to snow. The wind whipped the snow into stinging shards that irritated Saber's cheeks. The horse was tired from going against the wind, and she hoped the poor animal would make it to the ranch house.

They topped a hill, and Reese halted the horse. "Hold on. We're almost home."

Saber glanced at the log house with the wide front porch and shutters at the windows. There was a huge barn and several outbuildings that looked freshly painted, and the corrals looked in good repair. "Can we hurry?" she asked urgently. "I'm so cold."

He nodded and nudged the horse down the hill. He wondered what Saber's reaction would be to his small house. It was here that their differences would become apparent, and he would be able to distance himself from her; at least, he hoped that would be the case.

Saber hunched her shoulders and braced herself against his strong back. The horse was moving slowly, the tired animal had given its all. The only things she could think about at the moment were a good warm fire, a hot bath, and a soft bed.

Chapter Ten

Saber was so cold that Reese had to lift her down from the horse. As snow whirled all around them, he took her hand and led her into the house.

A rush of warm air hit Saber's face as she stepped inside. A cheerful fire burned in the fireplace, and Reese guided her to the warmth. He took a brightly colored Indian blanket from the back of a chair and placed it around her shoulders.

"Stay here where it's warm. I'm going to see to the horse."

Her teeth were chattering, and she could do no more than nod. She dropped down in front of the fire, basking in its warmth. When she was able to move, she glanced around the room. The log walls had been honed and smoothed and whitewashed. A woven Indian rug covered the plank floor, and several Indian artifacts hung on the walls. Three rifles hung over the fireplace, and a coatrack stood near the door. There was a small high-backed bench and two straight-backed chairs. A battered desk was the only other furniture, and she noticed the neat stacks of paper on top. A shelf attached to the wall held several books. There were no curtains at the two small windows, no womanly frills of any kind. It was a man's room, and surprisingly neat and clean.

She could see a bed through one of the doors, so she supposed the door to her left would lead to a kitchen.

Saber heard someone stomping the snow off his feet outside the kitchen and thought Reese had returned. But a young boy entered with an armload of firewood. She judged him to be no more than fourteen or fifteen.

He placed more logs on the fire and put the rest in a wood bin. Only then did he remove his hat, smiling brightly. "I'm Jake Kendrick, ma'am. Reese asked me to tell you he'd be in shortly."

He had sandy hair and soft brown eyes and a

shy smile. She could tell that he was nervous, because he kept shuffling his feet, so she tried to put him at ease. "I'm pleased to meet you, Jake. My name is Saber Vincente. Do you live here at the ranch?"

"Yes, ma'am. Me, Gabe Cooper, and Miguel are Reese's hired hands. Miguel's wife, Rosita, is the washwoman." He nodded toward the door. "We live in the bunkhouse, just beyond the barn, and Miguel and Rosita live in a small house just beyond that."

Saber smiled at the amount of information Jake imparted to her in such a short time. She'd already learned more from him than Reese had told her in all the time they had spent together.

Jake backed toward the door and planted his hat on his head, then touched the brim. "Ma'am."

Cold wind swirled through the room when he opened the front door. After he'd gone, she frowned thoughtfully. She knew so little about Reese; he never talked about himself. He had not mentioned anything to her about his ranch hands. But of course he'd have hired hands to help out on the ranch. Otherwise he could not have gone looking for her.

She was luxuriating in the blissful warmth when the door opened and Reese entered. He hung his coat and hat on the coatrack and came

141

toward the fire. She moved over so he could sit beside her.

"Storm's getting worse," he said worriedly. "I'll probably lose more cattle before it blows itself out. Gabe said we've already lost twenty head."

"I'm not surprised. It's been an unusually harsh winter. I'm so sorry about your cattle."

He tossed several more logs on the fire. "I keep forgetting you are a rancher's daughter." He gazed down at her. "Of course, your brother could lose several thousand head, and it wouldn't hurt him."

"It wouldn't hurt him now. But there was a time when Noble had to struggle to keep Casa del Sol from being taken for taxes." She looked into his eyes, suddenly feeling angry. "You don't have a very high regard for my family, do you?"

There was remorse in his silver eyes. "I know it sounds that way to you, but you are wrong. The Vincente name is well respected in the state. And you have my greatest respect."

"Then why do you—"

He couldn't tell her that he had to use every means at his disposal to keep her at arm's length. He knew he shouldn't strike out at her with cruel words, but he couldn't seem to stop himself. "I have lived too much away from civilization, and my social graces aren't what they should be. I don't know how to treat a woman like you."

"You treat a woman like me just as you would treat any other woman. Actually, you have been wonderful to me, except for the times when you imply that I'm spoiled and always want my own way. Who else would have gone right into the Miller brothers' hideout to rescue a woman he didn't even know?"

He touched her arm. "Sometimes I speak without thinking. Please forgive me."

A tender smile formed on her lips. "Of course."

"Have you ever had to do without anything you really wanted?" he asked, trying to understand her. He was feeling unsure of himself because he was all too aware of the shabbiness of his house now that she was in it.

She stared into the fire for a moment before answering. "I have known extremely hard times, Reese."

He cursed himself for a fool. She had been kidnapped, roughly handled, probably not fed well, and might have suffered other atrocities that she didn't care to share with him. He still wasn't sure if the Miller brothers had violated her. "I'm sorry," he said softly. "I shouldn't have said that. You have gone through an experience no woman should ever have to endure."

"I wasn't even thinking about the Miller brothers. It goes back much further than that. While Noble was away during the war, my father was dying, although I didn't know it at the time. He sent me to Georgia to live with my grandparents, not knowing they had died during the winter. He thought I would be safe with them."

"Your mother was already dead?"

"Yes. She died when I was small. I hardly remember her. There was a time when I thought everyone dear to me had died, even Noble."

Reese could only imagine what she had suffered. This was a side of her he had never suspected. He wasn't sure Matthew fully valued this woman he was to marry. "What did you do in Georgia?"

"My aunt was the only family I had living back there. Late in the war, the Yankees tore through Georgia, burning, killing, and destroying. The plantation house was burned, the valuables stolen, and the livestock confiscated by the enemy. My aunt and I sought sanctuary in the overseer's crude, empty cabin that was half the size of this room. We had no food, no clothing, and I believe we would both have died if I hadn't met Matthew."

"So that's how you met? Matthew never told me."

She ran a delicate finger over the knee of her

frayed trousers. "I imagined he would have told you that."

"No. He keeps a lot of his thoughts about you to himself."

She met his eyes and smiled. "I met you through the letters he wrote me. Matthew thinks very highly of you. To read his letters, one would think there is nothing you can't do."

He rose to his feet, and her gaze followed the line of his long, lean body. "I'll just fix us something to eat."

She stood up beside him and placed her hand on his arm. "I'll help you."

"Not this time. You have been through a lot in the past weeks. I'll take care of you tonight."

She looked so sweet with the firelight playing on her golden hair and reflecting in her blue eyes. Reese wanted to grab her and press her against his aching body. He suddenly felt empty inside, realizing for the first time how lonely his life had been without a wife. He hadn't thought this way before—hell, he'd had plenty of women over the years. He couldn't think of any woman he'd wanted that he couldn't get. But Saber was different. He could never have her. If fate hadn't thrown them together, they would never have met. If they had met on the street, she would probably have passed him without even noticing him.

He reminded himself that she'd been born to be the jewel of some man's heart, to be paraded around as a prize, and Matthew was that man. He allowed his mind to go further, and speculated on how it would feel to slide between her legs, to have her lips on his, to feel her breasts in his hands. He suddenly felt hot and shaken.

He had to stop thinking like this! He would never know the taste of those lips or feel her writhing beneath him in the heat of passion.

"Damn," he said, twisting away from her and striding out of the room. He'd never allowed any woman to get under his skin as Saber had. She was in his blood, tangled in his mind, and he couldn't get her out. It was going to be a living hell, being snowbound with her and being tempted every day.

Saber was puzzled by his strange change of mood. She walked to the window, peering out at the snow. It was a bad storm, and she couldn't see as far as the barn. It made her sad that Reese would lose some of his herd.

Closing her eyes, she leaned her forehead against the windowpane, feeling guilty because most of her thoughts were of Reese and not of Matthew. If Reese only knew how she saw him— he was her hero and always would be.

She moved restlessly about the parlor and then went to the bedroom and stood in the doorway. The room was small, it held only a bed, a night table with a pitcher and a lamp, and a slatted chair in the corner. She advanced into the room, thinking this room would reveal more of Reese's personality. She picked up a book and wrinkled her nose at the title: *Fielding's Technique of Animal Husbandry*.

"Well, Mr. Starrett, your reading habits give me very little insight into your character," she said aloud. "My brother has this book."

The bed was covered with an indigo and green Indian coverlet, and on the floor was a braided rug. She saw a bootjack and a pair of boots in the corner. There was a holster and a six-gun hanging from a wall peg.

There was nothing of the man here. Nothing to tell her who Reese was. There were no pictures of his family—no treasures from family members. She had the saddest feeling that he had no childhood memories to cherish.

She went back into the parlor and glanced at the books there. Running her finger down the titles, she smiled. Now these were interesting, but they puzzled her further. There was Homer's *Iliad*, poems by Thomas Hood, and Phillip Green's *Guide to Arabian Horses*. His choice of books was as complicated as the man himself.

When he called out to Saber, it startled her as if she'd been caught snooping. She quickly shoved the books back into the shelf.

"I have the kitchen warmed up. You can come to the table and eat."

She spun around, finding him standing behind her. "I'm starved."

He glanced down at her. "I have never known a time when you weren't hungry."

She entered the kitchen and observed that the room had an unused feeling about it. Reese's large size made the room feel even smaller, and he seemed uncomfortable in this setting. He moved to the stove, spearing bacon and placing it on two plates.

"I'm sorry about the food. The kitchen isn't my domain."

Saber sat in the chair he indicated and sniffed the air, taking the cup of coffee he handed her. "It looks delicious to me," she said, watching him, awkwardly scrape eggs out of an iron skillet.

Reese sat across from her, and they ate in silence for awhile. It seemed that now that they faced each other over a table, they were having a hard time communicating. Saber had so much she wanted to ask him, but her questions would be prying into his private life. Now was not the time to question him, she thought, taking a bite of the fluffy egg.

"I cook better on the trail," Reese said, watching her carefully.

"A man shouldn't have to cook, Reese. You should have a wife to do it for you."

He smiled slightly. "Now, I have never thought of food as a reason to take a wife."

"Well, a wife has more functions than just putting food on your table."

He paused with his fork halfway to his mouth. "Such as?"

"Well . . ." Her brow puckered. "I can't say you need a housekeeper, because everything is neat and orderly."

"Jake keeps the place clean for me."

"Well, you must want children. A man should have a son to carry on his name."

"Have you appointed yourself as a one-woman committee to get me married?" He took a bite of bacon and stabbed his fork into another. "I do very well without a wife, thank you. If I want a woman—" He broke off, somehow resenting her for thinking he needed a woman.

"I'm sorry," she said, standing up and gathering her dishes. "I know it's none of my business."

"Damned right it isn't!"

He rose abruptly and left the kitchen, returning with his coat and hat. "I'll be late. When you

are ready to go to bed, you can have the bedroom."

"I don't want to take your bed."

He stared at her for a moment. "I'll bunk with
Jake and Gabe."

He was startled when she lunged at him, and
he had to catch her in his arms.

"No, Reese. I don't want to sleep in this house
alone. I want you with me." Her stomach tightened in a knot, and she could hardly draw a
breath, she was so frightened. She shook her
head, confused by her own feelings. "What is it?
What have I done to make you so angry with
me?"

His chest expanded, and he reached out to
touch her cheek. "Everything about you makes
me angry," he answered harshly, with a cruel
slant to his mouth. "You don't have any idea
what you are doing to me, do you?"

She knew what he was doing to her, but she
didn't know how to answer his question. She
shook her head and replied softly, "No, I don't."

He could feel her trembling and realized that
she was really afraid of being left alone. He
should have realized she had not yet recovered
from her ordeal.

He captured her in a protective clasp. "Of
course you don't want to be alone. I just have
some chores to do. I'll be back before dark."

Saber touched his face, feeling the stubble of his beard, dazed by the pleasure she felt at being close to him. "You won't forget?" she asked in a throaty voice.

He dislodged her from his arms and walked toward the door. "No, I won't forget."

The house felt empty when he left. Saber began doing the dishes while she tried to conquer her fear. What if she spent the rest of her life frightened when Reese wasn't with her? She realized that not even her brother, Noble, made her feel safe the way Reese did.

Why was that? she wondered.

Chapter Eleven

Saber cleaned the kitchen, then went into the parlor, where she found a stack of quilts on the chair. She spread them before the fire so Reese could keep warm. She was so tired when she made her way to the bedroom. A smile lit her face when she saw that Reese had placed one of his flannel shirts across the foot of the bed. She was sure he wanted her to use it as a nightgown.

Cold air hit her when she undressed, but she still took the time to pour water into the bowl and quickly wash herself. Shivering, she pulled the soft flannel shirt over her head. She laughed when it fell to her knees and the sleeves covered her hands. She rolled up the sleeves and climbed into bed, hoping Reese would have a comfortable night on the pallet.

She buried her face in his pillow and sank into the mattress where his body usually lay. A strange contentment came over her, and she could see herself spending the rest of her life in this house . . . in this bed with Reese.

The truth had been there for her to see all the time, but she had been too confused to recognize it. She had fallen in love with Reese. Not the idealistic love of a young girl who had been overwhelmed by Matthew's handsomeness and his kindness to her when she needed it most. What she felt for Reese was the love of a woman who wanted to share her life with him, to have his children, to stand beside him in hard times and laugh with him in good times. She wanted to press herself into his arms and never leave him.

Reese was as different from Matthew as two men could be. Matthew was from a prominent Philadelphia family, always saying the right thing, his manners impeccable. He had the kind of looks that drew gasps from young ladies. Reese would never feel at home in a drawing room; his hands were callused from hard work. He was a man to fear if you were his enemy, but a man to be trusted if you were his friend. He was honorable, trustworthy, a man of the land.

Thinking about the cattle Reese would lose before this blizzard blew itself out brought tears to her eyes. She already knew he was not a man to give up. He'd fight on no matter what the odds. He'd work hard to rebuild his herd, and she wanted to be beside him and help him.

She rolled to her side and watched the snowflakes drift slowly past the window. Noble would respect Reese, because they were very much alike. She frowned, wondering if her brother would like Matthew when they finally met. She pulled the covers to her chin, relishing the feel of a soft bed. In no time at all, she was asleep.

Noble Vincente's dark gaze pierced Zeb and Alejandro. "Why in the hell did you leave my sister with that man? I don't know him, and I sure as hell don't trust him."

Zeb bit off a chunk of tobacco and let the *gran vaquero* of Casa del Sol explain Saber's actions to her brother.

"*Patrón*, it was Señorita Saber's wish to remain with Señor Starrett. She trusts him, and so do I. She is in no danger from him."

Noble paced the length of the hotel room and back again, stopping before Alejandro. "Did it occur to either of you that her reputation might suffer when it's learned that she's staying with him without a chaperon?"

Zeb ambled forward and fixed Noble with a sagacious glance. "I'm a-thinking that people will say what they want to no matter what. I've heard talk about her being alone with the Miller brothers. I don't like it any, but people'll always sink their teeth in gossip."

Noble's jaw clamped in a hard line. "What kind of talk, Zeb?"

"I didn't want to tell you, but I 'spect you should know."

"Just say it right out, old man," Noble insisted.

Zeb nodded grimly. "They're a-saying that she can't be pure if she's been with those Miller brothers. Tom Wade was saying they ain't the kind of men to leave her alone, if you know what I mean. I took me a swing at him and cracked his jaw a good-un. He won't be jawing for a time."

Noble seemed to loom over Zeb; his dark eyes held a murderous light. "Show me the men who have said anything about my sister, and they will die today."

Alejandro placed his hand on his patron's shoulder. "You can't kill the whole town. The talk will only grow worse if we call attention to it."

Zeb removed his hat and tossed it on the bed. "The way I see it, Miss Saber is safe with Reese

Starrett. And that frees us up to go hunting for the Miller brothers."

Alejandro's voice was raised in anger as he swooped toward the bed and grabbed Zeb's hat, tossing it to the floor. "You are loco, old man! You should know it's bad luck to put your hat on the bed, and we have had enough of that lately."

Zeb scooped up his hat and planted it on his head, seemingly undaunted by Alejandro's outburst. He knew everyone's temper was frayed, especially Noble's. He wished Rachel were there to calm the situation down. "We got us enough trouble and don't need to start a-fighting each other."

Noble walked to the window and threw the curtain aside. "When did you say Matthew Halloway and his family would be here?"

Alejandro produced the note that had been delivered to him earlier. "The note said by mid-morning."

Noble stared out at the darkened Fort Worth streets, feeling helpless. He wanted to ride out tonight and get his sister; he also wanted to find the Miller brothers and Graham Felton. He could be very patient when the situation called for it. He would take care of the men who had dared touch Saber. He just needed to know she was unharmed.

He glanced back at the two men who watched him expectantly. "While we wait for the Halloways, tell me everything you know about Saber's abduction and rescue by this Reese Starrett. And don't leave out any detail."

Reese bumped his knee on the stone fireplace and muttered an oath beneath his breath. As tall as he was, he was cramped on the small pallet. He turned until he found a comfortable position, knowing his restlessness had more to do with the woman who slept in his bed than the hardness of the floor.

He'd never brought a woman to his ranch. He tried to imagine a wife doing chores around the house, cooking, cleaning, and waiting for him when he got home. But no woman of his acquaintance fit that picture. His imaginary woman took on a form and a face—she was Saber. In his mind he could see her slowly undressing and coming to him naked to nestle in his arms.

He shot up to a sitting position and shook his head to clear it of the haunting vision. Saber hadn't been brought up to do housework or labor on a ranch. So she could cook—that didn't mean she would be willing to do without all the comforts she was accustomed to having. He recalled Matthew telling him that he'd hired a cook and a housekeeper to take care of the house where he and Saber would live after they were married. No, she would not be spending her life cooking in his small kitchen, and she sure as hell would never come to him naked.

He placed another log on the fire, watching sparks shoot up the chimney. Saber was getting under his skin. He didn't know how much more of this he could take. She had woven herself into his mind so tightly he couldn't think of anything but her.

He should have insisted that she leave with Zeb and Alejandro. He'd used the excuse that he could protect her here. Well, who was going to protect her from him if he couldn't control this burning passion that was ripping him apart?

When Saber awoke the next morning, she dressed quickly and went through the house, finding it empty. She was disappointed that Reese had already left. She found a cheerful fire in the parlor, and when she went into the kitchen, she found a pot of coffee on the back of the stove. After she'd eaten a thin slice of bacon, she set about making herself useful. She made her bed, swept, and dusted the house. She washed her dirty clothing and hung it before the fireplace to dry. She then bathed and washed her hair and dressed in the clean trousers and shirt.

Then she waited for Reese to return.

If he was anything like Noble, he'd be out all day trying to save as many head of cattle as he could. He'd need a hot meal when he got home. She rummaged through the well-stocked kitchen shelves until she found the ingredients to prepare a hearty meal.

She had been so busy she hadn't noticed that it was almost sundown. She went to the front door and stepped out onto the porch. The biting wind stung her face. It had stopped snowing, and the clouds had moved away; the brilliant sunset painted the land with a crimson glow. She considered going to the barn to see if Reese was there, but he would only scold her for coming out in the weather. She shivered and stepped back into the house, then went into the kitchen and began kneading bread dough.

Warmth surrounded her heart as she removed an apple pie from the oven and set it on the back of the stove. She was happy and felt as if she belonged there. It felt so right to be preparing a meal for the man she loved. A sudden rush of feeling assaulted her senses, and she found herself wishing that she had the right to be there, to take care of Reese as a wife should.

Her heart was racing so fast it was hard for her to breathe. She dropped down in a chair and lowered her head, overcome with shame and guilt. She should not be having such thoughts about Reese when she was engaged to Matthew. If only she could talk to her sister-in-law, Rachel, perhaps she would be able to figure out why she was having these disturbing feelings for Reese.

Saber was always one to face the truth about herself. She loved Reese, and she probably always would. But duty and honor burned deep within her, and that honor would bind her to Matthew. She was determined that when they were married she would be the best possible wife. She would hide her love for Reese, so Matthew would never know.

The hour grew late, and still Reese had not returned. She opened the door and stared out into the silent darkness. Loneliness pressed in on her, and she shivered from the cold.

Where was Reese?

She went to the kitchen, where it was warmer and laid her head down on the table; before she realized it, she'd fallen asleep.

Reese opened the door and was immediately hit by delicious smells. He removed his coat and hat, put them on the coatrack, and went to the kitchen.

Saber heard his heavy bootsteps and roused

herself. When Reese appeared in the doorway, she smiled. "You must be starved."

"What smells so good?"

Saber went about setting the table. "You might want to invite the others. I made plenty."

He had been thinking about her all day and wondering what she was doing with her time. He saw the apple pie on the back of the stove, and a steaming pot of stew bubbling in the large iron pot.

He moved to the back door and gave her a wide smile. "I'm sure Rosita has food waiting for Miguel, but I'll get Jake and Gabe."

Moments later, Reese reappeared with the other two men in tow. Saber dished up a generous serving of stew for each of them and placed a pan of fresh, hot bread before them.

"Hello, Jake," she said to the young boy who beamed at her. "I don't know how it'll taste. It's been warming for quite a while." Her eyes moved to the older man, who reminded her a lot of Zeb. He was gray-headed and bowlegged; his leathery face attested to the long hours he spent in the saddle. "You must be Mr. Cooper. Please sit and eat before everything gets cold."

"Yes, ma'am," Gabe Cooper said, straddling a chair and reaching for a knife to slice the bread. A warning glance from Reese reminded Gabe of his manners. "Excuse me, ma'am," the old cowhand said remorsefully. "It's been a long time since I feasted on food fixed by a female."

"You gentlemen go ahead and enjoy the meal. I'll just leave you to eat in peace."

"Aren't you going to join us?" Reese asked, holding a chair for her.

"I ate earlier." She smiled and moved to the door. "Good night, gentlemen."

It was quiet in the kitchen after she'd gone. The three men looked at each other and then hastily began filling their plates.

It smelled good, but Reese couldn't form a picture of Saber cooking on the old woodstove. Hesitantly he took a small bite of meat on his fork and tasted it, noticing that Jake and Gabe were already eating with gusto.

"Delicious!" Gabe pronounced with his mouth full.

"Yes, it is," Reese agreed, taking another bite and then another.

"Miss Vincente's a good cook," Jake said, reaching for his second slice of bread while eyeing the apple pie—his favorite.

Reese smiled to himself. He owed the lady an apology. Hell, he owed her many apologies. He'd been treating her like the spoiled sister of a Spanish grandee, when in truth she had acted with intelligence, kindness, and patience, and had never complained when she was cold and hungry.

After he'd eaten, he gave Jake and Gabe their orders for the next day. When they left he went into the parlor. He half feared Saber had gone to bed and he wouldn't get the chance to apologize to her for his rudeness the night before. He found her curled up in a chair, reading a book under the dim light of an oil lamp.

Saber glanced at Reese and laid the book aside. "Did you lose many head?"

He pulled a chair up beside her and nodded grimly. "Yeah. Close to fifty so far."

She moved forward and in a feminine gesture laid her hand on his. "I'm so sorry, Reese."

His hand closed around hers, and a knifelike sweetness swept through her. She wanted to comfort him, but would this self-assured man accept comfort from a woman? She somehow sensed that he needed it. "You will build your herd up again. I'm sure Noble will give you a sizable reward for—"

He jerked his hand free of hers and surged to his feet, standing over her with anger etched on his rugged face. "I don't need your brother's money."

"No, of course not. I just thought—"

Again he interrupted her. "My problems aren't yours, Miss Vincente." He moved to the corner, where she had neatly folded his pallet and carried the quilts to the fireplace.

"Now," he said, turning to her, "unless you want to watch me undress, I suggest you go to bed. It's been a long day, and tomorrow will prove to be an even longer one."

With as much dignity as she could gather, she stood, placed the book back on the shelf, and moved out of the room, closing the door behind her.

Reese stared up at the ceiling until he could gather his thoughts. Hell, what was the matter with him? He had seen the wounded expression in her eyes. He had meant to be nice to her, and all he'd managed to do was hurt her.

Without removing his clothing, he settled on the pallet and turned to stare at the flames burning low in the fireplace. He was a fool. Why couldn't he have just politely declined the offer of her brother's money and thanked her for the fine supper? Because, he told himself, he didn't want her to feel that she owed him. He would do anything for her and would stand between her and danger anytime. It wasn't for money—it never had been. His gun belt was gouging him, so he removed it and placed it near at hand.

Tomorrow he'd apologize to Saber for hurting her tonight.

The bedroom door opened, and he saw Saber's silhouette dimly reflected by the lamplight behind her. "I am going out with you tomorrow."

He raised himself up on his elbow. "No, you're not. It's too cold, and we'll be out all day rounding up any strays that may have survived the norther."

"You have no say in the matter. I don't care how cold it is. I am accustomed to riding every day, and I *will* ride tomorrow. Good night."

He could hear the determination in her voice. "Very well. But don't say I didn't warn you."

She stepped back into the bedroom and closed the door.

"Damn that woman!" he muttered. "She's as stubborn as a mule." Well, he'd just let her have her way and see how she liked it. She'd be begging to return to the house before the morning was over.

Chapter Twelve

Noble answered the knock at the door. Thinking it would be the Halloway family, his heart stopped when a beautiful woman with red-gold hair flew into his arms.

She nestled against him, fitting just right, as if she belonged there. Noble's arms tightened around her, and his heart filled with warmth. She had known he needed her and had come to him. Had any man ever had such a wife? "Rachel, what are you doing coming here at this time? If I know anything about you, you came alone."

"No, I didn't, because I knew you wouldn't approve. Teak and George came with me. I just had a feeling you might need me, so here I am." She turned her head up to his, and he raised her on tiptoe to receive his kiss. At last she broke away from him and went into the room. "I just couldn't stay at home worrying about Saber. Have you found her yet?"

He moved into the room and closed the door. He hadn't known how much he'd missed her until that moment. "I sent a man to the ranch with a message telling you all about it."

"We must have crossed paths. Have you found her?"

There was leashed anger in his eyes when he thought of what his sister had been through. "Yes. She's been found."

She went into his outstretched arms. "Thank God! I have been out of my mind with worry." She felt the tension in him. "She is all right, isn't she?"

"She's alive, but I don't know what she suffered at the hands of those bastards."

"Where is she? I want to see her."

Noble released his hold on Rachel and frantically paced the length of the room and back. "It seems she was rescued by a man by the name of Reese Starrett. Do you know him?"

Rachel frowned. "I've heard that name before. Wasn't he the man who stopped the Comanche from fighting with the army not too long ago? I believe he was hailed as something of a hero."

Noble stopped before her. "Did he? I hadn't heard that. Zeb told me that Reese has already killed one of the Miller brothers."

"Where is Saber now?"

"She's at Starrett's ranch. Zeb and Alejandro saw her and have assured me she is in good health."

Rachel shook her head. "I don't understand. Why is she at the Starrett ranch?"

He put his arms around her and drew her close. "Let me hold you, and I'll tell you what I know." He laid his face against hers and felt the familiar stirring of his body. "I have missed you, Green Eyes. I'm glad you are here."

She knew him so well, and she also knew he might go after the Millers and get himself killed. He was not a man to stand by idly while others hunted for the kidnappers. "What are your plans?"

"I'm leaving early in the morning. Some buffalo hunters claim to have run into the Millers just across the Mexican border."

She knew better than to try to talk him out of going, so she asked, "Who is going with you?"

"Five men from Casa del Sol."

"I want to come, too."

He eased her out of his arms. "You can't do that, Rachel. But it would ease my mind considerably if you would go to the Starrett ranch and find out about Saber."

She nodded in agreement. "Perhaps that would be for the best. I'll leave in the morning."

He drew her tightly against his body. "How did you know I needed you?"

She closed her eyes, loving her husband with her whole being. "I just know you so well."

He looked at the bed, wanting to lay her down and make love to her, but he groaned in frustration—that would have to wait until later tonight. "Matthew and his parents are supposed to be here at any time."

"What is the law doing to find the men, Noble?"

"You may well ask," he replied, his lip curled in distaste. "Sheriff Davis has taken a posse in the direction of the panhandle. That man couldn't find his own tail."

She touched her lips to his, and he forgot for the moment that he was meeting anyone. He pressed his body into hers and pulled her tighter against him.

Rachel knew that her husband needed comfort, and she knew just how to give it to him.

There was a knock on the door. Noble groaned and set Rachel away from him. "Later," he said, smiling.

A young soldier handed Noble a letter. "A message from Major Halloway, sir. He said to tell you how sorry he is that he and his parents can't come to Fort Worth today." The young man waited a moment. "Will there be an answer, sir?"

Noble felt irritated. "No. I have nothing to say to them."

When Noble closed the door, Rachel pulled him toward the bed. "I'm glad they aren't coming. Now we can be together."

It was still dark when Reese awoke and stretched his cramped muscles. He ran his hand over the bristles on his chin, thinking he should shave, but he didn't want to take the time. Every moment lost might mean more dead cattle.

He crammed his feet into his boots and tucked in his shirt. Glancing toward the bedroom, he was surprised to see the door open. On closer inspection, he discovered the bed was already made. He followed the delicious smell coming out of the kitchen and found Saber just taking biscuits out of the oven.

She noticed how tumbled his hair looked, and she noticed the tired lines beneath his eyes. He was working too hard, and she doubted that he'd slept very well on the floor.

"Something smells good," he said, sniffing the air.

A warm glow spread through her at the shared

moment of intimacy. She tried to remember that she was angry with him, but it was difficult with him looking at her with such a soft glow in those silver eyes.

"After you've washed and called the others, breakfast will be ready to eat."

"I didn't hear you get up. I thought young ladies of your station reclined in bed and had their breakfast served to them."

In a sudden rush of irritation, she now remembered why she'd been angry with him. Why did he always have to say such cruel things to her? "I have always been an early riser myself—and for your information, I never take my breakfast in bed unless I'm ill. As for you"—she shrugged—"it would have taken a stampede to wake you when I first got up."

The sight of her standing there with a smudge of flour on her cheek was so endearing that it made him smile. "I'll wash up," he said, going out the kitchen door with light steps.

Later, when the three men were seated at the table, Saber poured each of them a steaming cup of coffee, then sat down to drink hers.

"Why aren't you eating?" Reese said in a growl. "A good puff of wind would blow you away."

Her head swiveled in his direction, and her blue eyes glowed dangerously. "I ate while you were still asleep. I also washed your dirty clothing, hung it on the line, and made breakfast."

"Rosita does my laundry," Reese grumbled.

"Good. Then I won't do it again."

Jake and Gabe exchanged startled glances. Knowing Reese's temper and hoping to keep the boss from making a fool of himself, Gabe said quickly, "Ma'am, I guess you're just about the best cook I ever met. I ain't ate like this since I was a boy. My ma made biscuits like these."

"Why, thank you, Mr. Cooper. I don't know when I've had a nicer compliment."

Jake nodded, his eyes clear and honest. "I agree with him, ma'am, although I don't remember my ma's cooking."

Reese managed to look disgruntled, but he said nothing.

Saber took a quick sip of coffee and smiled at Jake. "I am riding out with you this morning."

Gabe nodded. "Bundle up good. It's still right cold, but I don't think we'll have anymore snow."

Reese scowled at the two men, resenting the fact that they made Saber smile. Hell, he resented any man who could make those sweet dimples appear in her satin cheeks! He shoved his plate away and stood. "You two ride to the high pasture. I'm going to take Miss Vincente and search in the valley so we won't be so far from the house."

172

"Yes, sir, boss," Gabe said with pretend seriousness, and received a frown from Reese for his trouble.

"I'll be in the barn," Reese said, his movements jerky.

Three pairs of eyes watched him stomp to the parlor, where his coat hung.

Saber sighed and stood. Taking the kettle of boiling water off the stove, she scraped the dishes and dunked them in soapy water. Reese could hurt her so easily. She paused as Gabe and Jake left, her mind made up. No man was going to treat her with such insolence. She had done nothing wrong. He was probably tired of having her around. She dried the plates and stacked them on the shelf. Yes, that must be what was wrong with him. Well, it had been his decision to bring her here, not hers.

Jake swung into the saddle and whispered to Gabe, "What's wrong with Reese—what's put a burr under his saddle? I've never seen him act like that before. The look he gave me when I complimented Miss Vincente on her biscuits would have curdled cream."

Gabe mounted his horse, laughing. "That little thoroughbred filly's what's wrong with him. She's got him twisted in knots. He ain't never seen her like before, and he's fighting to the end of his tether."

173

"Do you mean he's acting this way because he . . . wants her?"

Gabe laughed and spurred his horse on. "That's exactly what I mean."

Jake rode up to the older man. "Well, I'll be damned. Never thought the boss would go all soft on a woman."

Gabe gave him a knowing look. "Yes, sirree, he's a-bucking and a-rearing like a stallion caught in a barbed-wire fence. He'll not walk away from that little filly so easily. She's got spirit—real spirit!"

Reese noticed that his sorrel appeared to be favoring its left hind leg. On examining it, he discovered the horse had picked up a stone. He was concentrating on prying it loose, so he didn't glance up when Saber entered the barn.

She made her way to the stall where one of the mares was kept and opened the gate, patting the animal and receiving a friendly whinny in return.

He glanced at her and noticed she was wearing one of his old coats. It was rolled up at the sleeves and hung past her knees. She had also helped herself to a pair of his gloves, which were so big she was having trouble keeping them on her hands.

"Are you still set on riding out today, Saber?"

She gave him a lofty glance. "I need to get out of the house, and I am going."

He ground his teeth. "If you'll wait until I am finished here, I'll saddle that mare for you."

She led the mare forward, seething inside. "I don't need you to saddle my horse for me! I have been taking care of my own horses since I was no taller than your knee."

He gave her a doubtful glance, then watched as she aptly slipped the bridle over the mare's head and slid the bit between its teeth. He turned to help her, only to find that she'd already retrieved the saddle blanket from the stall railing. Dropping the gloves, she fixed him with a glare that stopped him short.

Saber slid the blanket in place and then heaved the saddle over her head. Reaching beneath the mare's belly, she fastened the cinch. After she'd adjusted the stirrups to her height, she rubbed the mare behind the ear and turned her glance to Reese, who was speechless.

"Mr. Starrett, my father was a firm believer that if you own an animal, that animal is your responsibility." She arched an eyebrow at him and asked in a purring voice. "Now, would you like me to saddle your horse for you?"

He turned away and began saddling his horse, hiding the smile that tugged at his lips. "I think I can manage."

175

"If you have any trouble, I'll be glad to help," she stated, jabbing her foot into the stirrup and mounting. Leaning over, she took a coiled rope from a peg and hooked it on her saddle horn. "I can rope, too, if you need me to help you today."

He swung smoothly into the saddle and looked into her eyes. "Ah, your offer of help warms my heart. Dare I hope that the lady begins to like me?"

"Banish any such hope, Mr. Starrett. The lady does not like you in the least." She nudged her mare forward and rode out of the barn.

Laughing, Reese rode after her, ducking his head when he came to the barn door. "Saber Vincente, you may be too much woman for Major Matthew Halloway," he said daringly.

She halted her mount and waited for him to join her. He saw the mischief reflected in her eyes and waited for her to speak.

"You see, it's the Spanish blood that's the problem. The part of me that is my mother will always do what is correct. But my father's Spanish blood causes me to behave irrationally. It's good if you understand this about me."

"I'll try to remember that," he said, nudging his horse forward at a gallop.

In spite of his earlier objections, Reese admitted to himself that it felt good to have her riding beside him. He had been well fed, and a beau-

Thrill to the most sensual, adventure-filled Historical Romances on the market today…

FROM 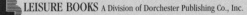 LEISURE BOOKS

As a home subscriber to the Leisure Historical Romance Book Club, you'll enjoy the best in today's BRAND-NEW Historical Romance fiction. For over twenty-five years, Leisure Books has brought you the award-winning, high-quality authors you know and love to read. Each Leisure Historical Romance will sweep you away to a world of high adventure…and intimate romance. Discover for yourself all the passion and excitement millions of readers thrill to each and every month.

SAVE AT LEAST *$5.00* EACH TIME YOU BUY!

Each month, the Leisure Historical Romance Book Club brings you four brand-new titles from Leisure Books, America's foremost publisher of Historical Romances. EACH PACKAGE WILL SAVE YOU AT LEAST $5.00 FROM THE BOOKSTORE PRICE! And you'll never miss a new title with our convenient home delivery service.

Here's how we do it. Each package will carry a 10-DAY EXAMINATION privilege. At the end of that time, if you decide to keep your books, simply pay the low invoice price of $16.96 ($17.75 US in Canada), no shipping or handling charges added*. HOME DELIVERY IS ALWAYS FREE*. With today's top Historical Romance novels selling for $5.99 and higher, our price SAVES YOU AT LEAST $5.00 with each shipment.

AND YOUR FIRST FOUR-BOOK SHIPMENT IS TOTALLY FREE!*

IT'S A BARGAIN YOU CAN'T BEAT! A Super $21.96 Value!

LEISURE BOOKS A Division of Dorchester Publishing Co., Inc.

GET YOUR 4 FREE* BOOKS NOW— A $21.96 VALUE!

Mail the Free* Book Certificate Today!

Get Four Books Totally
F R E E* —
A $21.96 Value!

PLEASE RUSH
MY FOUR FREE*
BOOKS TO ME
RIGHT AWAY!

Leisure Historical Romance Book Club
P.O. Box 6613
Edison, NJ 08818-6613

AFFIX
STAMP
HERE

tiful woman was next to him. What more could a man ask for?

By midmorning Reese had just about given up the hope of finding anymore strays. Suddenly he heard the frantic bellowing of cattle. Following the sound down to a deep gully, he and Saber located two cows that had been trapped in a high snowdrift.

Grabbing his rope, Reese shot forward, twirling it over his head, throwing it with precision, and catching one of the cows in his noose. When he wrapped his end of the rope around the saddle horn, the well-trained cutting horse pulled the rope taut and began to back up.

Saber loosened her rope and whirled it over her head. She had done this many times at Casa del Sol. She prayed that her aim would be accurate today. With a quick whirl, her loop sailed artfully through the air, slipping easily over the cow's horns. She did the same as Reese and wrapped her rope around the saddle horn. However, it took her only a moment to realize her mount was not trained to bulldog, so she would have to dismount.

Pulling the rope hand over hand, she found she could not budge the frightened animal. She soon felt Reese beside her, and his strong gloved hand slid over hers as he added his strength to hers. They pulled together until the animal was free; then Reese loosened the rope.

They both watched as the frightened animals ran up the draw.

"Where did you ever learn to do that?" he asked in amazement.

She looped her rope neatly and gave him her haughtiest look. "I grew up on a ranch, Reese. I know you think I did nothing but sit around and study fashion catalogs, but it's just not true."

His admiration for her was growing daily, and so was his desire to have her. He watched her mount her horse, noting the roundness of her hips. He wanted to take her down on the ground and grind his lips against hers and drive into that tempting body until she felt some of the hunger he was experiencing.

"What do we do now?" she asked, wondering what he was thinking as he looked at her so fiercely, his silver eyes catching the sunlight and burning right into her heart.

"We look for more strays," he said at last. "Are you cold?"

"No. Let's ride on."

He mounted, watching her ride ahead of him. He cursed the day he'd laid eyes on her. She was his torment, and his heart's mate. If he had never met her, he never would have known what he'd missed. No woman would ever satisfy him

178

now. If ever a woman had been created for him, it was Saber Vincente. But she didn't know it, and she never would.

She halted when she reached the top of the draw and stared about her. Everything was so peaceful and serene. "I love this land," she said dreamily. "It's so beautiful, Reese. No wonder you love it here."

He tried to see it through her eyes. It had been a long time since he'd really looked at his ranch. He'd been too busy working to keep from losing it. He could see for miles now because winter had stripped the trees of their foliage. A deep path, cut by hundreds of years of buffalo roaming, wound through the trees to the Trinity River. He saw deer tracks where a herd had fed and followed the river. There was no better grazing land in Texas than on his ranch.

"I suppose a woman like you would find it too isolated and lonely out here."

"No. I love living on a ranch. I would never fit in anywhere else."

"Not Philadelphia?"

Reese had hit on something that she had been struggling with. "Philadelphia is Matthew's home, and I assume he will one day want to return there. As his wife, I will, of course, go with him."

Silence fell between them, and Saber's gaze

traced the Trinity River until it disappeared around a butte. At last she said, "My brother always says that he who owns the water is master of his world. You have good water here, Reese, and a good ranch."

"Your brother is right about the water." He glanced down at her and found she was watching him. "I have heard that your brother married one of Sam Rutledge's daughters. That gave him the rights to both sides of the Brazos."

Saber laughed, her eyes filled with mirth. "If you knew my sister-in-law, you might say the woman who controls the water rights is mistress of her domain."

"Don't you like your sister-in-law?"

"I adore her. But Rachel is a woman who makes her own destiny, and I admire that about her. She can certainly handle my brother. No other woman could have made him as happy as she has. She rules him and makes him like it."

Reese was startled. "Your brother allows this?"

"He has no choice. Rachel is Rachel." She was thoughtful for a moment. "Actually, Noble encourages Rachel to be herself. He likes her just the way she is, and so do I."

"Why did he marry her?"

Saber gazed up at the clear blue sky and took a deep breath. "I hope I have a marriage as loving as theirs. They are deeply committed to each other. I have never seen two people who are more in love."

"Yet they come from two different worlds."

She smiled at him. "Noble once told me that crossing the river between their two ranches was the longest trip he'd ever made. I suspect he had to humble himself a bit to win Rachel."

"And you say you like her."

"Of course. She's the sister I've never had. She makes my brother happy, and I would love her for that alone, if not for herself."

Reese wanted to reach out and touch her face, to bring her against his shoulder and hold her until she realized that he would cross that river for her, brave any distance if it would bring her to him. But again his honor stopped him. "Let's ride on."

Saber followed him, wishing he'd look at her just once the way his brother looked at Rachel— or even notice that she was a woman. She doubted if he ever thought of her as anything but trouble. He had certainly never seen her looking like a woman. If only he could see her in something besides worn and baggy trousers. She wanted him to think she was pretty, and she blushed at that thought. She had never thought about impressing a man before, but then, Reese was not just any man.

She found him watching her. How would he feel if he could read her thoughts? "I believe it's growing warmer," she said, stating the first sensible thought that came to mind.

"Yes, it has. But it's come too late to save most of my herd."

"I know. I'm sorry."

He tightened his gloved hand on the reins and tapped his spurs against the side of his horse; Saber had to gallop to catch up with him. He didn't want her pity. The last emotion a man like him would want to evoke in anyone was pity.

"Let's try the left ridge," he said, guiding his horse over a slippery patch of snow that had iced in the shade cast by the cliff.

They found three dead steers and two dead bulls.

Her heart felt heavier. "When will it stop?"

He didn't bother to answer her. They both knew that the storm had killed most of his herd.

Saber's mood matched the colorless sky, and she pulled her coat tighter about her, huddling beneath the warm folds.

There was nothing she could do to help Reese, but she was glad she'd come with him today. At least she could share his misfortune.

Chapter Thirteen

If Reese had been by himself, he wouldn't have built a campfire when they stopped to eat the noon meal. Although Saber hadn't complained, he could see that she was cold. Being the stubborn woman she was, she'd rather die than admit to having any weaknesses. She huddled close to the fire, her cheeks rosy, her blue eyes sparkling.

"I love working with cattle." She glanced up at him. "Of course, Noble always tries to curtail what he terms my 'rambunctious nature.' I don't understand why he should object. I can ride as well as he can, and he admits that."

He handed her a plate of beans and a slice of

hardtack. "It sounds like you and your brother are very close."

"Yes, we are. After our parents died, it was only the two of us. Then Rachel became one of the family and brought joy to my brother. He had been very . . . sad for a time, but no one can be sad around Rachel." She studied the plate she'd placed on her knees. "I can't wait until they have children. I want to be an aunt." She gazed up at Reese. "I love children, don't you?"

In that moment Reese could not have felt worse if someone had hit him in the stomach. She would one day carry Matthew's baby in her body and give it life. She would hold the child in her arms and nurse it at her breasts. The pain of that vision was almost more than he could bear. He quickly glanced away, trying to remember her question, and for the life of him he couldn't.

"I'm sorry, Saber, what did you ask me?"

"I merely asked if you like children."

He thought for a moment. "I don't know any children. I've seen them around, but I don't think I have ever really spoken to one."

She threw back her head and laughed so hard, she almost fell off the log. "I can't believe you haven't been near children."

He frowned. "It's true."

"Then you have a wonderful experience waiting for you. Just wait until you have a child of your own."

"I don't plan on having children," he said dryly.

"You may feel that way now. But one day when you . . ." Her voice trailed off. He was the most solitary person she'd ever known, and she wanted so badly to make his life better.

"I met your housekeeper, Winna Mae," he said, changing the subject; talking about children was too painful. "What a formidable woman."

Saber's smile unfolded like the petals of a rose, and then her laughter went though Reese like no warmth he'd ever known. She had a fierce, unwavering spirit, and it touched him so deeply he wanted to always see her as happy as she was now. He'd never forget how she looked at the moment in her ill-fitting trousers with her golden hair crammed beneath a too big hat. He'd been watching her so closely, tracing the outline of her lovely face, it startled him when she spoke.

"You can't imagine how formidable Winna Mae can be. She came to the ranch with Rachel when she married my brother. She's the real dictator of the house." She smiled softly. "Actually, she's like family. I know she likes and respects my brother, and it wasn't easy for him to win her over because she is so fiercely protective of Rachel. It seems that somewhere along the way, Winna Mae took me into her inner circle and became my watchdog. She doesn't like very many people, and anyone who can win her respect is fortunate indeed."

Reese had formed that same opinion about Winna Mae the day he'd spoken to her in Fort Worth. "How do you feel about moving to Philadelphia and leaving your family behind?"

She studied the tip of her worn shoe. "I've tried not to dwell on that." Her eyes met his. "You know Matthew. Do you think his family will resent me because I am a Southerner? I wonder what they will say about my being kidnapped by the Miller brothers."

"Why should they think anything about it? It wasn't your fault."

"They are very proper."

He studied her carefully. "What are you saying?" He took her hand in his. "Did the Miller brothers do anything to you?" Anger flared within him. "Oh, God, did they hurt you, Saber?"

There was misery in her blue eyes. "I . . . don't know."

He tilted her chin up. "What do you mean? A woman knows if she's been . . . if a man's been intimate with her."

She lowered her eyes. "I was unconscious for two days while I was with them."

He frowned, trying to think what to say to her. It was possible that she had been raped. He certainly wouldn't put it past those bastards. He wanted to comfort her, but he didn't know how. "I believe a woman would know if a man did anything to her, even if she was unconscious."

Tears rolled down her cheeks. "I've tried to put the thought out of my mind, but it's always there. I just don't know what happened when I was unconscious."

He pulled her into his arms and cradled her lovingly, touching his lips to her temple and burying his face in her hair. "Matthew loves you. That won't change no matter what, Saber. If you belonged to me, I'd only love you more if you had been mistreated by those men."

Her chest expanded because of the tears she was trying to suppress. "A man would have to love a woman a lot to overlook her being used by other men."

"Not if the man loves the woman."

She pulled back from him. "Is there a way I can know for sure if they . . . if . . . ?"

"Yes, there is. But that would be for Matthew to determine after you are married."

"Is there no way I can tell before?"

He nodded. "There is. A doctor can tell." She

was in torment and had probably been carrying the fear of what the Millers had done to her from the beginning. He would have a talk with Matthew and make sure he handled this situation just right. He was sick with rage. He wanted to find the Millers and kill them with his bare hands. "When you see Matthew, he will prove that he loves you," he said in a gruff voice.

She moved away from Reese and picked up a slice of meat. She put it in her mouth to have something to do, but it formed a lump in her throat, and she had a hard time swallowing it.

"Saber, I—"

"No, Reese, I don't want to talk about it anymore. I don't know why I brought it up. It's just that . . . not knowing is so hard to bear."

"Is there anything I can say to make you feel better?"

She stared at him, thinking he was the only one who could make her feel better. He'd said if he loved her it wouldn't matter to him if she had been violated, and she believed him. But she wasn't sure Matthew would feel the same way. All the feelings she had been suppressing came rushing to the surface, but she said, "I am not going to burden you with my problems, Reese. You have done enough for me as it is."

"If you want to talk, I'm a good listener."

She sensed a new tenderness in him and wondered why she hadn't seen it before. "I know, and I thank you. But I have to face this alone."

He realized that she didn't want to talk about it anymore and changed the subject. "Since the weather has let up, I'm going to ride into Fort Worth tomorrow and find out what's happening. Would you like me to bring Winna Mae back with me?"

"I should go with you. I'll need to see Matthew."

"I can't let you do that, Saber. It's still too dangerous. You'll have to stay here until your brother or Matthew comes for you. But you needn't be afraid. Jake and Gabe will look after you."

She wanted to beg him not to leave her, but she knew from the stern look in those silver-gray eyes that he would have his way. "I would love to see Winna Mae—and could you bring my trunks?"

Reese had suddenly lost his appetite. He began clearing the remains of the meal away, then doused the campfire with snow. "Yes. I'm sure you will be glad to have your own clothing."

He watched her walk in the direction of her horse, wanting to crush her in his arms and never let her go. He didn't know how much longer he could keep his hands off her. Where was Matthew, damn it? She was his to take care

of. Surely Noble Vincente's men had informed
Matthew by now that Saber was here at his
ranch. Why didn't either her brother or her future husband come after her?

Reese swung into the saddle and urged his
mount into a fast gallop, and she kept pace with
him. In a way she hoped Winna Mae had already
gone back to Casa del Sol so she could have a
few more days alone with Reese. If only she had
the courage to tell him that she loved him.
Would he be horrified if she did? Yes, he was the
kind of man who would never think of touching
a woman who was supposed to marry his friend.

She was weighed down by misery as they rode
in search of more stranded cattle. In the late afternoon they came to a wide valley, and Reese
held his hand up for her to stop. She rode to his
side and gasped at the grisly sight that met her
eyes. The frozen carcasses of dead cattle were
too numerous to count.

Reese dismounted, removed his hat, and
stared in disbelief at the carnage around him.
He couldn't win against such odds. He exhaled
slowly, facing defeat. He felt a soft hand in his
and glanced down to see tears swimming in Saber's eyes. Without stopping to consider, he
turned her to him and held her tightly.

Saber pressed her face against the rough fab-
ric of his coat, loving him to the depths of her

soul. This was what love meant, she thought: to hurt for someone so badly that his pain became her own. "I'm so sorry, Reese," she murmured, unable to say more because of the lump in her throat.

He jerked her head up and gazed into blue eyes that swam with tears. Her lips parted, and his arms tightened around her, drawing her closer to him. His lips did not settle gently on her mouth but curved hard, urgently, ravishing, as he put all the frustration he felt in his kiss. His mouth punished and ground against hers, and her arms slid around his neck as she gave him access to her lips.

Reese's need for comfort quickly turned to desire for the woman in his arms. He took Saber to her knees with him. They were like two wounded souls, seeking the light.

"Oh, Reese," she cried, tearing her lips from his and kissing his rough cheek. "Reese."

"Shh, sweetheart," he whispered. "Shh."

He was taken aback for a moment. He'd never called a woman by any endearment. His body tightened as she pressed her face against him, trying to stop her tears. His hands moved beneath her coat and roamed up and down her back. He pulled her beneath his coat, and her breasts were flattened against the wall of his hard chest.

191

She made a small whimpering sound as passion and desire twined through her entire body like warm honey. When his hands went inside her shirt and she felt them settle on her bare breasts, she thought she would faint as he caressed them with such tenderness. His mouth covered hers again. She had not known that a kiss could be so wonderful.

When he broke the kiss, his chest was tight and he could hardly speak. Somewhere in the back of his mind he knew that what he was doing was wrong. But days of frustration, of wanting Saber, dulled his sense of right and wrong. He only knew he was touching her, and she didn't pull away.

Saber didn't feel the cold wind as he unbuttoned her shirt, but she was vaguely aware of the horses stomping and the jingle of their bits.

"Saber," he said softly against her ear, feverishly hungry to feel her soft skin against him. His lips touched just behind her ear and slid down her neck. "Saber. I need you."

"Yes," she answered in a whisper, placing her hands on either side of his head and pulling it down to her fully exposed breasts. She wanted to feel his lips there, and she almost screamed when his lips touched the curve and slid to the nipple.

She threw her head back, her lower body gravitating toward his. She wanted to be closer to him, to feel all of him.

Reese knew he should stop, but he couldn't. He quickly removed his coat and laid it on the snow, taking her down on top of it.

She moaned with pleasure when his weight pressed her to the ground, and he pinned her with his powerful thighs.

He bent his head and took possession of her lips, but this time less frantically and more leisurely. He nudged her mouth open with his tongue and slid inside. She seemed startled for a moment, so he slowly introduced her to the new sensation. Gently his tongue swept across hers, and he felt hers curl.

Saber was aware that a swirling fog had settled around them, and she could hardly see the horses. The world became enchanted, the fog only adding to her pleasure. She felt Reese's hand at the waist of her trousers, and she arched toward him, wanting him to free her of everything that was between him and his bare flesh.

His voice was deep and resounded through her consciousness. "I have wanted this for so long." He untied the rope that held her trousers up and pushed them over her hips. "I want to feel all of you."

Her flesh quivered when his hand spread across her stomach and moved downward. She felt hot all over and wanted to throw all her clothing off. When he gently spread her legs, she groaned with pleasure that was painful and glorious at the same time.

Her words came out in a breathless sigh. "Oh, Reese, I didn't think you even liked me."

His eyes were crystalline, and she could see her reflection mirrored there. "Like you?" he said softly, touching his lips to the shell of her ear, his hand moving between her legs. "I can't take a breath without thinking of you." He trembled, wanting her, and he realized that what he was doing was wrong. "I know what it feels like to stand at the door of Eden knowing you can't enter."

Desire lingered and played along her nerve endings, and she ached from the touch of his hand. "If I am Eden, I will take you in, Reese."

He suddenly stiffened. What was he doing? He moved away from her so quickly, she slid off the coat onto the snow.

He grasped her arms and surged upward, taking her with him, pulling her shirt together and lifting her trousers. "Saber," he said in a voice devoid of emotion, "you will have to forgive me. I lost my head for a moment. That's no excuse, and it won't happen again."

"Reese, I—"

"You are very desirable, and you made me forget your bridegroom is my best friend."

The implication of his words and the coldness in his tone cut her deeply, and her lashes swept over her eyes to hide what she was feeling. "If you think that I set out to seduce you, you are wrong, Reese. I have never allowed anyone to touch me as you just have."

He walked away from her so she could not see the dampness in his eyes. He shoved his boot in the stirrup and swung onto the saddle. "Mount up. I'll take you back to the house."

Saber quickly buttoned her shirt and straightened her trousers about her waist. She picked up Reese's coat and handed it to him without meeting his gaze. She was hurting so badly, she thought she would die from the pain of it. How could Reese make such an unflattering assessment of her character?

She mounted her mare and nudged the animal forward at an all-out run. Suddenly she felt cold and dead inside. She had offered herself to him, and he had rejected her in a humiliating way. She couldn't get away from him soon enough to suit her.

Her mare never slowed its rapid gait, causing a spray of snow to fly out behind her. Tears were wet against her skin, and she brushed them angrily away. She never wanted to speak to him again as long as she lived!

Chapter Fourteen

The sun was going down when they reached the house. Saber rode the mare directly into the barn and dismounted. She knew Reese had followed her, but she refused to look in his direction as she unsaddled the mare and put it in a stall. With her head held at a proud angle, she moved purposefully toward the house.

Once inside the front door, she allowed the tears to fall. She had most certainly acted in an unladylike manner. Why had she allowed him to take such liberties? How he must despise her! He would never have touched her if she hadn't encouraged him. And he would never believe that she hadn't set out to entice him.

Moments later Reese entered, and their eyes met. He noticed the forlorn expression on her face and knew he was responsible for hurting her again. She didn't know that by hurting her, he'd wounded himself to the very core of his being. At the time he had used the only means he'd had to fight against taking her there in the snow. He had forced himself to say those hateful things to drive her away from him, because if she had touched him one more time, he would not have been able to stop until he was inside her.

He came up to her and removed her coat, draping it over his arm while he led her to the fire. "You are cold as ice. I don't want you sick."

She shook her head, and her stomach tightened in a knot. She could hardly draw a breath, her heart was pounding so hard. "How can I ask you to forgive me for what I've done? I feel so miserable, and I most humbly ask for your forgiveness."

His voice was deep and strained, his eyes intense. "It wasn't your fault. Don't you know that?" he asked gravely.

"You said that—"

"Forget what I said. You are an innocent. You only reacted to what I was doing to you. I'm the one who should ask your pardon." He moved to the coatrack and hung the coat there, keeping his back to her. "Will you forgive me, Saber?"

She frowned and walked over to him, forcing him to look at her. "Tell me what you want from me."

"I think you know."

His eyes were like hot silver, and she could no longer look into them. "How can I know unless you tell me?"

Reese drew in an impatient breath. "Nothing. I don't want anything from you." He turned away from her, but not before she saw the muscles in his neck cord and his teeth clench.

Saber had thought that she was beginning to know him so well. But there was a part of him that he kept hidden from her.

"You certainly have nothing to blame yourself for," she said.

"Yes, I do. I knew what I was doing—you didn't." Frustration was reflected in his eyes. "Believe me in this, if you never believe anything else I say, Saber: I was manipulating you, so don't take the guilt that belongs to me alone."

She moved closer to the fire and held her hands to the warmth. "You are a gentleman, so therefore you are attempting to free me of my part in what happened." She glanced back at him. "It won't work." She licked her lips, deciding to tell him exactly what she had felt. "I liked what you did to me, Reese. I didn't want you to stop. You were the strong one—not me. It was you who stopped it before it went too far."

He took a step toward her, trying to ignore the desire to throw honor to the wind. He had made her desire him because he wanted her to. He knew just what a woman liked, and she had responded to his prowess.

Her eyes were wide and innocent, and he saw the hurt she tried to conceal. It had been his duty to protect her, and he had very nearly stepped over the line and become the one she needed to be protected from.

"We could talk about this all night and still come to the same conclusion. I instigated what happened, and that's the end of it."

She was silent for a long time, not knowing what to answer. There was no warmth coming from him, and no sign of the man who had held her in his arms and kissed her that afternoon. "Then I will say good night."

His voice stopped her as she moved to the bedroom. "Saber, I will be gone when you get up in the morning, and I don't want you to be in the house alone. I will leave instructions for Jake to sleep here by the fire. I trust him with my life, and you will be safe with him. Have you any objections to him staying in the house with you?"

She paused in the doorway and turned back to him, frowning. "Do you expect trouble?"

"Not really. But I will not take a chance on your safety." He forced a smile. "Matthew would never forgive me." His eyes suddenly took on a serious expression. "And Saber, I don't want you to go out riding alone. If neither Gabe or Jake can go with you, then stay near the house."

She nodded. "I understand." She gazed past him, unable to look into his eyes. "How long will you be gone?"

"I don't know. Several days, a week, maybe more. It's hard to say."

She turned away, feeling that any time spent without him would seem like a lifetime. "Good night, Reese. Have a safe journey."

"Good night, Saber." When the door closed behind her, Reese stood for a long time staring at nothing. He closed his eyes and lowered his head. The hardest thing he'd ever had to do was walk away from her today, and the second hardest would be to leave her tomorrow.

Saber had tried to keep busy cleaning house and reading, but the day stretched on endlessly. She made the evening meal for Jake and Gabe because it gave her something to do, and they were always so grateful.

When Jake came in with an armload of wood, she was reading by the dim lamplight.

The young boy smiled shyly as he placed the

wood in the bin. He stacked two logs on the fire before he spoke. "Miss Vincente, Reese said he wanted me to sleep in the house tonight, that I was to make my pallet by the fire."

"Yes, he told me, too."

She laid her book aside and smiled at him, trying to put him at ease. "Did you find anymore frozen cattle today?"

He nodded grimly. "Five head. We haven't checked by the mesa yet. I'm hoping some of the cattle took shelter there. It's enclosed on three sides, so they might have survived there."

She shook her head. "It is such a tragedy."

He eased his tall frame down beside the fire and folded his arms. "I'm sorry it had to happen to Reese. He's fought so long and hard to hold this place together. He's a good man and deserves better."

"Nature knows no friend when she's on the rampage, Jake."

"No, she don't," he agreed, bracing his back against the wall.

"Have you lived here long, Jake?"

"I'll be fifteen next month, and Reese found me when I was thirteen and brought me here to live." He looked pensive. "That would be two years come this April."

"You say he found you?"

"Yes, ma'am—that's exactly what he did. I

don't know what would have happened to me if he hadn't taken me in and given me a home. My ma and pa were dead, killed by a fever along with my brother and two sisters. I'd fallen in with a rough bunch who were bound for trouble. I had me a gun, and I wanted to prove that I was as mean as anyone."

She leaned forward, enthralled by his story. "How did you meet Reese?"

"He was fresh out of the war; in fact, he still wore his tattered gray uniform. Me and my three friends got drunk and rode into San Antonio, shooting out windows and yelling and whooping it up, thinking we was big men. I don't know how we kept from killing someone with a stray bullet, but I'm glad we didn't. As it was, a bullet hit Reese in the upper arm while he was mounting his horse. I saw right away that I was in trouble because it was my bullet that struck him. The sight of his blood was enough to make me think twice about what I was doing."

"What happened?"

"Well, Reese ignored my friends and came right for me with a look of murder in his eyes. You know how powerful his eyes can be when he's mad. Well, he was mad at me. He yanked me off my horse, drug me over to the horse trough, and doused my head. He held me under till I almost drowned, and then he pulled me up again, and then dunked me again. By the time the sheriff got there, I was nigh onto sobering up. Reese refused to have the doctor take the bullet out of his arm until he talked to the law about me. When he learned I had no family, he wouldn't let them lock me up, and he brought me here. I ain't never had no one care if I lived or died since my family was buried. I guess Reese is about the best man I ever met. I'd do anything for him—even die for him, if I had to." He grinned, feeling he was being too serious. "I guess the day I shot Reese was about the luckiest day of my life."

"That is extraordinary. Why do you suppose he cared what happened to you?"

"I asked him that very thing myself. He said I reminded him of himself as a boy. His ma ran off with his pa's most trusted friend, and Reese kinda raised himself and took care of his pa until he died. Reese was only fourteen at the time, but he kept this ranch. I can only imagine how hard he must have worked. He's been on his own since then."

Saber's heart wrenched inside her. Reese had never really had a proper family life; she could understand why the ranch was so important to him. If only he'd let her, she could help him. But he was such a proud man, he probably wouldn't take help from anyone.

She stood and replaced the book on the shelf. "Good night, Jake. I am comforted just knowing you are nearby."

"You don't have anything to be afeard of, Miss Vincente. If you need me, just call out, and I'll hear."

She smiled warmly. How perceptive of Reese to see that Jake only needed guidance and a home with someone to look up to as his hero. And it was clear Reese was the boy's hero. Just as Reese was her hero and always would be.

Saber closed the bedroom door and undressed. She pulled Reese's flannel shirt over her head and felt it fall softly about her like a smooth caress. She missed him so desperately. When she left here, they might never see each other again. How would she live the rest of her life without knowing what was happening to him?

It was a long time before Saber fell asleep, because for the first time in her life passion had stirred her body. She knew what it felt like to have a man touch her with such gentleness that she wanted to cry. She knew that she was capable of stirring that same passion in Reese. He'd wanted her; she knew that.

She felt strangely empty and unfulfilled. She was consumed by a desire and a need that she could not understand. But one thing she did know: NO other man, not even Matthew, could satisfy the hunger Reese had awakened in her.

She closed her eyes, imagining he was touching her. Then she turned her head and sobbed into her pillow.

Midnight had come and gone before she closed her eyes in sleep.

Reese left his horse at the stable and started for the hotel, where he expected to find either Matthew or some of his family. He hoped to hell Winna Mae was still there, because he could no longer trust himself alone with Saber after what had happened between them. He couldn't get the feel of her satiny skin out of his mind, or the way her blue eyes shone with passion when he had touched her breasts.

Thinking about her now made him want to get on his horse and ride back to the ranch. He paused at the door to the hotel. He had to have a woman to help him forget about Saber—he had to have one now!

He walked purposefully toward the saloon and thought of Edith with the large breasts that looked like they would fall over the top of her gown if she bent over. Then there was the redhead, Dotty, who had tempted him on occasion. Hell, he didn't care which one it was. He just wanted a woman!

When he entered the saloon, he found it

crowded. He walked directly to the bar and ordered straight whiskey. Edith came up to him, touching her hip to his and smiling alluringly. "Well, well, Mr. Starrett, what can I do for you tonight?"

Her cheap perfume made his senses revolt, and he remembered Saber's clean, sweet smell.

Edith pressed more tightly against him, her breasts brushing his arm. "I have been waiting a long time to get you into my bed. I have heard stories that when Reese Starrett loves a woman, she compares every other man to him afterward." Her eyes dilated with expectation, and she leaned closer to him, whispering in his ear, "I also hear you're big and thick. I'd like to find out for myself."

Reese felt nothing but disgust for her. This woman and ten others like her wouldn't ease what was bothering him. No one would ever satisfy him but Saber.

"Let me buy you a drink," he said to Edith, moving a bit away from her.

"Then afterward we could go to my room," she suggested.

He downed his whiskey effortlessly and threw money on the bar. "I'm not your man, Edith. Your hair's the wrong color, and your eyes are not blue."

She watched Reese leave the saloon, puzzled

and disappointed. Just what woman gave him his itch? Well, whoever it was, she wasn't going to get to scratch that itch for him—he just wanted the woman who was eating at his insides. She'd seen his symptoms before. Reese Starrett was in love, damn it!

Chapter Fifteen

A weak sun shining through a gray sky did little to banish the chill from the air. The people of Fort Worth were still pondering what had happened to Saber Vincente, and they were even more curious when they realized that her brother, Noble Vincente, was staying in town.

A group of women huddled near the general store watched Noble when he stepped into the sheriff's office. They put their heads together, each coming up with a valid reason for his visiting Sheriff Davis.

Noble found the sheriff asleep behind the desk. He leaned forward and said in a commanding voice. "Wake up, Davis. I hear you caught one of the Miller brothers."

The sheriff, Bud Davis, opened one eye and then the other. He thought the tall man dressed in Spanish trousers and a bolero jacket looked familiar, but he couldn't place him right off.

"Yeah. We got the youngest. Name's Sam, and he's plenty scared." The sheriff got to his feet, hiking up his holster where it had slipped beyond his ample belly. "And who might you be, stranger?"

"I'm Noble Vincente, and I want to question Sam Miller."

Bud Davis nodded, impressed by the importance of his visitor. "You got the right to talk to him if anyone does. You want me to bring him out here, or you want to go back to his cell?"

"Has he talked?"

"Nope. He's not saying much."

"Then I might want to spend some time alone with him. He'll talk for me," Noble said, his eyes narrowing.

"I'll take you back."

The front door opened, and Reese entered the jail. He paid little attention to the man talking to Sheriff Davis, because he had more important matters on his mind. "I hear you got one of the Miller brothers. I want to talk to him."

"Get in line," the sheriff stated with humor. "What do you want with him, Reese?"

Noble turned to meet the ice-cold eyes of the man called Reese. "Are you Starrett?"

Reese knew immediately that he was facing Saber's brother. "I am. And you must be Noble Vincente."

The two men took each other's measure. And Noble was the first to speak. "Is my sister with you?"

"No. I didn't think it would be wise to bring her out in the open just yet."

Noble took the two steps that placed him in front of Reese. "And you have appointed yourself the expert on what's best for my sister?"

"Hell, yes," Reese said with the heat of anger. He had expected the owner of Casa del Sol to be an arrogant bastard, and he was. "When I found Saber, you weren't around to ask how you wanted me to handle the situation. So, to save her life, I just acted on my own."

"How is my sister, and what measures have you taken to protect her?"

Reese stared into the dark eyes of Saber's brother. "She's taken over the running of my house—she's offered me her advice on how to saddle a horse. She's taken on the running of my ranch—she is the damnedest, most stubborn woman I've ever met! How is she? You might

better inquire how I've survived her instructions."

Sheriff Davis whitened. No one, not even
Reese Starrett, ought to say such things to Vincente about his sister. With trepidation, he
watched the two powerful men glare at each
other, and he wondered if their meeting was going to end in bloodshed. He couldn't let that happen, and was about to step between them when
he heard Noble Vincente laugh.

Noble extended his hand to a startled Reese.
"You have just accurately described my sister. I
can see now why Zeb was convinced that Saber
would be safe with you. Well done, Starrett."

Reese grinned and shook Noble's hand. "I
don't mind telling you, I dreaded meeting you
far more than the Miller brothers, with Graham
Felton thrown in for good measure."

Noble clapped Reese on the back. "You will
find the Vincente family grateful to you for what
you did. Come, let us question Sam Miller. I
won't rest until I have his brother and Felton
locked away or dead, and I'd prefer to see them
dead. I heard you had to kill Earl. Later I will
want you to tell me all about it."

The two tall men made their way back to the
cells, leaving Sheriff Davis to follow, scratching
his head in confusion.

*   *   *

Sam Miller looked more like a frightened boy than a desperate outlaw. There was misery on his youthful features, and he couldn't meet the eyes of the two hard-eyed men who entered his cell.

But when he saw Reese, his eyes brightened. "Mr. Felton, have you come to get me out?"

Noble spoke before Reese had a chance to. "And if he has, will you tell us where to find your brother Eugene?"

Sam glanced in confusion at the man he believed to be Graham Felton. "Eugene's looking for our brother Earl, Mr. Felton. I don't believe Earl'd run out with the money, but Eugene does."

Reese sat down on the empty cot across from the young Miller boy. "Earl didn't run out on you anymore than I'm Graham Felton. I had to shoot your brother to get the information I needed to find Miss Vincente."

Sam's eyes widened, and he swallowed several times. "Is Earl dead?"

"I'm afraid so. He gave me no choice." Reese crossed his legs and met the boy's gaze squarely. "You see, Sam, when you walk outside the law, bad things happen to you. I spoke to your ma. If you get out of this, I hope you'll go home and take care of her."

Sam lowered his head and began to sob. "Our

ma will be mightily grieved when she hears about Earl."

Reese suddenly felt pity for the boy. "I think she already suspects he's never coming home, Sam."

Noble had no pity for the boy who had assisted in kidnapping his sister. "You should have considered your mother's feelings before you chose your kind of life."

Reese held his hand up to silence Noble. "Miss Vincente has told me of your kindness to her. She said you kept Eugene away from her and protected her. I'm sure if you talk, the sheriff will look a little more kindly on your part in the kidnapping."

Noble frowned, not sure what in the hell Reese was trying to do. But he'd wait and see where the other man went with this.

Sam raised tear-bright eyes. "I couldn't let Eugene hurt her."

"No, you couldn't. I believe that your ma would be proud of you for protecting Miss Vincente, Sam."

Sam blinked. "Do you think so?"

"Yes. She was the one who told me how to find Earl, and that finally led me to Miss Vincente."

"Ma wouldn't help you against her own sons!"

"She was hesitant until I told her that the

213

three of you had kidnapped an innocent woman."

His face flushed with shame. "My ma knows what we did?"

Reese nodded. "She's hurt real bad, Sam. You might like to know that I made her a promise that I tried to keep. I told her I wouldn't shoot any of you unless you drew first."

He nodded in understanding. "Earl drew on you, and you had to kill him."

"Yes."

"And you'd keep your promise if you found Eugene?"

"I would. So far all the law wants you for is kidnapping. You haven't killed anyone yet. You'll probably spend time in jail, but it's better than being dead." Reese moved forward and lowered his voice. "Now, you have to understand, Sam, Sheriff Davis and Noble Vincente here didn't make your ma any such promise. That's why I think you should tell me where to find Eugene. If I can, I'll bring him in alive. You don't want your ma to weep over another dead son, do you?"

Sam was quiet while he considered Reese's words. At last he nodded. "I don't even know your name."

"Sam, my name's Reese Starrett."

The boy's eyes widened. "I've heard of you. If

Earl pulled on you, he didn't stand a chance. They say you're fast on the draw."

"But no one ever said I drew on an unarmed man or shot first, Sam."

"I heard that, too," Sam agreed. "I'll tell you where Eugene went, but only you."

"You'll have to tell Mr. Vincente, too, Sam. Saber is his sister."

Sam glanced into the cold, dark eyes of the Spaniard. "No. I won't tell him. He'll kill Eugene for sure."

"Damned right I will!" Noble said menacingly. "No one takes one of my family and lives to tell about it."

Sam hugged the wall, his eyes going to Reese. "If I tell you, you won't tell him, will you?"

"Think how you'd feel if someone kidnapped your sister," Reese told him.

The boy lowered his head, weighed down with shame for what he was about to do. But he had to try to save his brother. "Eugene's gone looking for Earl across the Mexican border at Los Lunas."

"What makes you think Earl is in Los Lunas?" Noble asked.

" 'Cause," Sam replied. "That was where we was to meet up with him if we got separated."

Reese stood. "You did the right thing in telling me, Sam."

Noble had trouble keeping his temper. But Reese had been clever in getting the information they needed. Noble reached out and gripped Sam by the shirtfront and slammed him against the wall. "I could kill you right here, you little weasel, and no one would blame me."

Reese clutched Noble's arm. "We have what we need from him. Let him be. He can't hurt anyone locked in here. And he did protect your sister as well as he could."

Noble dropped his hands to his sides and turned to leave. "If I find you lied to us, Miller, I'll be back, and no one can save you then."

Reese had reached the cell door when Sam's voice stopped him. "You'll keep your promise to my ma, won't you?"

"Yes, I will." He stepped through the cell door and watched as Sheriff Davis locked it. "I'll keep my promise to your ma if you'll make me a promise."

Sam looked startled. "What kind of promise?"

"That you'll go straight and stay out of trouble when you get out of this. And that you'll take care of your ma."

The young boy's eyes held an earnest expression. "I promise, Mr. Starrett. I'll never do anything outside the law again. I learned my lesson."

When Reese reached the outer office, Noble

was pacing the floor. "Just what was that little display all about?"

Reese shrugged. "You wouldn't get the boy to betray his brother with threats. He might not like his brother, but he would never hand him over to us if he thought we were going to kill him."

"So you made a promise that you aren't going to keep?"

"Wrong, Vincente. I made a promise I have every intention of keeping. The promise was to Sam's mother, and I won't go back on it."

Guarded respect appeared in Noble's eyes. "I made no such promise."

"No, you didn't," Reese admitted.

Sheriff Davis hung the keys on a hook and turned to his two visitors. "I'll get a posse together and head out for the border first thing in the morning."

Reese swung around to the man Winna Mae had accused of bungling everything the night Saber was kidnapped. "No. No posse," he said in a commanding voice. "We can't hope to get Miller and Felton until we have a plan. I don't want a bunch of shopkeepers and farmers riding about the countryside gun-happy."

Noble's respect for Reese was growing. He'd been damn clever the way he had rescued his sister from the Miller brothers. Noble was just beginning to realize how much danger Reese had faced to save Saber. And he agreed with him about the posse. It would only get in Noble's way when they went after Graham Felton.

"This isn't your fight, Starrett," Noble told him. "It's my fight, and I'll do it my way."

"The hell you will," Reese said angrily. "You don't do anything without me."

Noble stared at Reese for a long moment. He nodded to the sheriff and motioned for Reese to follow him outside, where they could talk in private. "So she got to you, did she?"

Reese didn't have to ask what Noble meant. "Yeah. Saber worked her magic on me."

Reese stepped into the street, untied the reins of his horse, and led it toward the hotel while Noble fell in beside him.

When they reached the other side of the street, Noble asked the question that had been haunting him since he'd heard of Saber's abduction. "Did the Miller brothers touch Saber in any improper way?"

Silver eyes looked into dark brown ones. Reese decided to say it right out. "I don't know. And worse still, Saber doesn't even know for sure. She was unconscious for two days after they'd taken her."

Noble was angry and grieved at the same time. "Even you won't stop me from killing them if I find out they touched my sister, Reese."

"If that turns out to be the case, I'll help you string them up without a trial," Reese answered.

The two men who loved Saber most shook hands in understanding. Each knew the other would do whatever was necessary to capture the men involved in kidnapping Saber.

Chapter Sixteen

The two days since Reese had been away seemed to drag by for Saber. On the third day, she decided to go riding to get away from the house. Gabe and Jake had ridden out before sunup, so they couldn't go with her. Even though Reese had told her not to ride out alone, she was going anyway!

In spite of the cold weather, there was a feeling of spring in the air. The breeze was sweeter, and tender sprigs of green peeped from beneath the patches of snow that still remained.

As she rode along the riverbank, she stopped to watch a doe with its fawn. Her heart felt lighter, and her troubles lessened when she was riding. Gabe and Jake had not found anymore dead cattle since Reese had gone, and that pleased her for Reese's sake.

She rode toward the cliffs, watching the way the river cut through a canyon, and she wished she could imprint this tranquil picture on her mind. She wanted to think of Reese riding here after she had gone. She wondered if he would lose the ranch. She couldn't let that happen. There had to be something she could do to help him.

It was almost sundown when she finally led her mount into the barn. She was glad to see that the stalls where Jake and Gabe kept their horses were empty—that meant they weren't back yet. She unsaddled her horse and gave him fresh hay. Her footsteps were heavy as she made her way to the house to face another evening alone. And to make matters worse, she'd forgotten to lay logs on the fire, so it had probably gone out; the house would be cold.

Glancing up, she saw smoke rising from the chimney, and she was puzzled. That was when she noticed the fashionable black carriage parked in front of the cabin. Her heart lightened—it belonged to her brother!

She hurried into the house and was met at the door by a worried Rachel. "Where have you been, little sister?" Rachel asked, hands on hips.

Saber rushed into her sister-in-law's embrace and hugged her tightly. "Just riding. But I'm so glad you are here."

Rachel met her eyes. "Are you all right?"

"Yes. But I wouldn't be if it hadn't been for Reese."

Rachel slid her arm about Saber's waist. She loved Noble's sister every bit as much as she loved her own sister, Delia. "I am sorry you have gone through so much. But it's over now. They will find the men responsible, and that will put an end to it."

Saber nodded. "I know they will. I just needed you here with me to cheer me up."

Rachel stepped back and looked her over from head to toe. "I'd say your wardrobe is not quite . . . in fashion. Whatever are you wearing?"

Saber grinned, remembering a time when Rachel had worn trousers, much to Noble's dismay. "You don't like my choice of apparel?"

"I should say not! It's fortunate for you that I brought your trunk, and even more fortunate that your brother can't see you like this." She smiled. "Although I would love to see Noble's face if he caught sight of you in that garb."

Saber looked miserably into Rachel's eyes. "I really need someone to talk to, Rachel."

"That's why I'm here." She glanced about the house. "Where is this Reese Starrett? When I arrived there was no one here. I have wanted to meet him ever since I heard he'd rescued you."

"He's gone to Fort Worth."

"That explains it. We may have crossed paths." Rachel walked around the room, examining the books on the shelf. "This house could certainly do with a woman's touch."

"That's what I think, too."

"Well, from what I've heard of Mr. Starrett, he would have no trouble getting a line of women to volunteer for that position. He's quite sought after, but has managed to elude matrimony thus far."

Saber removed Reese's coat and hung it on the coatrack. "I imagine you're right." She linked her arm through Rachel's and led her toward the kitchen. "I'm hungry, how about you?"

"Starved."

"Shall I make enough for the Casa del Sol hands who accompanied you?"

"It seems Reese's man, Miguel, took them off to the bunkhouse and settled them in."

"I'm surprised that Noble would let you come without him."

"He grumbled about it a bit, but in the end we both decided that you might need me, and I wanted to see for myself that you were safe."

"I am. Jake and Gabe have been looking out for me."

"Then let's eat. And afterward I want you to tell me everything that's happened."

Saber and Rachel were just about to sit down to eat when Jake and Gabe ambled in. After Saber fed them and sent them off to the bunkhouse, she and Rachel sat around the fire in silent companionship.

At last Rachel said, "Well, tell me about Mr. Starrett. What does he look like? What kind of man is he?"

Saber leaned her head back and thought for a moment. "He doesn't have the chiseled good looks that Noble has, and he doesn't have the boyish looks of Matthew. Reese's features are harsher, his eyes disturbing, as if he'd done and seen too much. I know that nothing can harm me when he's nearby. He's strong and lean, and when he looks at me I . . . I want . . ."

Rachel had been watching Saber closely. "I see. Tell me a little more about him."

"He's a man of the land, and the sky is reflected in his eyes. He's proud, honorable, and stubborn. I have never seen anyone with eyes the color of his. They can be dark gray when he's thinking, or they can be transparent silver when he feels something deeply."

"And did he feel something deeply with you, Saber?"

Saber met Rachel's questioning glance. "He feels passionate about this ranch."

"And?"

A painful lump formed in Saber's throat. "I love him." She buried her face in her hands and fought against the tears that threatened to fall. "I love him so desperately."

Rachel bent down beside her, brushing the hair out of her face and making her look up. "How does he feel about you, Saber?"

"I think—I know—he finds me nothing but trouble."

"Are you sure?"

"Yes, very sure. I am ashamed to tell you this, but I have to tell someone. I threw myself at him, and he wouldn't have me."

"Saber, you just said he was a man of honor. Perhaps if he liked you less, he would have taken you to bed."

"No. You are mistaken. He wants only to see the last of me."

"This is very serious indeed. What about Matthew?"

"Everything is in such a tangle. I can never let Reese know how much I love him, or he will despise me because Matthew is his friend. Matthew must never know, either. I will marry him as I planned, but I will always feel like I'm cheating on him, because I love Reese. Perhaps knowing I don't love him will make me a better wife. I'll be tolerant and thoughtful, and he will never know that I am dead inside."

Rachel gathered Saber to her. "Oh, my dear little sister—you are in love with Reese Starrett. I can only imagine the torment I would be living through if Noble and I had not settled our differences and admitted that we loved each other."

"I know. But there will be no such happy ending for me, Rachel."

"Don't give up so easily, Saber. Let me think on this for awhile."

"Do you believe I'm awful?"

"No, sweet little sister. I think you are a woman disposed to marry the wrong man, and I will never let that happen."

"But what can I do? Even if I don't marry Matthew, Reese still doesn't love me."

"We will put our heads together and see what comes of it."

Saber felt better for unburdening herself. "Even if I must marry Matthew, I can bear it. After all, Matthew is a wonderful man. The one thing I could never do is hurt him. I owe him so much for helping me in Georgia."

"You don't owe him the rest of your life, Saber."

The fire burned low, and soon Saber and Rachel went to bed.

"The first thing I'm going to do tomorrow is take a tub bath and put on one of my gowns."

"Yes, I believe that would be a good idea." Rachel's mind was reeling. She wasn't going to let Saber sacrifice herself in marriage. She suspected that Reese Starrett was in love with Saber. It didn't matter how honorable he was—if a woman with Saber's beauty offered herself to a man, he'd be hard-pressed to refuse her. No. Reese Starrett loved Saber and refused to take advantage of her while she was under his protection—that was what it was!

"Rachel?"

Rachel yawned. "Yes?"

"What are we supposed to do now?"

"Noble would like us to be at Casa del Sol, where you will be better protected, but he fears the journey would be dangerous. So he wants us to remain here until he comes for us."

"I have tried to think why I was kidnapped."

"Everyone would like to know that. The most likely reason is that you were kidnapped for money."

"Rachel, there is something I haven't told you."

Her sister-in-law stiffened, dreading what was to come. She had feared that Saber had been raped by her abductors—and she prayed it wasn't so.

"I was unconscious for two days after I was abducted. I don't know what they did to me in that time."

"Were there any signs that they . . . raped you?"

"I wouldn't know what to look for."

"There might have been blood, Saber."

"No. There was nothing like that." She raised herself up on her elbow. "Does that mean they didn't touch me?"

"No. Not really," Rachel said, knowing she had to be honest with Saber.

"How will I ever know?"

"Have you had your monthly?"

"Yes."

Rachel breathed a sigh of relief. "Then it's best not to think about it just now. When you are married, your husband will know."

"But I should tell Matthew. I couldn't let him marry me without letting him know that it could have happened."

Rachel pondered Saber's words. She didn't know what kind of a man her future brother-in-law was. "Let me think about it. We will decide what to do later."

Saber turned onto her side and closed her eyes. "This nightmare never seems to end."

* * *

The next day Rachel kept Saber busy so she wouldn't have time to dwell on her situation. When Saber had bathed and her hair had been washed and brushed until it hung to her waist in soft curls, she felt more like herself. She put on a yellow cotton gown and matching slippers. It felt wonderful to know that she looked her best. She wished Reese could see her now.

Jake and Gabe had ridden out early, and most of the Casa del Sol riders had gone with them. But Gabe had informed them that two men would stay behind to watch out for them.

Saber was rearranging her clothes in her trunk when she heard a rider approaching. Thinking it might be Reese, she ran to the window. The barn door was open, so one of the men must have returned.

She had an uneasy prickling sensation at the back of her neck.

"Rachel."

There was no answer.

Saber ran to the bedroom and lifted Reese's pistol out of the holster. It was unloaded! She had seen some boxes of shells under the bed when she'd been cleaning. Maybe there were bullets to fit this gun in one of the boxes. She took a steadying breath when she found that one of them did indeed hold the right bullets. She was going to feel foolish when the rider turned

229

out to be Jake or Gabe. But she had learned not to take chances.

She heard Rachel's voice as she opened the door to greet whomever it was. She wanted to call out a warning, but it was too late. She shoved bullets into the chamber and prayed the gun wasn't too rusty to fire.

"What can I do for you?" Rachel asked.

"I'm looking for work. Would you be the woman of the house?"

Saber cringed when she heard the voice that had haunted her nightmares. It was Eugene Miller!

"No, I'm sorry. You'll need to come back another time. The man who owns the ranch is away at the moment."

Saber heard the door open wider, and Rachel gasped.

"Who are you? What are you doing?"

Saber realized that the men left behind to protect them were not going to be any help. She squared her shoulders and moved out of the bedroom, the gun hidden behind her. She nodded to Rachel, and her sister-in-law moved aside.

"This is Eugene Miller," she told Rachel. "He's here because he and I have unfinished business," Saber said as calmly as if she were introducing a friend.

"That's right, pretty thing. Now there's two of you. Which one will I take first?" His hand went down to rest on his gun. "Don't either of you make any sudden moves. Miss Vincente, me and you will just go into the bedroom."

She backed toward the bedroom door, trying to draw him farther away from Rachel. "I'd hoped you were dead," she said with all the hatred she felt for the man. "I'm sorry you aren't."

"Now, I wouldn't want to leave this earth until I have me some of that sweet little body." He glanced at Rachel. "You stay put and don't call out for help, or I'll shoot Saber Vincente dead."

"Don't hurt her," Rachel said quickly. "I won't do anything."

Eugene glanced into the kitchen and was satisfied that there was no one there. "Is anyone else with you?" he asked, his eyes raking over Saber's soft curves.

"Yes, there is," she said, bringing her hands from behind her back, where she'd been hiding the gun. "Meet Smith and Wesson." She leveled the gun at his chest and watched a look of horror come over his face. She fired once, then again and again.

Chapter Seventeen

The dinner crowd at the hotel dining room fell silent as they watched Maj. Matthew Halloway limp toward Reese Starrett. Then people put their heads together, whispering, and the crowd's reaction was not lost on Matthew. He knew people were speculating about the kidnapping. Some of the gossip that had reached his ears was vicious, and he was not in a good mood.

Matthew leaned heavily on a cane and grinned at Reese before easing himself onto a chair.

After a few curious glances people went back to enjoying their meals, and Reese nodded toward the splint. "How's the leg?"

"It doesn't hurt much now, but it itches like

hell. I'll be glad to get this splint off. If the army doctor has his way, he'll keep me hobbled for the rest of my life."

"Yeah. I remember. My Confederate doctors were probably as inadequate as your Yankee doctors."

Matthew picked up a water glass and turned it around in his fingers. "There is no way I can thank you for what you did, Reese. I don't know what would have happened to Saber if you hadn't gone after her."

"You don't owe me any thanks," Reese replied gruffly. "I am sure you're aware that she's at my ranch. I thought it would be the safest place for her until Eugene Miller and Felton are caught. But she would be safe enough if you took a company of your men and escorted her to Fort Griffin."

Matthew dropped his gaze, seeming to pay particular attention to the water glass. "I don't think it would be a good idea to bring her to Fort Griffin at this time. She's better off where she is."

Reese looked puzzled. "What do you mean?"

"I . . . my mother and father have heard the gossip that's been circulating around town about Saber. They . . . we think it would be better to let it die down some before she comes back. After all, we don't really know what the

233

Millers did to her. It could be somewhat difficult to explain to our friends back in Philadelphia."

"What the hell are you talking about, Matthew?" Reese asked, jerking the glass out of Matthew's hand and slamming it on the table, drawing attention to them again.

Matthew lowered his voice. "Well, that little demonstration caught everyone's attention. We can't talk here."

"No," Reese said, barely able to control his temper. "We wouldn't want anything we said getting back to Philadelphia."

"Reese, don't say anymore. Let's get out of here. I sent word to her brother to meet us in my hotel room. He's probably there by now with my parents." Matthew awkwardly rose to his feet. "Suppose we finish this conversation there."

Reese tossed money on the table and followed Matthew out of the dining room and up the stairs. When they reached Matthew's room, Noble was already there, talking to Matthew's mother and father.

Mrs. Halloway was a prim woman with a high-necked lace gown and several strands of pearls that hung almost to her waist. Mr. Halloway was an older version of Matthew, with gray hair and boyish blue eyes.

Mrs. Halloway was speaking when Reese entered. "Mr. Vincente, I have heard nothing but praise about your family. I understand that your Casa del Sol is one of the largest ranches in Texas."

"There are others bigger," Noble was saying, his eyes meeting Reese's. "But here's the man you really want to meet, Mr. and Mrs. Halloway—Reese Starrett, the man who saved my sister's life."

Reese nodded stiffly and turned to Matthew. "Tell Saber's brother what you just said to me downstairs."

Matthew grinned uncomfortably and offered his hand to Noble. "We meet at last, Mr. Vincente. Saber has written me so much about you, I would have recognized you had we met on the street."

Noble looked puzzled. "What are you supposed to tell me?"

"Go ahead," Reese prodded. "Repeat what you said to me."

"I merely pointed out to Reese that it might be better if Saber remained at his ranch until the gossip died down."

Noble understood why Reese appeared so angry. He had not expected this from the man his sister was going to marry. "Saber has suffered enough, Matthew. I believe my sister would be better off with the people who love her. If we

235

keep her isolated, she will think we are ashamed of her."

"What my son means," Mr. Halloway interjected, "is that your sister might suffer embarrassment if she heard what was being said."

"Just what *is* being said?" Noble insisted on knowing.

Mrs. Halloway lowered her eyes to avoid the probing glance of Saber's brother. "I don't know if you are aware of it, Mr. Vincente, but our son is planning to run for political office when he leaves the army. Any breath of scandal may well end his hopes in that direction."

Noble's eyebrows met across the bridge of his nose. Had the people in the room known him better, they would have recognized that he was angry. "It seems to me that my sister is the one who has suffered. I don't give a damn about some future political career your son might aspire to."

"Now, now, let's not be hasty," Mr. Halloway said jovially. "The wedding will take place. We just need some assurances."

"What kind of assurances?" Reese asked in a cold voice. But he knew what was coming—he just didn't believe anyone could be so insensitive as this family. He'd thought of Matthew as an honorable man, but if he let his parents hurt Saber, Reese would have no respect for him at all.

It was Mrs. Halloway who answered. She linked her arm through her son's as if to steady him. "I know you are a good friend to my son, Mr. Starrett. He's told me that you wouldn't even accept money for what you did. That's why I feel I can talk plainly in front of you, knowing you will be discreet about this sensitive situation." She smiled, but there was no warmth in her expression. "Mr. Vincente," she said, turning to Noble. "I hope you will understand that we would like to have a doctor examine your sister."

Reese's hand came down hard on Noble's arm, and he stepped in front of Saber's brother. "At the moment, I don't think you can expect Mr. Vincente to respond to such a hideous notion, so I'm speaking for him. Saber will not be put through the humiliation you are suggesting."

Noble's fists were clenched, and he took a step toward Matthew. "And my sister won't be marrying you, you bastard!"

Matthew's face paled, and he shook his head. "I love your sister. I want her to be my wife."

"It will not happen, because you do not treasure her as she deserves to be treasured. I would never allow her to marry into such a family."

"You mistook our good intentions," Mr. Halloway blustered. "I have heard my son say on many occasions how respected the Vincente family is. That's why I think you will want to clear this nasty business up once and for all. I can't tell you how my wife and I have been looking forward to meeting dear Saber."

Noble barely kept his temper in check, and Reese took his arm and steered him to the door. He was angry enough himself to tear into Matthew, but it wasn't his place. "We are all upset by what's happened. After you have had a chance to think clearly, maybe we can talk this out."

Noble wrenched his arm free from Reese's grip and stalked to the door. "I have nothing more to say to any of you."

Reese followed him downstairs and outside. Noble stood for a long moment, letting the cool air hit him in the face. "What did you make of that, Reese?" he asked at last.

"About the same as you did."

Noble gripped the hitching post and leaned over, drawing in several deep breaths. "Saber is special. It's not because she's my sister. She's kind and loving; she cares deeply about those she loves. She would never understand what was said in that room today."

"I believe Matthew loves her."

Noble turned to Reese. "That's not the kind of love she deserves. Money and position mean nothing to her. Hell, Saber is wealthy in her own right, and as for position, she has my father's respected name, and our mother came from a fine old Southern family. No, I will not have her put through what they suggested."

"I agree with you on that."

Noble glanced at Reese. "You are Matthew's friend. Why have you sided with me in this?"

"I'm on Saber's side. Like you, I don't want to see her hurt, and she would be if you told her what was said in that room today. Matthew is being influenced by his mother and father. He's not usually like that."

"I need a drink," Noble said, stepping into the street and heading for a saloon. "Come on."

"Yeah. I need one, too," Reese agreed.

They were only halfway across the street when Reese heard a rider galloping right for them. He recognized Jake, and his blood froze. His gaze went to the horse Jake led, and the body that was draped across it.

"What's happened, Jake?" Reese asked, while Noble stopped and watched worriedly.

Jake slid from his horse, his youthful face flushed and excited. "It's Eugene Miller, Reese!"

Reese pulled back the canvas that covered the body, took a handful of hair, and peered at the dead face. "Yes. That's Eugene, all right." His stomach muscles tightened in fear for Saber. "What happened?"

"He came to the house, Reese. I know you told

me to keep an eye on Miss Vincente, but her sister-in-law came. I didn't think that anyone would bother them in the daytime, and we left two men behind to watch after them."

Noble's hand fell heavily on the young boy's shoulder. "My wife, my sister, has anything happened to them?"

"No, sir," Jake said, immediately recognizing Noble Vincente. "They ain't been harmed."

"For God's sake, Jake, tell me what happened, now!" Reese demanded, losing patience. "Tell me or I'll choke it out of you."

"It was Miss Saber that did it!" His youthful eyes were full of wonder. "Miller was coming for her and making threats, and she shot him deader'n dirt."

"Saber did?"

"She used your old gun from the bedroom, boss."

"I'm none too happy with you, Jake. She should never have been forced to defend herself," Reese said, his voice shaking.

"Our men heard the shots and ran to the house, but she didn't need them by then, other than to clean away the blood. She's some woman, Reese! There we was wanting to protect her, and she took care of herself!"

Reese and Noble exchanged glances. "Take the body to the sheriff and tell him what happened," Reese said. "Come on, Vincente; we got some riding to do!"

Chapter Eighteen

Although it had been two days since Saber had shot Eugene Miller, her hands still trembled, and her knees went weak when she thought about it.

Gabe and Jake had been wonderful. Gabe had insisted that Saber and Rachel leave the house while he cleaned up the blood, and Jake had taken the body to Fort Worth.

She walked into the bedroom, hoping she wouldn't cry again. Rachel had been so compassionate and understanding, but Saber didn't want to burden her any more than she had to.

She took one of Reese's shirts and held it against her face, knowing in her heart that she wanted his arms around her at that moment, holding her terror at bay and giving her comfort.

Rachel heard riders and glanced toward the rifle Gabe had loaded and placed near the door should they need it. But when she saw who it was, she flew out the front door, crying her husband's name. Noble was off his horse and had enveloped her in his embrace even before the animal halted.

Reese's glance went past Rachel, anxiously searching for Saber. He had almost ridden his horse to death to get to her, knowing she must be frightened and needing him.

Rachel untangled herself from her husband and walked up to Reese. She offered him her hand, and he grasped it firmly in his. "I don't have to ask who you are, Mr. Starrett. You are exactly the way Saber described you."

Reese was anxious because Saber hadn't come out to meet them. "How is she?"

Rachel frowned. "It is difficult for her, Mr. Starrett. Go on in and talk to her. You'll find her inside."

Noble started forward, but Rachel stalled him. "Let's get the horses taken care of. It looks like you tried your best to run them into the ground."

Noble shook his head. "I need to go to Saber."

"No, you don't." She nodded at Reese, who

was hurrying into the house. "He'll take care of her."

Noble frowned, and his jaw went rigid, the way it always did when he was angry. "What is that supposed to mean, Rachel? Why should Reese Starrett take care of her?"

She slid her arms around his waist and gave him a heart-shattering smile. "Because he's the one she wants right now." She tilted her head back and laughed at the confusion on his face. "You men are always the last ones to know. How simple it would be if we women just told you outright that we loved you."

"What? Are you saying my sister loves that man?"

"Of course. If you were a woman, you'd understand why. He is extraordinary looking."

Noble still looked confused and a little jealous that his wife found another man handsome. "Are you saying Saber loves Reese, and he doesn't know it?"

"That's exactly what I'm saying," she answered, taking the reins of Reese's horse and leading it toward the barn. "And you aren't to say anything to him. That will be up to Saber to do."

Noble had no choice but to lead his horse and follow her. "I won't have this, Rachel. First she's going to marry Matthew—although I refuse to let her marry him, and now she loves Reese Starrett. What's going on? What?"

"I don't know Matthew Halloway, but I like Reese Starrett, just from what Saber has told me about him. He isn't wealthy, and he doesn't have an aristocratic name, but he's honorable, and if it weren't for him we wouldn't have Saber."

Reese stood at the door with his hat in his hand. "Saber."

She hadn't heard him ride up because she'd been locked in her private hell. When she heard Reese's voice, a sob escaped her lips, and she walked out the bedroom door, wanting to be in his arms.

Reese could only stare at the beautiful vision in a long-sleeved pink gown with golden hair tumbling down her back to her waist. He had never seen anything that touched him so deeply. He wanted to rush to her, but this was not the Saber he knew. This was the polished and exquisitely dressed Miss Vincente.

But Saber took the decision out of his hands. She ran to him, throwing her body against the hard wall of his, and his arms went around her like a protective shield.

"Oh, Reese, Reese. I . . . took a life. I killed Eugene Miller!"

He buried his face in her hair and held her

tightly so his body could absorb her sobs. "I know, Saber. I know. But you had to." His lips touched her cheek, and he closed his eyes, loving her to the depths of his soul. "Don't think about it. It's over and done with."

She buried her face against his rough shirt and slid her arms around his shoulders. "I wanted you here with me. I knew you would make the nightmares go away."

He raised her chin and stared into tear-filled blue eyes. "What nightmares, Saber?"

"Every time I close my eyes, I see his dead eyes staring at me. He didn't think I'd shoot him, Reese. But I had to—I had to!"

He cradled her head against him. "It's over, sweetheart. He can't hurt you now."

"Yes—you're here now, and everything will be fine again. For the first time since you left, I feel safe."

He knew that she had come to depend on him, and that was more painful to him than if she were indifferent to him—because he would have to let her go, and soon she wouldn't be his to take care of.

He looked at her dainty hand with its slender fingers and delicately shaped nails, and he dipped his head to press his lips against that hand. For this moment she was his. But soon the world would come through that door in the shape of her brother, and he would have to let go of her forever.

She raised her head and looked into those silver eyes that were softened by gentleness. "Promise me you will never leave me again, Reese!"

There was agonizing regret in his heart. "That's one promise I can't make, and you know it, Saber."

She stepped away from him and raised her head to that proud tilt that he recognized so well. "You are right, of course. Since I no longer have to worry about the Millers, I can leave now."

"Your brother has come to take you away."

"Noble?" She started for the door. "Where is he?"

"I suspect he's talking to his wife."

Saber rushed out the door, looking about for Noble. Then she ran toward the barn. She needed her brother. Oh, she needed him so desperately!

Saber and Rachel were in the bedroom packing her trunk while Reese and Noble were sitting by the fire in the parlor. Reese was cleaning his rifle, and Noble was quietly pondering something in his mind.

At last Noble said, "I'm going to say something

to you, and I don't want you to misunderstand."

Reese glanced up quizzically. "I believe we have come to know each other in a short space of time. You can say what you will to me."

Noble grinned. "Remember you said that when I make my proposal to you."

"If you are going to offer me money, stop right now."

"No. It isn't money, it's something more valuable, and it will help us both out. I like what you've done with this ranch. You've had a bit of hard luck, but that can change."

Reese looked at him warily. "And you are going to tell me how I can do that?"

"Well, I wouldn't have put it quite like that, but, yes."

Reese finished oiling the rifle and set it aside, crossing his arms over his chest. "Go on. I'm listening."

"I purchased four bulls from England and seventy-five head of cattle from Spain. I want to crossbreed them and see if I can come up with a healthier and beefier herd."

Reese nodded. "It might work."

"Well, here's the rub," Noble said, glancing into the fire. "I have been looking for someone who is willing to throw in with me."

"Why? And in what way?"

"I want to split the herd and the bulls, run half

of them on Case del Sol and the other half with someone I find capable of such an endeavor."

"That someone being me?"

Noble leaned forward. He respected Reese Starrett as much as any man he'd ever met, and he had saved Saber's life. Furthermore, if Rachel was to be believed, Saber loved Reese. He certainly liked Reese better than he liked Maj. Matthew Halloway. "I told you, I've seen what you've done here, and you are the right man to split the herd with me. You've got the river and excellent grazing."

"I don't think so, Noble. This is just another way for you to offer me money."

"That's where you are wrong. I don't intend to give you my cattle, and what I propose will take a lot of work. I am prepared to split any offspring that come from the breeding. Fifty-fifty."

Reese leaned forward with sudden interest. "You know I lost most of my herd. If we have another bad winter, I could lose your herd as well."

"I'm a betting man sometimes. And I have this gut feeling that we won't have two bad winters back-to-back."

"Can I think about it?"

"There's not that much time. We have already missed most of this year's breeding season. You need to decide soon, Reese—now, today. The

249

cattle arrived two weeks before I left Casa del Sol. It will take at least three weeks for my drovers to herd them here."

Reese had lived his life as a loner, never quite trusting anyone—but he trusted Noble Vincente. He rarely let anyone get close to him or touch the world he'd created for himself. But Saber Vincente was banging on the door, and he knew there had been moments when he'd wanted to throw it open, if she would have him. He thought of her brother and how close she was to him. For the first time in his life, he wanted that kind of closeness in his life. He wanted children—he wanted Saber to mother his children.

"Well?" Noble asked. "What do you think? As I said, we would be helping each other."

Reese nodded. Saber would soon be leaving, but if he and Noble went into partnership in this, he'd still have a connection to her. "I'll do it."

Noble grinned and extended his hand. "It looks like I have a partner."

After a long silence, Reese said, "I assume you'll be taking Saber to Casa del Sol. When will you leave?"

"Early in the morning. We've taken advantage of your hospitality long enough. But I won't be taking her home just yet. Saber needs to settle this thing between her and Matthew. We Vincentes have never run from—or ignored—our troubles. No matter if Mrs. Halloway wants to keep my sister hidden away, I will never allow that. I will put her out there for the world to see."

"Noble, Matthew loves Saber. When he's not under the influence of his mother and father, he's an entirely different person."

"I like a man who is consistent. But that will be my sister's choice; only she can decide."

Reese stared back at the fire again and spoke in a hard voice. "I just want you to know that you need to look out for Graham Felton. He's not in Mexico, or Eugene would never have shown up here. I suspect he's still after Saber. I'm going to track him if I can."

"It's not your place, Reese. I will take care of Mr. Felton."

"It is my place. I started this, and I'll finish it."

Noble nodded, knowing Reese would do what he said. "I agree, on one condition."

"And that is?"

"If you find him, send me word. I want to be there, too. I have to know why he did this to my sister, or I'll never have any peace of mind."

"I'll let you know, if there's time. But if it means losing his trail, I'll go it alone. I don't intend to kill him unless I have to. I want to know myself why he had Saber kidnapped."

Noble looked into Reese's eyes and nodded. He understood more than Reese thought he did. Reese was going after Felton because he loved Saber, and for no other reason.

Chapter Nineteen

Saber wore a gray wool gown that matched her mood. She glanced about the bedroom, knowing she was seeing it for the last time. She would have been so happy here if she could have slept in that bed as Reese's wife.

Her footsteps were heavy as she moved into the tiny parlor and found Jake and Gabe waiting for her there.

"We wanted to say good-bye, Miss Vincente," Jake said, running his fingers around the brim of the hat he clutched in his hand.

Gabe grinned. "It's been a pleasure to know you, Miss Vincente. I'll miss your cooking."

She went to Jake and kissed his cheek. "Take care of yourself, Jake."

He blushed and looked pleased.

She then moved to Gabe and brushed her lips against his leathery skin. "You look after Mr. Starrett, Gabe."

He grinned and held his face where she'd kissed him. "Yes, ma'am, I'll surely do that, but a man like him takes a powerful lot of looking after."

She smiled, fighting the urge to cry. "We are in agreement on that." She hurried out the door and walked in the direction of the barn, wondering if Reese would be there. He would probably be happy to be rid of her, since she'd brought him nothing but trouble.

The inside of the barn was dark, but Saber saw Reese pitching hay to the horses. He didn't look up as she approached, but she knew he was aware of her presence.

"I couldn't leave without saying good-bye to you, Reese."

He paused, leaning a gloved hand on the handle of the pitchfork. "I'm sure you are anxious to see the last of this place." He didn't quite meet her eyes.

She placed her hand on his arm. "I have been contented here, Reese. You gave me a time to heal, and I will always be grateful to you for that.

254

You have done so much for me. I owe you more than I can ever repay."

He gave her a piercing gaze, and his light eyes turned silver. "You don't owe me a damned thing. I told you, Matthew paid me for what I did for you."

"Yes, but—"

He removed his gloves and tossed them aside. "Damn it, Saber, go to Matthew and talk to him—tell him how you feel. He loves you."

Tears welled in her eyes. "I'll just say good-bye then, Reese." She stepped closer, still unable to leave. "Hold me, Reese. Just this one last time."

A deep growl escaped his lips, and he grabbed her, clutching her so tightly she could hardly breathe. It felt glorious to be in his arms. If only he knew how much she loved him—if only he loved her, everything would be perfect!

He had managed to keep a tight rein on his feelings so far, but his control was slipping rapidly. His lips were hard and demanding as he ground them against hers. His tongue slid between her lips, and he groaned, backing her against the wall and lifting her, bracing her weight against him. He settled his hardening erection against her, and he fought against shoving her underclothes aside and driving into her.

Saber thought she would faint from the excitement he aroused in her. She forgot everything but the touch of his hand against her skin.

His mouth moved to the front of her gown, and he moved it against the material, kissing, nudging, making her cry out with awakening desire.

"Why couldn't you have just left without saying good-bye, Saber?"

His words barely penetrated her consciousness. She tossed her head back and whispered his name when he pushed her gown up and spread her legs. She bit her lip to keep from crying out. His hand moved between her thighs, and he slid his finger inside her, causing her to arch and buck against him.

"Reese, oh, Reese."

His neck muscles corded, and his breathing came out in a hiss when his finger reached through her hot tightness until he came to the barrier he'd hoped to find. His body trembled, and he gritted his teeth.

Saber was still a virgin!

She had not been violated. He wrestled with the temptation to break through that barrier, but he slowly withdrew his hand and set her on her feet.

His voice was deep and harsh. "You can assure Matthew that the Miller brothers didn't violate you while you were unconscious."

She blinked her eyes as she came back to reality. "I . . . what?"

He straightened her gown and gazed into her confused blue eyes. "I have just felt the proof that you were untouched, Saber."

"I don't care about that. It doesn't matter any longer."

"It will matter when you see Matthew again, Saber. Although, if I were you, I'd tell him your memory came back and not admit to what I just did to you." He pushed her tumbled hair away from her face.

She looked into his eyes and saw torment and hopelessness. "Why did you stop, Reese?"

He glanced up at the rafters as if he were having a hard time speaking. "It was difficult to touch you and let you go, Saber. You will never know how much that cost me."

Her mouth went dry, and she felt pain rip though her with such intensity that she pressed her hand against her heart.

Reese loved her!

She saw the love shining in his eyes—how could she not have seen it before now? She knew the reason he had avoided her since he'd returned: he didn't trust himself around her.

But the realization of that love brought her only momentary happiness, because he would never admit to her that he loved her. He would never take a woman who belonged to his friend. Why did he have to be a man of such integrity and honesty?

Loving him as she did, she could do no less than he was willing to do. She could never admit to him how deeply she loved him, because it would only bring him torment, and he would be burdened by the knowledge.

"Reese, do you think love lasts forever—I mean, real love, the kind that comes along only once in a lifetime?"

He breathed deeply and reached up to tie a bow that had come undone on her gown. "Yes. If love is real, it will last forever and perhaps beyond." He turned her toward the door. "So you see, you have nothing to worry about. Matthew will be waiting for you with all the love a man can give a woman."

Her eyes were sad and teary. She softly touched his lips, and he closed his eyes. "I will remember what you have told me. Love is forever."

His voice was deep, strained, his eyes still intense. "You had better leave, Saber."

She nodded, turned, and ran from the barn. She was running away from the man she would always love to marry a man she could never love.

An hour later they were ready to leave. Rachel was seated in the carriage, and her brother was mounted on his horse. When Saber approached from the house, Noble dismounted and helped her into the carriage.

"Ready to go, Saber?"

"Yes. Take me away from here."

She settled back against the cushions, and Rachel placed a lap robe over her. "We'll be in Fort Worth before sundown," she said.

Oh, Reese, she cried silently as the carriage pulled away from the ranch house, why must life be so unfair?

After they had been traveling for some time, Rachel knew she had to tell Saber what Matthew and his parents had requested of her before the marriage. But when she had done so, Saber did not react with the indignation Rachel had expected.

"Do you understand what I'm saying, Saber?"

"Does Reese know about this?" Saber asked.

Rachel frowned. "Yes. Noble said he was furious. You can imagine what your brother's reaction was. In fact, Noble wanted to take you directly to Casa del Sol and tell the Halloways to—well . . . go to hell. But I managed to persuade him that this was your decision and that you had to see Matthew and talk to him yourself."

Saber's voice was calm because she was remembering what Reese had said to her in the barn. Now it all made sense. What he'd done for her had been because he loved her and didn't want to see her suffer the indignity of being examined at the Halloways' request.

Rachel settled back against a fluffy pillow and looked thoughtful.

"If you don't love Matthew, you will be doing him a great disservice by marrying him, Saber. You could end it, you know."

"Sometimes we get caught up in a situation that we can do nothing about. If Matthew still wants to marry me, how can I refuse?" After a while, she added softly, "Reese loves me."

"I am so relieved he told you. Now you can do something about it."

"He didn't tell me. You have to understand the kind of man he is and why he's that way. We can never be together—never."

Rachel shook her head, thinking about the tangle that awaited them in Fort Worth, and the one they had just left behind.

It was a little after dark when they reached town. Noble took his sister straight to the hotel and had dinner served in her room. Then he went in search of Matthew.

Reese lifted the pan off the stove and muttered a curse, dropping it back down and rubbing his burned hand. Nothing was going right. But what did it matter—what did anything matter since Saber had left?

He remembered how confused she'd been in the barn that morning. She was so young and innocent. She'd been caught in a situation not of her making. If she hadn't been kidnapped, he would probably have gone to her wedding and watched her marry Matthew without feeling any emotion toward her at all.

He shook his head. No. Even meeting her for the first time on her wedding day would not have kept him from loving Saber. It had been meant to be that he should love her, and nothing could change that. He knew that he would never love another woman—that his heart would always belong to her.

He walked out of the kitchen, grabbed his coat, and headed for the barn. He was going to Fort Griffin, knowing Matthew would have reported back to duty by now. He couldn't go on wondering what was happening to Saber. And he was determined to keep an eye on her and to make sure Graham Felton didn't get near her. Felton was a desperate man. Saber wasn't safe as long as he was on the loose.

Chapter Twenty

Matthew had been ordered to report back to Fort Griffin, and his parents had accompanied him there. He lay upon his cot, staring into the darkness. Everything was in such confusion. All he'd wanted to do was marry Saber. He loved her, but he also wanted a career in politics—he wanted both. He had a sterling reputation as an army officer, and that would go a long way toward helping him when he ran for office.

He hadn't wanted Saber to be examined by a doctor, but his mother had convinced him it was necessary. What if she had been raped? What if one of the men had impregnated her? He certainly didn't want to give his name to one of the

Miller brothers' by-blows. He remembered Saber as she'd been in Georgia, a beautiful and innocent young girl who had gotten caught up in a war she didn't understand. He'd fallen in love with her at that time. But that had been over two years ago. He still pictured her as that young girl, and sometimes he had trouble remembering what she looked like.

He shoved the covers aside and went to the window, staring out into the gathering light. He tested his leg and was glad it was no longer painful; the doctor had removed the splint.

He frowned; his mind was in a quandary. He couldn't marry Saber. After all, they really didn't know each other. But how could he offend the sister of one of the most powerful men in Texas? It was quite simple: HE would have to make her reject him. And the means to that end might already have been set into motion. All he had to do was insist that she go through with a doctor's examination.

Noble Vincente had sent word that he would be bringing Saber to Fort Griffin tomorrow. The commanding officer of the base had been so impressed by the Vincente name that his wife had planned a welcoming party and invited all the officers and their ladies. He could feel the trap closing around him.

He pulled his trousers on. Tomorrow night he

would be free of Saber. A strange ache touched his heart as he remembered the beautiful young girl he'd pictured as his wife. He had to let her go and then forget about her.

Matthew heard the sound of the bugler playing assembly. It was too early for formation, so something must be wrong. He hurriedly tucked his shirt in and pulled on his boots, then thrust his arms into his coat. Running for the parade ground, he found the returning patrol leading riderless horses.

"Indian attack at several ranches between here and Fort Belknap, Major Halloway, sir," the pockmarked sergeant informed him hurriedly. "Colonel Washburn's ordered us to ride out at once, sir."

Matthew was somehow relieved as he later rode out the gate at the front of his patrol. He'd never been accused of lacking courage, but he would rather face the Indians than Saber and her formidable brother.

Rachel entered Saber's room and spun around in a circle. "It's amazing that a dress from your trousseau would fit me. What do you think?"

Rachel looked beautiful in the green silk creation. "I never thought about it, but we are of the same height."

"I confess I had to let the waist out a bit," Rachel said, laughing. "You have such a tiny waist."

Saber slipped her white gloves on and met Rachel's eyes. "I am not looking forward to this party. I would sooner have ridden home to Casa del Sol."

"I understand, Saber. But your brother and I will be beside you." She tilted Saber's chin up. "Just remember who you are."

Sadness touched Saber. "I never forget who I am. After tonight I want to go home."

"Are you sure?"

"Yes. Very sure. I thought I could marry Matthew, but you were right when you said I would be cheating him since I don't love him."

Rachel slid her arm around Saber's waist, feeling pity for Noble's sweet sister. "Whatever decision you make tonight, your brother and I will stand by it." She frowned and took Saber's hand. "Take that worried look off your face. Noble thinks the party is a good idea. We will sail in and act as if nothing is amiss."

"What if Matthew is still on patrol? I'll have to face his mother and father alone."

Rachel fastened a strand of pearls around Saber's throat. "No, you won't. I told you that Noble and I will be with you. And we Vincente woman are dressed for battle."

Saber smiled and nodded. "Stay near me tonight."

Reese stood across the room, his arms folded over his chest, his eyes on the door that Saber would come through when she arrived. He felt different from everyone else in the room, but he somehow needed to be there. Since he'd scouted for the army and was known to be a friend of Matthew's, he was welcome at these functions. But he had never attended until tonight.

He caught a glimpse of Matthew's mother and father mingling with the officers and their wives. They were apparently enjoying being the center of attention. There was a stir at the door, and Matthew entered, the gold leaves on his dark blue dress uniform signifying he was a major. Reese watched as Matthew greeted everyone and then finally made his way across the room to him.

"I heard you had Indian troubles, Matthew."

"Nothing much. Just a few renegades who got liquored up and caused a disturbance. They are sobering up in the guardhouse, and we'll let them go in the morning." He stared at Reese, who looked uncomfortable in a black suit. "I'm surprised to see you here tonight. I know you were not too happy with me the last time we met in Fort Worth."

"I won't deny that I was angry at the time." Reese glanced around the room, wondering what he was doing there. "But you are still my friend."

"I hope I'll still be your friend after tonight." Matthew's face whitened, and he stiffened, his gaze focused on the doorway. "They're here!" His glance moved from the beautiful redhead to the breathtaking woman with hair the color of summer wheat. She wore a shimmering blue gown that left her shoulders bare. "She has grown even more beautiful," he said in amazement. "I am just reminded how much I love her."

Reese was speechless as he watched Saber standing between Rachel and Noble, looking so proud and yet so frightened. He had never seen anyone more beautiful than she was at that moment. Did anyone but him know how apprehensive she was? He was once more aware of their differences. Saber would never be his, even if she didn't marry Matthew. She was quality, and he was a dirt-poor rancher who could never offer her the kind of life she was accustomed to. "You are a lucky man, Matthew," he said through the thickness in his throat.

Matthew stared at Saber as if he'd never seen her before. She was an angel, a goddess. In that moment he forgot his earlier plan, knew he must have her for his wife.

Constance O'Banyon

Reese watched Matthew cross the room to Saber. It was at that point that he overheard a young first lieutenant speaking to his companion. "What a beauty! I'd ride to hell and walk back just to see her smile at me."

"Yeah, me, too. But that smile is for the major; and no one else. You could only reach as high as Saber Vincente's shoelaces."

Reese shoved himself between the two officers and cast them a threatening scowl. "You couldn't even reach her shoelaces," he muttered.

The lieutenant spoke to his friend in a puzzled voice. "Now, what do you suppose got Reese Starrett's dander up?"

"Maybe he wants the lady to smile for him. They did spend a lot of time alone together, remember?"

Both men snapped to attention, and their faces became flushed when Colonel and Mrs. Washburn walked past them. The look the colonel gave them made them fall silent.

Saber's hand was resting on her brother's arm, and he felt it tremble. Noble gave her a soft look of encouragement. "You have been to grander balls than this, Saber."

She nodded, watching as an elderly man and woman approached her; she wondered if they might be Matthew's parents. The woman was wearing a black lace gown, and her gray hair was piled on top of her head. Her skin was unlined, and she looked the part of the perfect matriarch.

Noble greeted the Halloways and presented them to Rachel, and then to Saber.

"My dear," Mrs. Halloway gushed, "you are simply lovely. I now know why my son is so taken by you."

"You are too kind," Saber said politely.

"Not at all." Mrs. Halloway's gaze settled on Noble, and she bestowed her most charming smile on him. "I have learned, Mr. Vincente, just how important you are in this state. Why didn't you tell me your family is descended from Spanish nobility? I had to find it out from Colonel Washburn."

"I don't believe that a useless honor settled on my ancestors is of any importance, Mrs. Halloway. I am an American, and I have no ties to Spain or any of its titles."

"Whyever not?" Mrs. Halloway said with conviction. "An uncle of mine, by marriage on my mother's side, was related to George Washington, and I am proud of it."

"If it makes you feel more important to claim some distant kinship, then by all means, go to it," Noble said coolly. Rachel could feel his anger stirring, and she moved to his side and gripped his arm. She was grateful when Matthew appeared, and everyone's attention turned to him and Saber. After being presented to the major, she gave Saber an encouraging nod.

Matthew bowed before Saber, his eyes never leaving her face. "I thought this day would never come." He held his hand out to her. "Shall we dance?"

She allowed Matthew to lead her across the floor, her eyes on his face as she searched for the young officer who had come to her rescue in Georgia. "I'm glad to see your leg has healed."

"It is as good as ever."

He had changed but little, still handsome and still the gallant gentleman she remembered. "How fortunate it healed so quickly." She was reaching for something to say to him. She hadn't known this first meeting would be so awkward for her.

Matthew's gaze moved across her face, and he felt his heart quicken. "Before you were a lovely young lady; now you are a breathtaking woman."

She could not help smiling at Matthew. He certainly was charming. "You are much the same as I remember you."

Reese stepped out the door, unable to watch Saber in Matthew's arms. It was as if he had been ripped apart and was bleeding inside.

"I wish we could be alone," Matthew said, squeezing her hand. "How unfortunate that our first meeting after all these years should be in a crowded room."

"I would like very much to talk to you alone. Perhaps we can meet after the party."

His eyes gleamed. "Yes, of course." His chest swelled, and he knew he was the envy of every man in the room. "I'll arrange it."

Saber was soon separated from Matthew and found herself dancing with Colonel Washburn and then several other officers. Her mind was not on her dance partners; instead, she was practicing what she would say to Matthew when they were alone. She was glad when her last partner returned her to Noble's side. She didn't want to dance, but she knew she'd be obliged to, if asked.

"Miss Vincente, may I have the next dance?"

Saber turned at the sound of the deep tone. Her eyes met Reese's, and she seemed to float into his arms. Her heart was beating so fast it was keeping time with the music of the lively dance.

"You seem to be the belle of the party."

"Do you think so?"

"You know you are beautiful, and everyone in this room knows it, too."

She could smell whiskey on his breath and

knew he'd been drinking. "Pretty words, Reese," she said, trying to make light of the situation.

He scowled at her, pulling her closer, his breath teasing her mouth, and her lips opened as if to receive his kiss.

Hot desire surged through his body, and his lips hungered for hers. "God help me, I have thought of nothing but you since you left me."

Tears gathered in her eyes because she knew she was hurting him. "I thought you would be happy to see the last of me."

His silver eyes narrowed, and his hand gripped her waist tightly. "When I saw you with Matthew, I knew you belonged together."

She wanted to lay her head on his shoulder and tell him that she belonged with him. But she couldn't, not yet.

Reese raised her hand to his cheek and closed his eyes at the satin touch. She sucked in her breath when he turned her hand over and placed a kiss just above her glove, sending a tingling sensation down her spine. She realized that Reese was half-drunk, and everyone was staring at them. She had to make him stop, or he would hate himself tomorrow. "Don't, Reese. Don't do this."

His head snapped up as if he realized what he had been doing. "Yes. You are right. I've had too much to drink. A man can't be held responsible for what he says when he's been drinking."

"It's not like you to drink, Reese."

"It seemed a good idea tonight."

His silver eyes seared her, his touch burned her skin, and she wanted to touch him, to tell him that she was as tormented as he was. She wanted him to touch him, to hold her, to do everything a man did with the woman he loved. But the image of Matthew stood between them like a flaming sword. She was glad when the dance stopped, and she hurried across the floor to Noble.

For the rest of the evening she danced with her brother and Matthew. Reese didn't approach her again, although she could feel his eyes on her.

Around midnight Reese left, and Saber wondered if she would ever see him again.

Chapter Twenty-one

Seeing Saber's ashen face, Noble turned to Matthew. "I believe my sister is tired. I am going to take her to the hotel."

"May I call on her tonight?" Matthew asked.

Noble pulled her protectively to him, his eyes holding a warning. "It depends on what you have to say to her," he said, lowering his voice. "She's been through enough."

Matthew smiled at Saber. "I believe she and I have a wedding to plan, don't we, Saber?"

"Do you?" Noble asked in a deep tone that would have intimidated most men.

But Matthew seemed to be lost in a pair of blue eyes. "Yes. We most definitely do," Matthew answered. "And my parents have asked if you would all attend a luncheon they are giving tomorrow."

Rachel glanced at Saber. "Are you too weary for visitors tonight?"

Saber nodded her head. "I am weary, Matthew. Perhaps we could talk tomorrow."

"Then we will say good night," Noble said, leading his wife and sister out of the building.

Saber leaned her head on her brother's shoulder. She couldn't think straight. She had realized tonight that if she married Matthew, she would destroy Reese, and she wasn't willing to do that.

Matthew found Reese standing in the shadows of the porch and clapped him on the back. "I am perfectly content that everything will end well for Saber and myself. I owe it all to you."

Reese swirled whiskey around in his glass, his eyes boring into Matthew. "Did you settle the part about having a doctor examine her?"

"That was all my mother's idea, and on thinking about it, I'm not willing to demand such a thing of Saber."

"A wise decision," Reese replied, his hand tightening on the whiskey glass.

Saber was dressed only in her nightgown and robe when someone knocked at her door. She expected it to be either Noble or Rachel, so when she opened the door and found Matthew there, she was shocked. "I thought we agreed to talk tomorrow."

He stepped around her and glanced about the room, looking for Noble or Rachel, and was relieved that they were alone. He smiled, taking her hand and raising it to his lips. "We have a lot to discuss, my sweet."

"You shouldn't be here, Matthew. Noble won't like it when he finds out about it."

"There's nothing wrong with my being here. I'm going to be your husband. And soon that brother of yours will have nothing to say about what we do."

She decided this was as good a time as any to tell him what was on her mind. "I don't think we are suited for each other, Matthew. I'm begging you to leave now."

"We're suited, all right. Any doubts I might have had disappeared the moment I saw you tonight." In a quick motion he drew her into his arms. "I want to sample some of what will soon belong to me."

She smelled the liquor on his breath and froze in fear. This was not the Matthew she had known and trusted. His arms tightened about her, and she tried to wedge her arm between them. "Let me go!" she said, pushing at him. He reminded her of Eugene, and terror curled inside her. His lips were wet when he pressed them against hers. His hands went up to cup her breasts, and she cringed inside.

"I don't know you," she said, turning her face away from his. His eyes were glazed with passion, and his breathing was heavy—she knew why he had come here, and it wasn't to talk.

Saber managed to push him away. "Please don't do this."

"You're mine. You belong to me."

He reached for her, but she managed to dodge out of his way. "You are drunk!" She felt sick inside—the back of her throat burned from the bile that rose there. "And I'm not yours. I could never marry a man who treated me the way you have."

He shook his head as if to clear it. "I was sitting at a table drinking straight whiskey, and I knew what I had to do."

She moved a safe distance from him. "What?"

"It's very simple. I'll take you to bed and find out for myself if you've been ruined. If they got to you, Saber, you will lose nothing by letting me make love to you."

Sudden tears stung her eyes, and she clasped her hand over her mouth. "You have a very low opinion of me, Matthew, if you believe I'd let you touch me. Get out and leave me alone!"

"I'll have you now, or I won't marry you at all."

Obviously he was past reasoning. "Noble's just in the next room," she warned him, "and if I call out to him, he'll hear me. If you don't leave now you'll have to face my brother, and believe me, you don't want to have him mad at you."

"You don't understand. It's eating me up inside thinking someone else had you before me. You're not the innocent I wanted to marry."

"And you are not the man I thought you were." She moved to the door and opened it. "Leave—now!"

"Saber, I want to recapture the love we found in Georgia. Everything has gone wrong, but I'll make it right." He reached out his hand and touched her hair. "You're like a well-bred filly and need to be handled gently. The only thing that would spoil it for us is if the Miller brothers sullied you."

She opened the door wider as she prepared to tell the first untruth of her life. "Then you are going to need to hear what I have to say if you feel that way."

Matthew was beginning to sober, to see the results of his actions. There was fear reflected on Saber's face. He loved her—didn't she know that? "Your brother told you I wanted you examined by a doctor, didn't he? That's what we'll do. You will do that for me, won't you, Saber?"

"I'll never submit to such an indignity."

He drew near her and turned her slowly to face him. "I see now that all this has upset you. I was wrong to come here tonight, and I'm so sorry. Say you'll forgive me."

"You have every right to know what happened to me while I was with the Miller brothers, Matthew. What would you do if you knew for certain that they raped me?"

He swallowed several times. "I love you. We would work it out somehow."

"How do you work out something like that? Would you resent me later on because I was violated by them?"

"I want you for my wife, Saber."

"Would you resent me later on?" she asked again, looking into his eyes to glean the truth.

"I had always thought the woman I married would come to me pure," he answered honestly. "I don't want you touched by any other man."

Saber remembered Reese telling her that if the woman he loved had been treated badly, he would only love her more. "You would feel that way even though the situation was none of my doing, Matthew?"

He felt crushing pain. "The way you are talking, Saber, makes me think those bastards did rape you."

She ducked her head. "I will say only that I am

not untouched, Matthew. Don't ask me anything more. I will not speak of it to you ever."

He lowered his head. "What if you . . . if you were to have a baby?"

"What if I did?"

He shook his head. "This is more than I can live with, Saber. I love you, but I can't give my name to you. I don't think I could make love to you without thinking of another man touching you."

"That is the way I thought you would feel. I release you from your promise, Matthew. You can say anything you want to save face with the other officers. I will remain silent on the matter."

"No one will ever hear about this from me, Saber." He staggered past her and stood in the hallway.

He didn't love her with the unselfish love she wanted from the man she married. "I think this is good-bye for us, Matthew."

He clasped her head between his hands. "When I saw you tonight, I remembered how much I loved you. I wanted you to be beside me the rest of my life. But I can't accept this, Saber. Try to understand."

"I'm trying. And you have to understand that after your conduct tonight, I could never marry you." There was sorrow in her blue eyes.

When he walked slowly away, she closed and securely locked the door, leaning against it. Tears of misery spilled down her cheeks. It was done.

Already Matthew was regretting the way he had acted with Saber. If only he hadn't been drinking when he'd gone to her room, it might have been different. He was haunted by the look of disgust on her face. How would he ever make it up to her for the things he had said to her?

Saber smiled sadly, hoping as time passed she would think of Matthew as the dashing calvary officer who had come to her rescue that year in Georgia. She went to the window and watched him mount his horse and ride away. "A young girl's dream," she said softly. "Not a woman's love."

Reese was sober when he walked to the livery stable to saddle his horse. The cold air helped to clear his head. He had only one thing to do now, and that was to find Felton and bring him in. That was the last thing he could do for Saber.

The barn was dark, with only a single lantern hanging from the rusty nail beside the front door. He made his way to his horse, which had been placed in the back stall. Throwing the blanket over the horse's back, he then lifted the saddle into place.

Constance O'Banyon

"Reese . . ."

Reese spun around to find Saber standing behind him. For a long moment he stared at her, unable to speak. "Should you be here?" he asked at last. "It's late to be out."

"I saw you from my hotel window and followed you here."

"I'm sure if you leave now, no one will be the wiser."

She ran her hand over the neck of his horse. "I need to talk to you."

He placed the saddle back on the railing. "I see you will have your way in this." He folded his arms over his chest. "Go ahead—talk. I'm listening."

"Reese, I lied to Matthew tonight. Not in words, really, but I led him to draw the wrong conclusion."

He couldn't see her face very well in the muted light, so he stepped closer to her. "What about?"

"I let him think that I'd been raped."

He grabbed her arm and pulled her closer. "Why would you do something like that? You know it isn't true—I told you it wasn't."

She decided not to tell him how badly Matthew had behaved in her hotel room. Reese didn't need to know how reprehensibly his friend had acted tonight. "He didn't love me

282

enough, Reese. Not the way a woman wants to be loved."

"I know he loves you, Saber. Surely he told you that."

"Yes, he did. But I am a rancher's daughter. I don't want the kind of life Matthew wants. I would not make a good politician's wife."

"It sounds like you didn't love *him* enough, Saber."

She moved closer and touched his cheek. "There is truth in that, Reese. I was so young when we first met. I guess you could say neither Matthew nor I loved each other enough."

Against his will he pulled her into his arms, feeling the softness of her cheek against his. "I'm sorry, Saber. I believe you and Matthew were right for each other."

"What about you, Reese? Will you ever marry?"

He set her away from him and reached for his saddle, so he'd have something to do with his hands. "No woman would want a broken-down old cowboy like me, Saber."

She laughed. "I see a tall, handsome man with wide shoulders who makes the women swoon when he passes by."

He frowned. "Surely not you."

"I don't know, cowboy. You stomp around in those boots acting tough, but I have seen the softness in you. And that's what I like most about you."

He drew in an agitated breath. "Is there a point to all this, Saber?"

"Yes, I was getting to that. If a man touches a woman intimately, do you think it's his duty to marry her?"

He let out his breath and dropped the saddle. "Damn it, Saber! I know where you are going with this. Is that why you wouldn't marry Matthew, because I touched you?"

She could have said yes, but it wasn't true, and she had already told one lie tonight. In truth, she wanted him to take her to the ground right now and fan the flames that he'd ignited in her that day in his barn. "You are the only man who has touched me. I think if my brother knew, he'd insist you marry me."

"Hardly. I don't think I'm what he has in mind for a brother-in-law."

"I would never feel right with any another man, Reese."

He glanced upward, trying not to lose his patience. "I shouldn't have done what I did, Saber. But your virginity is still intact. You are as pure as the day you were born."

She stepped closer to him. "Didn't you like touching me, Reese?"

He stepped away from her so fast she might

have thought her touch burned him. "You'd better leave now, Saber. A man can only take so much."

She moved even closer, standing so near she could feel his breath on her cheek. She leaned her head on his shoulder and felt him stiffen. No one had ever given her the comfort she drew from being near him. She loved him, and she was sure he loved her. But he would never ask her to marry him. He had the mistaken notion that he wasn't good enough for her. How could she make him see he was wrong?

"Hold me, Reese."

His arms went around her, crushing her against his body. He kissed her cheek, ran his lips across her lashes, and then lifted her, crushing her mouth with his. Saber had never known that a kiss could be so consuming. She felt as if she would faint. She never wanted him to stop, but he did.

He drew back his head, on the brink of losing control completely. "If you don't leave now, Saber, I'll have you in that hay in another minute, and there won't be any doubt that you have had a man."

She dropped her cape and unhooked her gown while he watched helplessly. He burned and swelled for her, and when she took his hand and placed it on her exposed breast, he went slowly to his knees, taking her with him. His lips were on her mouth while he caressed her breast—but he wanted more.

Saber hardly realized he had laid her on the hay. He lowered his head, his mouth closing over her nipple, and she wanted to scream from the unbridled passion that tore through her. He pushed the bottom of her gown upward and moved her legs apart.

Reese had wanted her for so long, he couldn't stop himself now. He rolled her to her back and lowered his body on top of her.

He pressed between her legs, and she could feel him even through his trousers. Saber squirmed, trying to get closer to him. She didn't want anything between them but bare flesh.

"Be still," he said in a growl, "or I'll have all of you, Saber."

She arched her back, pressing herself against the swell of him.

Reese groaned, pushed her undergarment aside, and caressed her urgently. "Is this what you wanted? Is this why you came here?"

His words were angry and like a cold dash of water in her face. She braced her hands against his chest, feeling the laborious beating of his heart. "I didn't have this in mind when I followed you. But once inside the barn, I decided I wanted you." She pushed against him, and he released her.

"Your plan worked. My hands were all over you, Saber."

He gripped her arm, but she shoved his hand away. "You have nothing to reproach yourself for tonight, Reese. The fault is all mine."

She scrambled to her feet and tugged her gown into place. Reaching down for her cape, she slipped it around her shoulders and hurried toward the door. But she had not gone far before she came up against the solid wall of Reese's chest.

She was near the lantern, and he could see tears on her cheeks. "God, Saber, why are you doing this? What do you want from me?"

She shook her head, suddenly feeling ashamed of her actions. "I will say good-bye now. I don't think our paths will cross again, Reese."

His hands dropped away. "No. I don't think they will, Saber. There is just one question I want to ask you, but I really don't have that right."

"You can ask me anything you want to."

"Would you marry a broken-down old cowboy?"

"Would that cowboy be you?"

"You didn't let me finish, Saber. Could you so

easily turn away from Matthew, who has loved you for years and has spoken of you every day I've known him? Could you leave him and marry me?"

She was about to tell her second falsehood of the night. "I suppose you are feeling guilty, but you don't need to, Reese. It's not necessary for you to make me respectable by marrying me. Nothing really happened between us."

He was silent for a long time. "Would you have me for a husband, Saber?" His hand trembled when he touched hers. "Would you?"

She wanted him to reach inside himself and admit he loved her. "Why?"

"For whatever the reason, I'm asking you to be my wife." He had not intended to ask her to marry him; the words just seemed to slip out. He expected her to refuse his offer and to be horrified that he would dare ask her to marry him. He felt a deep, empty void inside as he waited for her to reject him. After tonight, he'd go back to his ranch and take up his empty life. Nothing would have any meaning because the golden-haired woman who'd made him fall in love had left him.

"Yes," she answered without further hesitation. "I will have you for my husband, Reese."

He reeled in shock at her acceptance. At first he thought he must have misunderstood. Maybe she wanted to punish Matthew by marrying his friend. Whatever her reasons were, they didn't matter to him. He'd take her any way he could get her.

"What do we do now? Do I go to your brother and ask for your hand?"

She was willing him to take her in his arms and confess he loved her, but he seemed to be in a daze. "I will tell Noble."

They stared at each other, both having so much to say, but neither willing to mention the love that burned within.

"I have something I have to do first," he said at last. "In two weeks' time, I'll come to you at Casa del Sol to ask if you still want to marry me."

Saber didn't know what she'd expected from Reese, but it certainly wasn't this cold indifference. "I won't change my mind. I'll be waiting for you," she answered, rushing past him into the night. He went to the door and watched her until she was safely inside the hotel.

He braced his back against the door frame and stared up at the night sky. This day, which had begun so miserably, had ended in his getting the one woman in the world for him.

But could he make her happy? He would sure try his damnedest. Even if he could keep her only a day or a week, he wanted her so much it ripped him apart inside.

289

He went back inside to finish saddling his horse. Just the thought of giving her his name, then taking her to bed, cut his breathing off.

Two weeks was a long time to wait when he wanted to be with her so desperately!

Chapter Twenty-two

Spring burst across the land. The prairie grasses had turned green, and new foals were frolicking in the fields among the wildflowers at Casa del Sol.

Saber shoved an apple through the fence to entice a young colt on wobbly legs to come forward. The colt nudged the apple and then backed nervously away. The mare, however, was accustomed to Saber's bringing treats and pushed her head forward to take the apple, devouring it in a short time.

Noble appeared at her side, grinning. "You have always had the Vincente touch with animals."

Constance O'Banyon

She turned troubled eyes on her brother. "Noble, do you think Reese will lose his ranch?"

"Not if he can help it. He's a fighter, Saber, and won't give up easily."

"You admire him, don't you?"

"Yes, I do. But that doesn't mean I want you to marry him."

"I love him, Noble."

He had balked at the idea of his sister marrying Reese. He had nothing against the rancher, but it was only a short time ago that she believed she loved Matthew. Rachel had calmed many of Noble's fears, and he did feel that Reese would be good to his sister. "He won't accept help from you, Saber. He's too proud to live on his wife's money."

"But I want to help him. There must be some way."

"We will think of something." He slid his arm around her shoulder. "It's a funny thing—I was not all that willing to give you up to Matthew, and I'm still not sure I know all that happened that night of the dance."

"I realized I couldn't marry him because I loved Reese."

He tilted her chin up. "Has he told you he loves you?"

"Not in words. But I know he does."

He grinned. "That's why we men don't have a

chance around you women. You always know what we're thinking."

"Rachel certainly can read your mind." She threw back her head and laughed. "Your little redhead is the perfect woman for you—just as Reese is right for me."

He moved toward the stable and called over his shoulder, "See you at dinner."

Saber turned back to the house, knowing that Reese would be arriving any day. She watched and listened for him and could hardly sleep at night for thinking about him. She couldn't wait to go back to his ranch and make it a home for him. She could hardly breathe when she thought of the night she would go to him as his wife. Saber was determined to be the best wife possible. Reese had been alone for so long, and she wanted to take care of him. She wanted to give him a family and to make him happy.

She watched as three wagons pulled up to the house—more supplies for the wedding. Noble had insisted that his sister marry in the Vincente style, and Rachel had agreed with him. Invitations had gone out all over Texas, and most of those invited would attend.

Reese rode through the gates of Casa del Sol and looked about him with the eyes of a rancher. Fat cattle grazed on plentiful grass, with an occa-

sional bundle of hay dotting the land. Water was
plentiful, fed by the double fork of the Brazos
River. There was a peacefulness and serenity
here. He galloped underneath huge trees that
arched over the road. When he topped a rise, he
gazed at the magnificent Spanish ranch house
with the red-tile roof. There were barns, stables,
outbuildings, and bunkhouses. Blooded horses
ran behind the white rail fence near the corral.
This was the kind of life Saber was accustomed
to. What kind of life could she expect to have
with him? There was nothing he could offer her
that her brother didn't have more of.

As he rode up to the stable, Zeb came hobbling
toward him. "I was told you was coming, Mr.
Starrett. There's quite a to-do up to the big
house." He cast a sideways glance at Reese.
"You're taking the rose of Casa del Sol. I 'spect
you will look out for her and treat her well."

Reese had to smile at the crusty old cowboy.
"I'll do my best, Zeb."

"I knowed you would. I heard you're a good
man; leastwise, Rachel says so, and she ain't
never wrong about people."

Reese dismounted. "I'll have to remember to
thank her for the kind testimonial."

At that moment Rachel came across the yard
with a welcoming smile on her lips. "Reese. I'm
glad you're here at last." She could tell he was

startled when she kissed his cheek and linked her arm through his. "I'm afraid you are going to have to suffer through a long bout of singing and dancing tonight. We at Casa del Sol know how to celebrate a wedding in fine style."

Reese removed his hat and paused at the door. "Saber still wants to go through with this?"

Rachel looked into Reese's slate gray eyes. She saw there the anxiety he was feeling. "I don't think you can get away from her now, so you'd better get ready to settle down and become a married man." Impishness danced in her eyes. "Father Delion has already arrived to perform the ceremony."

He ran a hand through his hair nervously. "What can I offer her compared to all this?" He made a wide sweeping motion with his hand. "You've seen my house."

"Saber will have it turned into a home before you know it. And as for what you can offer her?" She shook her head and laughed. "I'd be willing to bet half the women in the state of Texas envy her because she has caught the elusive Reese Starrett."

He grinned at the woman who would soon be his sister-in-law. "You always know the right thing to say, don't you?"

She opened the door and went inside with him. "Practically always." She looked thoughtful. "Nobel might argue the point with you."

Reese glanced around the entryway with its elegant furnishings and was struck by another moment of doubt. He saw movement on the wide stairs, and Saber seemed to float toward him. She wore a pale yellow gown, and her hair was swept on top of her head. Every time he saw her, he realized she was the perfect woman, and it scared the hell out of him!

Saber approached him, smiling, and a sweet scent that he had come to associate with her assailed his senses.

Rachel moved toward the door. "I'll turn him over to you, Saber. I want to make sure they hung the Chinese lanterns in the courtyard." She paused in the doorway and said, "Don't monopolize him, Saber. I know your brother wants to show him some cattle."

Saber laid her head against Reese's chest, and his arms slid around her. She was so fragile and delicate. It frightened him that he would be responsible for her well-being and happiness.

"I would like to have you to myself, but for now it's not possible." She sighed and went up on her tiptoes to brush her lips against his.

His eyes dilated, the dark irises becoming passionate swirls. "Saber, do you still want me for your husband?"

A teasing light came into her eyes. "You

haven't found someone else you'd rather marry, have you?"

"Not likely."

"Then you'll have to marry me." She led him toward the courtyard, where Rachel was instructing several workmen. "If you have changed your mind, you'd better run now, because at precisely seven tonight I come down the stairs wearing the most beautiful wedding gown you have ever seen."

He stopped near a fountain and stared at the bubbling water. "It isn't the same gown you were going to wear if you had married Matthew, is it?" He didn't know why he should care, but he did.

"No. That was donated to one of our vaqueros who had a sister getting married. She was most grateful for the gift."

"What happens after our wedding? I didn't want to make any plans until I spoke to you."

"Rachel and Noble will be spending the night at the Broken Spur with her sister and her husband. We will have this house all to ourselves. Of course, there will be dancing and singing all night."

"The Broken Spur was Rachel's ranch, wasn't it?"

"It still is. Her sister and her husband run it, but it's Rachel's all the same."

Before Reese could say anything more, guests started arriving. He was introduced to Rachel's sister, Delia, and her husband, Tanner. The guests just seemed to keep coming. Reese met so many people he didn't even attempt to keep their names straight.

Rachel finally rescued him and showed him upstairs, where he could escape until Noble got home. "Zeb brought your things upstairs. Your suit has been pressed and is waiting for you."

He smiled and said, "The perfect hostess."

She opened the bedroom door and waited for him to go inside. "Reese, I know you are feeling overwhelmed at the moment. Men don't do weddings well. But you see, we women sail right through them—and we seem to need them to feel really married."

"Are you telling me that all grooms suffer from trembling hands and this same tightening in the throat?"

"Yes. I believe most of them do. But the disease is not fatal, and I feel sure that you will recover soon after the priest pronounces you married."

While Saber prepared for the wedding, Reese spent the rest of the afternoon with Noble, looking over the cattle from Spain. Then Rachel, who seemed to direct everything with ease, came for Reese. He was fed and ushered upstairs to get ready himself.

When he came downstairs, dressed in a black suit, he was introduced to even more guests. The elite of Texas were paraded before him and congratulated him. He blinked in astonishment when Governor Pease shook his hand and told him he was walking away with the rose of Texas. The governor leaned closer and said in a low voice, "I want to talk to you when we get the chance."

Reese felt his stomach knot, and he didn't know what to do with his hands. But his nervousness fled, and his heart stopped when he was positioned beside the priest and the music began. Saber appeared at the top of the stairs, dressed in white, and Reese couldn't take his eyes off her. She looked like an angel with a filmy veil floating about her head.

Noble met her at the bottom of the stairs and offered her his arm. He kissed her cheek. "Be happy, little sister."

Tears sparkled in her eyes. "I shall."

He led her forward and placed her small hand in Reese's, then stepped back.

Reese glanced down at his bride and felt the wonder of knowing she would soon belong to him. There was no doubt in the blue eyes she turned up to him, only trust and gentleness. His hand tightened on hers, and he hardly heard what the priest was saying.

He mouthed the appropriate answers to the wedding vows and slid a plain gold band on Saber's finger, wishing it were a diamond.

The priest was smiling. "I now pronounce you man and wife."

Reese's lips brushed his bride's, and he wished all the people would go away so he could be alone with her—but that was not to be.

She beamed up at him. "I have you now, Reese. You belong to me."

He looked at her with a funny expression. He'd never belonged to anyone, and no one had ever belonged to him. Warmth started around his heart and spread throughout his whole body.

"Yes," he murmured in her ear, the power of possession taking over. "You belong to me."

Saber was ripped out of his arms by her brother, and Noble hugged her to him, while Rachel hugged Reese.

"We're your family now," Rachel said with feeling, knowing that this man had not had a family in a long time.

Reese attempted to absorb all that had happened to him in this one day, but he was confused by what it meant to belong to a family.

Soon the newly married couple were surrounded by guests and were led out to the courtyard, where music and dancing began. The bride and groom were soon separated by well-wishers. Reese was slapped on the back and his hand shaken in friendly greeting until everything was a blur.

Saber threaded her way through the crowd to her husband. There were tables set up and piled high with food of every kind.

Reese was surprised to find himself seated next to Governor Pease. "Reese, you don't mind if I call you by your first name, do you?"

He was stunned. "Not at all, sir."

"I've got an undertaking for you that we'll talk about some other time. But I want to sound you out on an idea and see how you feel about it."

"I would be glad to listen to you, sir."

"How would you feel about supplying the army with beef?"

Reese frowned and glanced down the table, where Noble was watching him. He knew that his brother-in-law was already reaching out to help him through the governor. "I would be willing to talk about it, Governor Pease."

"Good, good! Noble has told me you are reliable and honest, and that you have land enough to support this endeavor. You will benefit by this, and so will Texas. You won't have to drive your cattle to a railhead, and the army will have

a dependable supply of beef. This is big, Reese—
real big!"

"How many head are we talking about, sir?"

"I'm not privy to that information. I presume
it would be thousands of head a year." Governor
Pease grinned and attacked his food. "We won't
spoil your wedding with business. Someone will
call on you at your ranch within the month."

Reese gave a startled glance at his brother-in-
law, and Noble raised his glass to him and
smiled. Reese had some thinking to do—he
wasn't sure how he felt about the offer. Apparently this was what it meant to belong to a
family.

Chapter Twenty-three

The remnants of dinner and all evidence of the wedding cake had been cleared away, and soft Spanish music filled the courtyard. Saber clasped Reese's hand as she thanked each guest for attending. Reese was still in a daze. He hoped he was making all the right responses to the good wishes that were bestowed upon them. What he really wanted to do was escape with his bride.

The governor appeared beside them, laughing boisterously. "Saber, I have rarely seen anything that gave me more pleasure than watching you dance. Will you dance for us?"

She shook her head. "Let someone else dance tonight."

Suddenly a chant was picked up by the crowd, urging her to dance. She glanced at her brother, and he nodded, smiling.

Saber laughingly agreed. She smiled at her husband and said, "Tonight, I dance only for you."

The Spanish guitarist strummed slowly, and Saber raised her hands over her head in a graceful arch—she tapped her feet and whirled. The music began to build in intensity, becoming faster and louder. Saber moved her feet to the rhythm. Reese watched, fascinated, as his new bride tapped her feet, clapping her hands and whirling with a grace that took his breath away. How could such an ethereally lovely woman belong to him? He thought of her growing up at Casa del Sol, wanting for nothing. Then he tried to imagine her in his small house, and his heart plummeted.

Saber clapped her hands and moved slowly toward Reese, her hips keeping time with the music. Her blue eyes seemed to pick up the fire from the Chinese lanterns overhead.

A new emotion took possession of Reese—an emotion he'd never felt before.

Jealousy!

Reese quickly glanced around and observed

the other men watching his wife with admiration, and he didn't like it. By now Saber had reached him and whirled around him, stamping her feet and arching her body, her gaze never leaving his.

Suddenly the music stopped, and she went to her knees in front of him. "That was my wedding present to you, Reese," she said, smiling.

Reese stood and brought her up beside him, his eyes filled with something she didn't understand. "You will never dance like that again, unless it's for me."

Her eyes gleamed with a mischievous light, and she challenged him. "I have been dancing that dance since I was old enough to walk."

"I won't have you dancing for other men," he said heatedly, his eyes defying her to disagree with him.

Saber recognized his jealousy, and she decided not to tease him any further. "If that is your wish, I will never dance for anyone except you."

He had expected an argument, and when she gave in so easily he was left with nothing else to say. The music was slow now, and she squeezed his hand. "Is it permitted for me to dance with my husband?"

His arms went around her, and he felt his anger melt away. He would probably never know

305

why this exceptional woman had agreed to marry him, but she belonged to him, and right now all he wanted was to hold her.

As if she had read Reese's thoughts, Rachel came up to them and took Saber's hand. "This party will go on all night. I'm taking Saber upstairs: a little later you can follow."

He watched Saber move through the crowd and disappear into the house. His hands were shaking so badly that he crammed them into his pockets. What he needed was a strong drink, and he wasn't thinking of the punch that had been served all evening.

Again it seemed his thoughts were anticipated. Noble appeared at his side with a drink. "You must be confused by all this."

"I'm confused by a lot of things," Reese said, taking a deep swallow of the smooth brandy.

"The Spanish customs that are part of the Vincente heritage have always been accepted by us. You will grow accustomed to them in time."

"I don't mind telling you, Noble, I'm scared as hell that I can't make Saber happy."

"Would you like to tell me why you feel that way?"

"Isn't it obvious? This is where Saber was raised. Her life with me will be a hell of a lot different."

"There is something I will tell you about the

Vincentes that very few people realize: WE love only once and with our whole heart. Trust Saber. You might be surprised what she is willing to do for the man she loves."

"She thought she loved Matthew—she certainly doesn't claim to love me."

Noble started to comment and then paused and said simply, "Give it time."

Reese stared at a blue Chinese lantern overhead, which was swinging in the breeze. "I will try to make her happy, Noble."

"That is the only thing I'll ask of you, Reese. Be good to her."

"I will."

"I know that, or I never would have given her to you. It seems her happiness lies with you now."

Suddenly Rachel walked past, and Reese was stunned by the radiance that came into Noble's eyes. Rachel turned her head and glanced at her husband with eyes so soft and loving, Reese felt a stinging in his own eyes. That was the kind of love he wanted from Saber. One day he wanted her to look at him the way Rachel was looking at Noble tonight.

Rachel turned to Reese and whispered in his ear, "You should go upstairs now. It's the third door on the right at the top of the stairs."

He felt as nervous as a schoolboy anticipating

his first kiss. As he climbed the stairs, he could still hear the music and laughter. He paused halfway up and leaned on the polished banister. He hadn't known it was possible to love a woman as much as he loved Saber. Slowly he climbed to the top and paused at Saber's door before knocking softly.

Saber was standing at the window when Reese entered. She turned slowly toward him, and the look in her blue eyes told him she was uncertain what was to happen next.

Staring at the transparent nightgown she wore, he wondered if she knew he could see through it. Her slender body was clearly out-lined, and he could see the rosy tips of her breasts. He removed his coat and draped it across the back of a chair. Then he looked about the pink-and-cream room. The bed had a high canopy, and the rug beneath his feet was plush and full. "I've never seen such a room," he said, loosening his tie and jerking it free of his shirt.

"I never looked at this room from a man's view. I suppose I outgrew it a long time ago—I just didn't notice." She smiled. "Don't worry, I won't put frills on our bedroom at home."

"Say it again," he said, walking toward her.

"What?"

"The part about our home."

"From this night forward, for the rest of my life, Reese, your home is my home."

He paused as warmth rushed through him. His hands were trembling, and he drew in a deep breath. To slow his heart rate, he sat down in the chair and removed his boots; all the while his eyes were on Saber's face. "Don't be afraid of me. I won't hurt you, at least, no more than is necessary."

"I could never be afraid of you, Reese. It's just that I don't know what I'm supposed to do."

Her eyes were wide and confused as he pulled his shirt from his trousers and began unbuttoning it, revealing curly black hair against his tanned and muscled chest.

Saber's knees went weak, and she gripped the back of a chair to keep from collapsing. A tremor shook her, and she wanted to press her cheek against that muscled chest.

He knew that she was feeling shy and frightened, so he blew out the lamp and went to her. The room was cast in shadows, and he turned her face up to his and stared into her blue eyes.

"You knew what you were doing when you danced for me tonight."

"What do you mean?"

Slowly he drew her resisting body closer to him, keeping his grip on her arms light. "Your dance stirred my blood, Saber. As long as I live

I'll never forget how you looked tonight, my little seductress." He held her away from him. "You do understand what is going to happen between us tonight?"

She felt his warm maleness surround her. She knew only that he would bring her pleasure beyond anything she could imagine. "Rachel told me that there would be some pain, but it would not last long."

He closed his eyes, pulling her against him, dazzled by the soft scent of her. "I will be as gentle as I can with you, Saber."

His grip tightened about her waist, and he lifted her off her feet, bracing her body against his. "I have dreamed of this moment a hundred times, but I never thought I would have the right to take you with my body."

Saber couldn't believe this wonderful man was her husband. She had been having her own dreams about him, and she ached for him to make her his. She could feel the swell of him against her, and she moved her hips to get closer.

"No, don't do that." He took a deep breath, trying to steady the urge to satisfy the desire that burned in his loins.

She laid her head against the dark mat of hair on his chest. "You will have to show me what to do."

He placed his hands on both sides of her face and raised it to him, staring into her wide, blue eyes. He dipped his head and touched his lips to her cheek, tasting the saltiness of her tears. Was she crying because he was her husband and not Matthew? It didn't matter; she belonged to him, and he knew just how to make her want him—but winning her heart would be another matter.

He lifted her in his arms and touched his lips to hers ever so gently, while all the love he felt for her spilled from his heart. Couldn't she feel the heat of that love?

He laid her on the bed and unbuckled his belt, sliding out of his trousers. Saber tried to breathe as she looked at his muscled body, but something had cut off her breath.

He was magnificent!

Her gaze dropped to his erection, and her eyes widened with fear. Surely he was too big for her!

Reese came down beside her, pulling her gown upward until he lifted it over her head and dropped it to the floor. In the soft moonlight he feasted on her beauty—a beauty that no man but him had ever beheld.

Her breasts were high and firm, her waist tiny—her hips were rounded and her stomach flat, her legs long and shapely. He ran his hand across her shoulder, feeling the satiny skin beneath his fingers. "You are beautiful, Saber."

Her eyes sparkled with pleasure. "You are glorious," she said, touching the muscle that bulged at his forearm.

He laughed softly. "I don't think a woman has ever said that to me before." He knew the moment the words had left his mouth that he'd made a mistake. He saw her brow furrow, and she pulled away from him.

"Saber, forgive me. I spoke before I thought." He touched her lips and allowed his finger to trail down her throat. "I have to accustom myself to a woman's softer ways."

There was a pout on her lips. "I don't want to be reminded of the other women you have known."

His hand moved to the curve of her breasts. "As far as I'm concerned, there has never been anyone except you. The others were nothing."

"You might as well know this about me, Reese: I will never live with a man who wants other women. To me that would be dishonorable, and I could never have a husband without honor."

He paused, studying the soft mound that begged to be touched. "Is that the way you think of me?"

"No. I just think we should say these things here and now. You don't want me to dance for other men. I don't want you to—"

He closed her mouth with his finger. "When a man has a river, why would he desire a puddle?"

She wasn't sure, but she thought he might have just given her a compliment. It was hard to think, because his finger was tracing a line around her nipple, and an impatient cry escaped her lips. Every move he made tantalized her. Gently rolling the nipple between his thumb and forefinger, he enticed her until heat rushed through her.

But that was only the beginning of the pleasure.

When he dipped his head to take the rosy tip into his mouth, she ran her fingers through his hair, dragging air into her lungs.

His tongue swirled around her nipple; then he gave the same attention to the other one. Saber couldn't keep her body still. She threw back her head and moaned.

Reese moved to her lips and smothered a cry with his mouth. The kiss was drugging, and she felt like screaming when he pulled her naked body against his, absorbing the shocks that went through her.

He had never been so excited with a woman before. Beneath Saber's innocence a fire was smoldering, and he was the one who would bring it to full flame!

Chapter Twenty-four

Reese's eyes glittered silver, and Saber caught a glimpse of an expression she had seen before; she didn't know how to interpret it. It was fierce and gentle at the same time, yet somehow primitive. What was he thinking? she wondered.

But he didn't give her time to think about it. Her body quivered wherever he touched, and he touched her everywhere, his hands trailing sensuously across her breasts and over her stomach. He then moved downward, slowly parting her legs, kissing her all the while.

Saber wanted him to say he loved her; in fact, she was sure that when he was making love to her, he would finally tell her how he felt about her.

At last he broke off the kiss and raised his head, asking in a husky voice, "Are you sure I'm not frightening you?"

Saber licked her lips, wanting more from him than he'd given her up to now. "How could I fear the man who has stood between me and harm so many times?" She touched his cheek and tenderly smiled. "No, I don't fear you."

He touched his lips to each eyelid and slid down to her mouth, all the while spreading her legs apart.

He could feel the tenseness in her and wanted to put her mind at ease. "What will happen between us has been going on since the beginning of time, Saber." He gently touched his mouth to hers and groaned when she pressed more tightly against him. He covered a gasp as his hand touched her intimately and slowly slid into her female core. "No, don't stiffen, sweetheart. Just let yourself feel."

She suddenly tried to move upward to escape the intrusion into her body.

"Easy. Try not to move," he murmured in her ear. "Let me lead you to a world of touching and feeling."

All she could do was nod, but she was still stiff,

so he caressed the inside of her, feeling her begin to move restlessly.

She arched her hips, trying to get closer to the hands that were now giving her pleasure. She groaned, she whispered his name, and then her arms stole around his shoulders. Now she trembled with joy; her body felt more alive than it ever had. She waited for each new touch, each new sensation that went throbbing through her. Through the open window the faint sound of music drifted into the room, but she heard only the murmuring of her name on his lips.

Reese was on the verge of losing control completely. The sensuous manipulation of his finger plunging into her was driving her crazy and stirring his own need to the breaking point. His tightly muscled body pressed her into the mattress, and she gasped at the wonderful feel of him.

His eyes closed for a moment as desire went through him like the lash of a whip. She was ready for him now, so he nudged her legs farther apart and slid his erection into her.

Saber gasped and tried to arch upward again, but he stilled her with his hand. "No, sweetheart, don't do that. It will only hurt you if you take too much of me at once."

"I want . . . I feel . . ."

He breathed against her lips, and they quivered. "I know what you want. Just trust me, Saber."

Her hands laced in his midnight hair when his lips touched hers. As he deepened the kiss, he inched into her slowly. He was trembling from the effort it took to gentle his movement, feeling as if he'd explode at any time—throbbing hardness slid into hot velvet, melding, joining, becoming as one.

Saber still felt him holding back, and she wanted more. There had been no pain, as he had warned. She slid her hands to his waist and raised her hips upward, taking more of him into her.

Again he stilled her. "Don't do that, sweetheart. Don't tempt me too far, or I might hurt you."

"I don't understand," she said, moving her head back and forth feverishly.

"Sweetheart," he said between kissing her throat and then her breasts. "I'm large, and you are small. I have to be careful."

Pleasure rippled through her as he eased forward just enough to make her feel as if her insides were being filled by him. She let out her breath in a sigh as he paused at the wall of her virginity. With a quick jab he broke through, and she stiffened.

"No, Reese!" she cried. "You are too big."

His mouth cut off her protest, and he moved gently back and forth. "I will go no farther," he promised, gritting his teeth to keep from filling her completely. He tasted the saltiness of her tears and felt a stinging in his own eyes.

"Let this be the first and the last time I hurt you." And then he proceeded to take her mind off the pain by bringing her pleasure beyond her wildest dreams. His mouth was on her breasts, sucking and stimulating. His hands fit under her thighs, lifting her for his forward thrusts. Then he parted her lips and slid his tongue between hers, and she could taste the brandy in his mouth.

Suddenly her hips moved in time with his, causing warmth and pleasure to spread through her whole being. She twisted her head, reared her body, and shook with tremors as something magical happened to her.

A low groan issued from his lips, and his body found pleasure beyond any he'd ever felt. He had craved her for so long, and now she was his in every sense of the word. He surged into her, emptying his seed. He had never felt this way before, and he was sure it was because he loved her.

Her arms slid around his back, and she kissed his cheek and then his lips. Reese was amazed when he felt himself responding again so soon, and he grew hard.

He wanted her anew.

He would never have enough of her. Now he had stood at the gates of Eden and been allowed to enter.

Her hand trailed down his back, and she was lost in the wonder of what had just happened between them. "I didn't know it would be like this."

He swallowed deeply and eased most of his weight onto his elbows, then kissed her tenderly. "Are you all right?" he asked in concern.

She touched her lips to his rough cheek, loving the feel of him still inside her. "Yes, I am more than all right. It was just so . . ." She searched for the word. "Beautiful."

"Yes," he said softly against her ear. "Beautiful."

Her fingers trailed up to the back of his neck, and she nipped at his lips with her teeth.

Reese's eyes widened. She was being playful, and he was beginning to be fiercely aroused again. It was too soon—he didn't want to hurt her. His arms went around her, and he held her tightly, wishing he'd never have to let her go.

"I want it to always be like tonight, Reese."

He threw back his head and laughed. "I have many more things to show you that will be even better, my little bride. We have just begun."

She gazed into his silver eyes and was touched by their warmth. "When will you show me?"

"You little wildcat." He laughed, rolling her over until she was on top of him. "I just introduced you to the pleasures of the flesh, and you want more." Warmth and happiness filled him. He had always thought that married women looked upon going to bed with their husbands as their duty. But not Saber. She had given herself to him without holding back, and she had met his lovemaking with a passion to match his own.

"It's the hot Spanish blood in me. You can't say I didn't warn you about that side of me."

Reese had never thought of himself as having any weaknesses, but Saber had become his weakness. He would do anything for a smile from those lips. He had wanted to be inside her every time he looked at her. Now he was buried in her sweetness, and he never wanted to withdraw. But he did. He was afraid he would hurt her if he took her again so soon.

She stretched her silken body alongside his and nestled her head on his shoulder, her fingers running through the hair on his chest. She was entirely comfortable with the fact that they were both naked. He liked that about her.

"What do we do now?" she asked pensively.

He arched his brow at her. "You mean right now?"

She laughed. "No. I mean in the morning."

"What do you want to do?"

"I want to go home."

His throat tightened, and he couldn't speak for a moment. "Home?"

"Yes, to our ranch." She raised her head and looked at him. "Can we? We have a lot of work to do."

"Yes, of course. If that's what you want."

"What do you want to do, Reese?"

"I want to take my wife home." He held her so close he could feel her intake of breath. "How soon can you pack?"

"I have a lot of things that belonged to my mother that I will want, Reese. But we can always send for them later when you build me a bigger house."

He had been waiting for this. Would she want something in the grand style of Casa del Sol? She must know he couldn't afford this kind of house. But she had money—perhaps she would want to use it to build a house. No, he would never allow that. "What kind of building are you speaking of, Saber?"

"I think another bedroom, and perhaps we can enlarge the living room. What do you think?"

He felt himself relax. Her gentle understanding touched him deeply. "That won't be for some time, Saber."

"I know. Then all I will need is one trunk for now. Later Noble can transport the rest."

"What kinds of things, Saber?"

"The piano, linens, laces, dishes—it's an endless list. But Noble will keep everything here until we have room."

"I like to hear a piano. Can you play?"

She tossed her head back so her golden curls swirled around him. "I play better than I dance."

He shook with laughter. "Then God help me."

He ran his hand over her hips, still amazed by the silkiness of her skin. Her hair was soft and smelled wonderful, and her lips were so kissable. He had never thought she would be his, but she was, and he pitied any man who tried to lay a hand on her!

She moved her finger over the creases in his forehead. "What are you thinking? You look so serious."

"I want you again, but it's too soon." He moved her aside, stood up, and walked to the window. "I know it's too soon."

He dropped down in a chair and enjoyed the sight of her stretched out naked on the bed. She was beautiful in every way. Rachel had been right when she'd said that Saber was special.

She was sweet-natured—well, most of the time—
as well as loving and understanding.

He watched her swing her legs off the bed and
walk toward him, moving her hips enchantingly.
He stopped breathing when she slid onto his lap,
and he swelled painfully.

"I'm your wife. You can have me anytime you
want me."

He groaned as she settled on his erection. He
threw back his head as she placed her hands on
his shoulders and squirmed until he was inside
her.

"I don't want to hurt you, sweetheart."

She nipped at his ear and whispered, "Don't
hurt me; just love me."

He arched upward, out of control, driving
deeply into her tightness. He lifted her and laid
her on the bed without withdrawing from her.

"Saber," he said in a choked voice, his body
driving into hers. "Saber."

She met his thrusts and fell into his rhythm.
Her body trembled with release, and Reese cried
out at the sensation of being surrounded by wet,
hot honey. He quaked with total satisfaction and
fell forward, drained of strength. He had never
known such fulfillment, and Reese knew he
would have her again, because he was still swollen inside her.

Chapter Twenty-five

The room reflected the soft, rosy glow of sunrise, and it fell on Saber's sleeping face, fascinating her new husband. He'd been watching her for some time, and he still couldn't believe his good luck. She had chosen to marry him. But why? Someone like her would never fall in love with a man like him.

He wound a golden curl around his finger, fascinated by how alive it felt. He had awakened her passion, and he had satisfied it as well, but he wanted what Rachel and Noble had. He wanted to fill her belly with his seed. He wanted her to say the words that he'd almost cried out last night while in the throes of passion—he wanted to hear her say she loved him.

He looked at the richly furnished room, knowing he would never be able to give her anything like this.

Her lashes fluttered open, and he looked into the blue eyes he loved so well. She smiled and stretched like a cat before a warm fire. The sheet slid down to her waist, and he had a good view of her satiny breasts.

He groaned, wanting her again, and knowing she must be sore. She made a dive for him, wrapping her arms around his neck and pressing those breasts against his hard chest.

"Is it morning already?"

He trailed a finger down her cheek. "Uh-huh."

She raised her mouth to be kissed, and he laughed, hugging her to him. "You're as affectionate as a kitten," he said, giving her the kiss she wanted.

She broke off the kiss. "Do you mind?"

"Not me. I like everything about you. Don't change anything."

Saber stared into silver eyes that made her feel weak all over. She could get lost in those transparent depths. He had been magnificent last night. He was a gentle lover, except for the time she had taunted him into madness. She smiled at the memory, pleased that she had such power over him. She rubbed her breasts against him and nibbled his ear.

He growled and pulled her under him. "You won't be able to walk for a week by the time I get through with you. I had good intentions of making love to you only once."

She smiled slyly. "If I can't walk, we'll just have to stay in bed, won't we?"

His lips covered hers, and he spread her legs, sliding into her. He wanted her every time she looked at him. What would he do when they got home? He'd never get any work done.

She bit her lower lip as he rocked with her, thrusting, pulling back, and thrusting again. They rode the wave of passion, and afterward lay locked in each other's arms.

She closed her eyes, so grateful that she had married the one man in the world who would make her happy. She thought of how close she had come to marrying Matthew and hugged Reese tighter. Reese needed her—he might not know it yet, but he would find it out eventually. She almost purred as he dipped his head and took her nipple in his mouth. If she'd never known Reese, her life would never have been complete.

"I'm hungry," she said, pulling away from him. She stood and went to the bellpull, tugged on it, then turned to find Reese watching her.

"We'd better get dressed quickly, because within five minutes the maid will come knocking on that door." She pulled on her robe and belted it at the waist while he got dressed.

The expected knock came, and Saber called out, "Come on in, Lupe."

A middle-aged Mexican woman and her younger daughter entered, the mother carrying a heavy tray, which Reese took from the woman and placed on a small table.

Both women bobbed a curtsy, smiling cheerfully. "Do you need anything else, Señorita Saber?" the elder one inquired.

"*Sí*. In an hour we will both want to bathe. After lunch we will be leaving, and I will want the traveling coach loaded and ready."

"*Sí*, señorita, er, I forget, señora."

Lupe's daughter approached Reese. "Señor," she said in accented English, "a man brought to you this letter. He said I was to give it into your hands."

He nodded and waited for the two servants to leave before he spoke. "You issued orders to the servants with the ease of someone accustomed to doing it all her life."

"I have. But I was taught by my father to treat the servants kindly and with respect. I hope I have always done that."

"I wasn't implying otherwise. I just want you

327

to remember you will have no servants at Star-rett Ranch."

She frowned, troubled. "I know that, Reese. It seems to bother you more than it bothers me."

"If you had married Matthew you would have had servants."

"I know. But I didn't want to marry Matthew."

He held the chair for her to be seated. Then he sat across from her, still studying her closely. His eyes dropped to the breakfast before him: coffee, tea, sweet rolls, biscuits, fluffy scrambled eggs, ham, bacon, and fresh fruit. It was a feast big enough to feed six people. What was he doing taking Saber away from all this?

"Aren't you going to read your letter?" she asked with interest.

He nodded and opened it, scanning the pages. "Just business," he said in answer to her unspoken question, poking it into his pocket.

She was aware of his troubled thoughts and poured him a cup of coffee. "I recall you take your coffee black and strong."

He took the cup from her and raised the hot brew to his lips. "You have arranged our baths and our travel plans."

She set the coffeepot down and looked at him. "I did. If there is anything you want to change, I'll inform the servants. Would you rather leave tomorrow?"

He placed the dainty china cup down, his appetite gone. "No." He leaned back in the chair and stared into her eyes. "Why did you marry me, Saber?"

"What made you think of that now, Reese? This is a question you should have asked before we were married."

"Seeing you in this environment"—he waved his hand around the room—"has brought me a clearer understanding of your life."

She had known he'd soon start to question her reasons for marrying him, and she wondered how she should answer him. Should she pour out her heart and tell him that she had loved him almost from the first time she saw him? "What if I told you I loved you, Reese?"

"You thought you loved Matthew."

"Yes, but I was young when I met him."

"My mother thought she loved my father until she discovered how hard it is being the wife of a rancher. She left with a man who could offer her more."

She felt sick inside. "Are you comparing me to your mother? Do you think I would leave you just because of hard times? If we had a son, do you think I could leave him like your mother left you?"

He stood up and moved toward the door. "You'd better think about what you're doing before you leave here, Saber. You had better think about what you are giving up."

"Reese?"

He glanced at her through lowered eyelids. "Yes?"

"Don't you want me to live with you?"

Want her? He wanted her so damned bad he felt shredded inside. But to build his hopes and dreams on her as his father had done with his mother, only to have her leave him, would break him. "I want you. But understand, if you come with me, your life is going to be hard, Saber."

"I have married you knowing this. You may think I am an empty-headed, spoiled daughter of a wealthy rancher, but I can assure you, Reese, I am much more than that."

"Yes, you are much more than that," he agreed. "But you are accustomed to the comforts of life."

She wasn't going to let him leave this room until they settled this between them. "What have I ever done that you should have such a low opinion of me, Reese?"

His hand paused on the door handle. "I have a very high regard for you, Saber. Any man would have."

"I refuse to apologize for the way I was brought up. It's true that I have had many advantages. But my brother and I were taught that we must work for what we have and never leave it to others."

How could he explain to her the growing doubts that possessed his mind? "I have to leave you this morning, Saber. I don't want to, but this letter is important, and I have to ride to Fort Worth on some business. I think it would be safer for you to stay here."

She turned away from him, but she kept her head high, and her shoulders straight. "My home is with you, Reese. I want to go with you. I made a vow to you just last night." Her voice dropped to a whisper. "We Vincentes always keep our word."

"You are a Starrett now," he reminded her. "And I want you to stay here until I come for you."

"What can be so important that it must take you away at this time?"

"It's nothing you need to worry about, Saber."

"Good-bye then, Reese."

He wanted to gather her in his arms and carry her away with him. He hated to leave her, but he couldn't take her with him to Fort Worth, and what he had to do now was very important.

"Think very carefully about what I have said, Saber."

She heard the door close behind her and turned to find him gone. She ran to the window and watched until he emerged from the house and made his way to the stable. She watched until he mounted on his horse and rode out of sight.

"You aren't going to get away from me that easily, Reese Starrett," she said with determination. "You have never come up against a Vincente before. But you are going to know you have a war on your hands with me."

Reese dismounted at the Broken Spur and rapped at the door. Rachel welcomed him and ushered him inside.

Reese held his hat in his hand. "I can see why you love this ranch, Rachel. It's something to be proud of."

"It was once my whole life. But not anymore. I'm content to let my sister and her husband take over here." She steered him toward the library, where Noble was going over the ledgers.

Noble glanced up and frowned. "I didn't expect you here today. Is Saber with you?"

"No. I got this a while ago. I think you'd better look at it." He handed the letter to Noble. "I'm leaving for Fort Worth immediately."

Rachel left the two men alone while Noble quickly read the letter. "So Sheriff Davis thinks Graham Felton is hiding out in Dallas."

"So it would seem. I want to talk to the sheriff

332

and find out what he knows. Then I'll go to Dallas and see what I can discover there. Saber will never be safe as long as that man is on the loose."

"Did you tell her?"

"I didn't see any reason to upset her. I told her to stay at Casa del Sol until I return."

Noble nodded in agreement. "That sounds like a good plan."

Reese took the letter and headed for the door. He paused. "Thank you for the wedding, and for everything you've done for us."

Noble smiled. "It was our pleasure. We are family now." He stood up and walked Reese to the door. "Send me word. If you need me, I'll come at once."

Reese nodded and placed his hat on his head. "I'll do that."

He turned his mount and rode away, leaving Noble to wonder how Reese had managed to convince Saber to remain at Casa del Sol.

He went back to the desk and tried to work at the ledger, but his mind kept drifting to his sister. Suddenly he jumped to his feet. Knowing her so well, he knew she would already be making plans to leave.

He ran through the house calling for Rachel. "I've got to get back to the ranch! Saber is probably about to do something dangerous, and I have to stop her."

Chapter Twenty-six

As Reese rode within sight of his ranch, the failure of his mission lay heavily on his shoulders. Graham Felton was clever, and Reese always seemed to be one step behind him. He dismounted and led his horse into the barn.

Jake found him there unsaddling his horse. "Boss, you never said anything to me and Gabe about your getting married. We were plumb surprised when we found out. Congratulations."

Reese threw the saddle over the railing and looked at the young boy. "It happened suddenly. There wasn't much time to let everyone know."

"Did you have any luck finding Felton, Reese?"

"No. But how did you know I was searching for him?"

"Mr. Vincente told me. He brought Mrs. Starrett home, but then he had to leave. Said he wanted to catch up with you."

Reese's heart leaped with joy. "She's here?"

"Yes, sir. She and a dozen men from Casa del Sol. This place is like an armed fortress. Mr. Vincente instructed us all to be on the lookout for strangers," Jake told him.

Reese took a deep breath. Noble hadn't been able to keep Saber at Casa del Sol, but he had made sure she was protected. He liked his brother-in-law more every day.

"There's some kind of government man up at the house talking to Mrs. Starrett."

Reese walked to the barn door and glanced at the house. He'd been so buried in his thoughts that he hadn't noticed the buggy. With purposeful steps, he strode toward the house with Jake walking beside him as far as the front yard. "We bedded down all Mr. Vincente's men in the bunkhouse, boss. It's a bit crowded, but they ain't complaining. There's an old man with them named Zeb who does the cooking for us. His food ain't so bad, but his coffee would wake the dead."

Reese grinned. "I know that character. You

might as well get ready for him to settle in for a long time. He probably won't leave Saber."

"That's kinda what he said. I like him, and he's full of tales that he swears are true."

"How is my wife?"

"Reese, she's mighty fine. She's had me and the others moving furniture and toting water, and she even had Gabe help her hang curtains. She's surely a wonder."

Reese frowned. He probably wouldn't even recognize the place when she got through with it. Well, he supposed women liked fixing things up, he admitted to himself grudgingly.

"Just keep a close lookout for any strangers, Jake."

"We'll watch things for you, boss. Don't you worry about Graham Felton getting near the place."

When Reese opened the door, his eyes went first to Saber, and then to the stranger. Saber had served the man a cup of coffee and was sitting on the chair across from him. Reese wanted to go to her and tell her he was sorry for the way he'd left her, but that would have to wait until later.

"Reese," Saber said. "I'd like you to meet Mr. Williams. He's come all the way from Austin to see you."

Reese shook hands with the elderly man, who

was dressed in a brown suit and cowboy boots. "Would that be Carl Williams?"

The older man smiled. "That would be me."

"I've heard of you. You work for the governor."

"I do. And it's at his request that I'm here."

"I'll leave you gentlemen to talk," Saber said, moving to Reese and brushing a light kiss on his cheek. "I'm glad you're home."

He stared into her eyes, not knowing whether to hug her to him or turn her over his knee. He had wanted her to stay at Casa del Sol until Graham Felton was found, but he couldn't be sorry that his wife was home.

After Saber left the room, Reese drew up a chair and sat down. "You've come a long way, Mr. Williams."

"I think you'd better start calling me Carl if we are going to be doing business together."

In half an hour, Carl Williams had outlined the proposal that the government was offering Reese. "How does all that sound to you?"

Reese gazed about the room, noticing the changes Saber had made. There was a green rug on the floor and darker green curtains at the windows. There was a comfortable new brown sofa that matched the two new brown-and-green chairs. There were other touches scattered about the room that made it warm and inviting.

He hadn't known that the house could look this good. His mind went back to the man before him. "It sounds like my brother-in-law had a hand in this somewhere."

"Not as much as you'd think. Oh, the governor spoke to him about you, but only because he'd heard you had enough land to support our endeavor. On poking into your background, we discovered that you're an honest, hardworking man. This comes to you by way of your own reputation, Mr. Starrett." Mr. Williams smiled. "And your ranch is close to most of the forts."

"I don't suppose it hurts any that my wife is a Vincente." Reese looked skeptical. "Does it, Carl?"

Carl Williams looked sheepish and nodded. "It doesn't hurt a damned bit. You married into Texas royalty, and that's a fact. But not even that would have helped you if we in the State House didn't think you were the man we have been looking for." He stood and held out his hand. "What do you say? Do we have a deal?"

Reese stood as well and clasped Carl's hand in a friendly shake. "We have a deal."

"Good. You'll be hearing from me right away. We'd like you to get started as soon as possible. Can you start delivering cattle to the forts by early fall?"

"It will be done."

"Give my salutations to your charming wife. I want to be at the Barley ranch before sundown. Me and Ted grew up together, and I like his wife's cooking."

Reese walked Carl to his buggy, and after he'd gone he went back into the house. He could hear Saber humming in the kitchen, and he hurried toward her.

She had been setting the table for lunch, and she turned toward the door when she heard Reese's footsteps.

The kitchen was the biggest surprise. A round table had taken the place of the rickety old one he'd used for years. There was a white cloth on the table, along with candles and fancy blue dishes. "I'm glad you're home," she said, watching him closely.

In two strides he was across the floor, folding her in his arms. His head dipped, and he covered her lips with a searing kiss. She clung to him, returning his kiss, her arms going around his broad shoulders.

"Reese," she said, breaking off the kiss, her cheeks flushed. "I missed you so terribly. Did you miss me just a little?"

He swelled with desire and wondered how she could doubt it. His hand went to her breast, and she snuggled closer to him.

"I'm going to take that as a yes," she said, smiling.

He lifted her in his arms. "I'm taking you to the bedroom, if it's still where I left it."

"Wait," she said, reaching toward the stove. "That will burn."

He shoved the pot to the back of the stove in his haste to get her to bed. After carrying her into the bedroom, he set her on her feet and unbuttoned her gown, revealing her breasts. He lowered her to the bed and pinned her beneath his body.

Saber pulled the back of his shirt out of his trousers and ran her hand up his bare skin. "I have been thinking about this for days," she admitted.

Her honesty touched him deeply. Most women would be coy and flirtatious, but Saber was not ashamed to show her feelings. She was just the right woman for him.

He moved her gown upward, feeling her silken skin. "The whole time I was gone, I couldn't think of anything but you," he told her, his eyes closing as he touched his lips to her exposed breast. "You feel so good."

Moments later they were both naked, and his hands were roaming at will over her body. His lips became more demanding, his hands more insistent, and she gave him everything he asked for.

When he finally entered her, she met his thrusts with earth-shattering moves of her own. Reese knew that if he died at that moment, he would have really lived. Saber had given her sweetness to him, and he had taken it hungrily.

Exhausted from their lovemaking, Saber lay in Reese's arms, watching a gentle breeze stir the curtains at the window. She gave him a radiant smile that went right to his heart.

"I'm afraid your lunch is cold and probably inedible."

He nuzzled her neck and let his lips explore a creamy breast. "Who can think of food when I have you in my arms?"

She snuggled closer. "I was afraid you might not like the changes I made in the house. I know I should have consulted you first, but—"

He silenced her with a quick kiss. "This is your home now, Saber. I leave you to do whatever will make you happy." He pulled back and said in a decisive voice, "But please, no pink or lace."

She trailed a finger through the mat of hair on his chest. "You make me happy, Reese."

He lifted her hand and kissed the palm. "You are only intrigued by me for now because you've never met a man like me."

She knew he was still unable to accept that she loved him, and telling him would not help convince him. She would have to show him over the days, weeks, and months to come. But he would realize it in the end. "You're right about one thing, husband: I've never met a man like you before. But I'm beginning to know you." A gleam came into her eyes. "And I like what I know."

Her hand went lower, and she clasped him until he swelled in her hand. Reese groaned and pulled her beneath him. "You little hellcat, I may not live long enough for you to get to know the real me. You are probably going to kill me in bed."

Their bodies melded into one, and he sank into her, catching her moan beneath his kiss. She caught her breath with each forward lunge and let it out in a groan when he pulled back. Her nails dug into his back, and she raised her body to meet his powerful thrusts.

Much later, he kissed her damp forehead and pushed her hair away from her face. "I need you, Saber."

She closed her eyes, knowing what it had cost him to make that admission. But she would be satisfied with nothing less than a full declaration of love. He would come to trust her one day and confess his love for her. On that day he would know that she loved him more than her own life.

Chapter Twenty-seven

Reese sat across from Saber at the breakfast table, watching her carefully. They had been living together for three weeks now, and in that time she had been the perfect wife in every way. She rose early every morning and cheerfully made his breakfast and a lunch to take with him when he couldn't get home. The house always smelled of lemon oil and wax, and she had made it a home. When they went to bed at night and he took her in his arms, she fulfilled him as no other woman could. But he still couldn't beat down the uncertainty that lingered at the fringes of his mind.

Saber had never said that she loved him. Hell,

for that matter he'd never told her how he felt, either. Somehow he just couldn't seem to say the words that would reveal so much of himself.

"I got a letter from your brother yesterday," he said, taking a drink of coffee.

"I know, he mentioned your letter in mine."

"Then you know that he wants to sell me cattle below the market price?"

"No. I didn't know that. But he's done that with our neighbors before. He still comes out ahead, Reese, because he doesn't have the trouble and expense of driving them to the railhead, losing a fourth of the herd, and running their weight off on the drive."

"I don't want handouts from him, Saber."

"Reese, it isn't a handout. We are family. This is what families do. We help each other. If Noble needed you, wouldn't you be there for him?"

"Of course, but this is different. I have survived on my own since I was young. I can still do it."

"You aren't alone, Reese. You have me."

He scooted his chair back and glared at her. "I don't know what it means to have a family, Saber. I don't know how to be what you want me to be!"

She felt the start of tears and was determined not to cry. She hurt so much for him; he didn't know how to show his love, and he didn't know how to trust and accept the hands of love and friendship that were being held out to him.

She just had to show him the way.

"Noble reminded me in his letter that I should talk to you about my inheritance. He sent the deeds and documents, and I thought perhaps you might want to go over them. I have no head for figures, Reese."

His expression was grim. "What holdings and what deeds are you talking about?"

"I am sole owner of all the property in Georgia, but we should probably sell it, since we will never live there. Noble says that someone has made a generous offer for it. I also own several thousand head of cattle, Reese. Noble has looked after them for me. But I am sure he would like it if you took them off his hands."

Reese's voice was cold and without feeling. "Is there anything else you need to tell me about your holdings?"

She could hear the anger in his voice and didn't understand the reason for it. "I . . . Noble says that I have five hundred thousand dollars in a bank in New Orleans."

Reese shot to his feet, anger and indignation burning inside him. "I don't want your cattle, Saber, and I damned sure don't want your money! You can do what you will with your property in Georgia—it doesn't concern me."

"But I—"

"This conversation is over." He walked out of the room, grabbed his hat, and headed for the door. He had to clear his mind. He'd known that Saber had money, but he hadn't imagined it would be so much, and he hadn't expected that he'd be asked to handle it for her.

Saber tried to stay busy all day. She was still puzzled by Reese's reaction to her money. He must have known she had vast holdings; everyone else did.

She was making the bed when a heavy knock came at the door. Removing her apron, she went to answer it, thinking it might be Zeb. She stepped back when she saw Matthew standing there.

Neither of them spoke for a long moment. Then he removed his hat and tucked his gloves into his belt. "May I come in, Saber?"

"Reese isn't here."

"It's you I came to see."

She stepped back so he could enter. "I thought we had said everything we had to say at Fort Griffin."

He towered over her, his face set in a stone mask. "Why did you do it, Saber?"

"I assume you are asking why I married Reese."

"Yes. You belonged to me. We just had a misunderstanding. I was going to let you stew for a little while, and then I thought we would settle everything between us."

"I'm sorry for what happened between us, Matthew, but you didn't really love me, and you know it."

He advanced farther into the room. "How can you know how I feel about you?"

She wanted him to leave before Reese came home, so she didn't offer him a chair. "If you had cared about me, you would not have behaved as you did that night."

"I'm sorry for that, and I always will be. I went to your room the next morning, but you had already left. My mother urged me to ride to Casa del Sol and bring you back, but I thought I'd just give you a few weeks to think over our situation."

"Matthew, it didn't take me a few weeks to think about it. I realized when I saw you that we didn't love each other."

He reached out and grabbed her, dragging her resisting body against his. "For years I have thought of nothing but you. I wanted you for my wife. I wanted to spend my life with you. I don't care if you are married to Reese; you still belong to me!"

She struggled, trying to push him away, but

he held her fast. "Matthew, let me go. You're hurting me!"

"I'll never let you go," he said in a growl, holding her head between both hands and covering her mouth with his.

She struggled and pushed at him, but he forced her mouth open and crammed his tongue inside. He lifted her, fitting her most intimate part to his swollen loins. He trembled and held her there by sheer force. No matter how much she struggled, he would not let her go.

Finally she tore her mouth away from his and started pounding him on the chest. "Reese will kill you for this, Matthew!"

"You're mine! You have been since that first day I saw you in Georgia." He held her close to him as he spoke. "I was wrong; I know that now. But you shouldn't have married Reese."

"I love Reese. What I felt for you was affection and gratitude for helping me and my aunt when we needed it. I was too young to know my mind at that time, Matthew."

"You can't love Reese—you still love me!"

"Reese is my husband. Take your hands off me!"

Both of them heard the door open, and Saber twisted toward Reese and saw the murderous look in those cold, gray eyes. "Let her go, Matthew."

Matthew's arms only tightened around Saber. "You had no right to marry her. You knew she belonged to me."

Saber pushed against him. "I don't belong to you. Let me go!"

Reese grabbed Matthew's arm and, with sheer force, pried Saber away from him. He shoved her behind him and faced his friend. "You had no right to come here like this, Matthew. I'm going to ask you to leave now."

"I thought you were my friend," Matthew said bitingly. "I trusted you to rescue Saber from the Millers, when all along I should have been worrying about you seducing her."

"Leave now, Matthew. And I don't ever want to see you here again," Reese said in a quiet voice. Saber would not have known he was angry if she hadn't been watching his eyes.

"You owe me an explanation before I leave here, and so does Saber."

"I might owe you something, but my wife doesn't," Reese said.

"What did you do to make her turn from me to you?"

Reese guided Saber to the bedroom door. "You need to leave while I explain some things to Matthew."

"No, I won't," she stated stubbornly. "This concerns me, and I'm not leaving!"

Constance O'Banyon

Matthew stared at Saber. "You would settle for living in this hovel when I was willing to lay all Philadelphia at your feet? Reese isn't anything like you and me. He has rough ways, and he—"

"That's enough!" she declared. "Reese is my husband, and this is our home." She was trembling, she was so angry. "You asked some impossible things of me, Matthew. I could never have married you after that night." She paused. She'd never told Reese about the things Matthew had said to her in the hotel room after the dance.

Matthew turned to Reese. "I was drunk. I said and did some things I'm not proud of. Apparently she still holds it against me."

Reese's gaze went to Saber. "What kind of things?"

Matthew could not believe that Saber hadn't told Reese about what had happened. "Reese, you know a man will do and say things when he's drunk that he'd never say sober."

"What kind of things?" Reese demanded a second time. "Matthew, you'd better tell me now."

Matthew shrugged. "I kissed her."

Reese turned back to Saber. "That's all?"

"No," she said. "That's not all. I wasn't ever going to tell Reese, Matthew, but since you've brought it up, tell him the truth, or I shall."

Bitterness crept into Matthew's blue eyes. "I would never have done anything to her, Reese. I may have made some threats and touched her in an ungentlemanly way, but I'd never have gone through with it. I'm not like that. I would never have raped you, Saber."

Reese reached out and pulled Saber to him. "Get out, Matthew. This ends our friendship. Don't ever come here again."

Matthew's face went red. "I really came here to help you. But when I saw Saber, I lost my head and my temper."

"Say what you came to say and then go," Reese told him.

Matthew met Reese's icy stare. "Graham Felton has spread it all over Fort Worth, so you'll hear about it soon enough anyway. I just wanted to be the one to tell you first, since it concerns me."

Reese's voice was still cool. "I'm listening."

"We wrongly suspected that Felton had Saber kidnapped for her brother's money."

Reese's eyes narrowed. "What are you saying? You'd better explain yourself."

Matthew lowered his gaze because he could no longer look into Reese's cold eyes, and he was too ashamed to look at Saber. "Felton had her kidnapped to get back at me."

Constance O'Banyon

Reese's fists balled at his sides. "What for? There has to be a reason."

"I had seen Felton's sister, Gwen, several times." His gaze went to Saber. "It meant nothing to me. She just made too much out of it."

"Go on," Reese urged, feeling Saber stiffen beside him. She must be feeling sick inside at Matthew's confession.

"It seems Gwen Felton expected me to marry her, which, of course, I had no intention of doing. She knew I was going to marry Saber."

"So this is why Felton had Saber kidnapped," Reese said with doubt in his tone. "It doesn't sound like a good reason to me. He went to a lot of trouble just to punish a man who wouldn't marry his sister."

"There's more to it," Matthew admitted, studying the floor. "It seems the girl . . . killed herself. She left a note that said she didn't want to live after I rejected her. It wasn't my fault that she had this crazy infatuation with me."

Saber closed her eyes and leaned heavily against Reese. "Mr. Felton wanted to punish you for his sister's death. How very tragic."

"The whole family is crazed, if you ask me," Matthew stated. "Since Felton's spread this story around, my reputation has suffered. I'll not be seeking public office after this."

"Then it's all over, and Felton will leave Saber

352

alone, since she's married to me," Reese said angrily. Matthew was not the man he'd thought he was. He had fooled a lot of people, including Graham Felton's pitiable sister. "You've told me what was on your mind—now you can leave."

"It's still not over, Reese. Felton's saying that he's coming after Saber because he knows I still love her."

Saber ran from the room, feeling sick. She closed the bedroom door and fell across the bed. Oh, that poor woman, she thought. It was such a pity that the man she had died for didn't seem to be as concerned about her death as he was about his own reputation. She felt pity for the poor unfortunate girl who had loved so unwisely. After this day she'd never be sorry for Matthew again.

She didn't hear Matthew leave, or Reese ride away.

Reese rode toward the high country. He needed to think. He remembered how strangely Saber had acted that night in the livery stable. Now he knew why. Matthew had tried to rape her. His lip curled in anger. He should have killed Matthew.

He rode up a mesa and stared out over his land. "Why didn't you tell me, Saber?"

He knew the answer. The woman he'd married had been brought up with honor. She hadn't told him about Matthew because she didn't want to cause trouble between him and his friend.

That was some woman he'd married. He wondered if he'd be worthy of her.

His gaze went to the south. If Felton came, he'd come from that direction. He had to do more to protect Saber. She must never be left alone.

He nudged his mount forward, suddenly needing to see Saber. So far she had done everything right, and he'd done everything wrong. He just didn't know how to be a husband. He knew he loved her so damned much it hurt.

He suddenly needed her soft arms around him. He needed to hold her and know she was safe. One thing was sure: Felton was a very dangerous and unpredictable man. If he said he'd be coming after Saber, then that was exactly what he'd do. But when and where? That was the question.

Chapter Twenty-eight

It was long after sundown when Reese reached the house. He unsaddled his horse, and when Jake came into the barn, he told the boy to finish for him.

Reese didn't see Jake smile when his boss hurried toward the house. Everyone on the ranch knew Reese was burning for his beautiful wife.

When he entered the house, Saber wasn't in the parlor. He went into the kitchen, and she wasn't there either, but she had left him a plate of food warming on the back of the stove.

It seemed to him that the harsher he was to her, the kinder she was to him. He didn't understand a woman like her. Why was he doing his best to drive her away when all he wanted was to keep her with him?

He walked into the bedroom and found her curled up in bed asleep. Her hand was resting against her cheek, and he reached out and touched her face.

Saber awoke instantly and smiled at him. "Did you eat?"

He sat down on the bed and removed his boots. "I wasn't hungry."

"I don't like it when you don't eat, Reese. When a man works as hard as you do, he needs food."

He unbuttoned his shirt and then stripped off his trousers, sliding into bed beside her.

"Reese," she said, moving closer to him. "Don't be mad at me because I didn't tell you about Matthew."

"I know why you didn't tell me." He turned his head toward her. "For the noblest of reasons. You knew he was my friend."

She smiled. "You know me too well to place a halo on my head, Reese. I think, if I'm truthful, I just didn't want to tell you or anyone how unworthy he was of a woman's love. We certainly saw proof of that today."

"Yes. Yes, we did."

She looked unsure. "Are you still angry with me?"

He pulled her into his arms, and she curled up to him like a warm kitten. "I was never mad at you, Saber." His hand trailed down her arm. "I was mostly mad at myself for not seeing what Matthew was like. I should have protected you from him the night of the dance. I knew he'd had too much to drink." He looked at her and arched an eyebrow. "I'd had too much to drink that night myself." He traced the outline of her chin. "Tell me what he did."

"It isn't important. I don't want to talk about him anymore," she said, pressing her breasts against his bare chest and making his eyes dilate with passion. He lowered his mouth to hers and fit her to the length of his body. They had become accustomed to each other in a short time, and they seemed to fit together as if nature had intended them to find each other.

"You may have been too drunk to remember that I tricked you into marrying me," she said, running her fingers through his thick black hair. "I was out to catch you, cowboy, and I did."

He burst into laughter, his whole body shaking with mirth.

She raised herself up on her elbow and looked puzzled. "What do you find so funny about that?"

"The fact that someone who looks like you, someone who was born a Vincente, would have to trick a man like me into marriage. I'd liken that to a man being invited into paradise and told his every wish would be granted."

She felt warm all over. "Is that how you see it?"

He tugged at her gown and swiftly had it off. His hands moved over her, pulling her against him. He lifted her just a bit so she fit snugly against his throbbing erection. "When I take you, it's always like being given my fondest wish," he muttered in her ear, his mouth working its way to her breasts.

Their lovemaking was frantic, and so intense that afterward they were both exhausted. She rolled her head against his hard chest, feeling completely fulfilled as a woman.

"Are you ever sorry you married me, Reese?"

His hand gripped her shoulder, and he moved forward to bury his face in her golden hair. "I can't think of anything I have to regret."

"I'm glad. I want to make you happy."

He closed his eyes, gathering her to him, gently stroking her back. "I don't know why you would want to bother with me. I know there have been times when I have said things to hurt you, and I haven't always been easy to live with. I don't know why I've been this way with you. You are the last person in the world I'd ever want to hurt."

She moved her head up and rested her cheek against his. "I know why."

"Then you'd better tell me, because I sure as hell don't know."

She could have told him that he loved her, but she wasn't sure if he had realized it yet. "A woman has to have some secrets," she said, drowsily closing her eyes.

She fell asleep in his arms, and he held her to him as if she was the most precious gift he'd ever been given. He was more confused than ever. Saber could have had any man she wanted—and yet she had chosen him.

He touched his lips to her forehead and felt her steady breathing against his neck. "I love you," he whispered. "I love you so much it's tearing my guts out."

Saber slept on, unaware that her husband had just declared his love for her.

Reese awoke before sunup and found Saber still snuggled against him. One creamy breast was above the cover, and he dipped his head to touch his lips to the rosy tip.

Her eyes opened, and a smile curved her lips. "Is it morning already?"

His hand went to her other breast, and he gently circled it with an exploring finger. "It's time to get up."

She climbed on top of him and sat up, drawing a gasp of wonder and delight from him. She guided him inside her and settled him deeply. "Of course, if we don't have time for this . . ." she taunted.

He growled and rolled her over, losing control completely. "You little tormentor. I don't know how I have the strength to keep you satisfied."

She laughed and kissed his lips. "That's because I feed you so well."

His silver eyes gleamed, and then drifted shut as her velvety softness closed around him. "I seem to live for the times I can get inside you," he whispered. "You have me just where you want me, don't you?"

Desire was coiling inside her, and she could hardly think past the pleasure he gave her. "Yes, cowboy, I have you just where I want you."

Afterward, as they dressed for the day, Reese asked Saber, "How would you like to ride into town with me today? I have business at the bank."

She beamed with pleasure. "I'd like nothing better. And I could do with some supplies."

"Then be ready by nine. I'm going to have several of the men ride along with us just to be safe."

She knew he was worried about Graham Felton, and for that matter, so was she.

* * *

Reese had chosen Jake, Zeb, and three of Noble's *vaqueros* to ride with them into Fort Worth. They hadn't ridden very far from the ranch when he realized they were being followed. He had seen the flash of the sun off a rifle or something shiny. He met Zeb's gaze and realized that the old-timer had seen it, too.

Not wanting to alarm Saber, he halted his horse, and the others did the same. "I'm going to backtrack for a mile or so. The rest of you ride on, and I'll either catch up with you or meet you in town." Reese motioned for the other four to close ranks around Saber, and he lowered his voice so only Zeb could hear. "Don't stop for anything and don't spare the horses."

Zeb nodded. "I'll take care of her. You just look to yourself. If it's that Felton fellow, I hear he's not quite right in the head."

Reese spun his horse around and galloped away from them while Saber frowned worriedly. "I want to wait for him," she said.

"Nope," Zeb told her, waving the others forward. "Reese said we'd ride on, and that's what we'll be doing."

After they had been riding for a short time, Zeb started on one of his long tales, trying to distract Saber.

But Saber was no fool. She knew Reese suspected someone was following them, and she was afraid for him. Everyone said he was the best tracker in the state, and he certainly wouldn't ride into another man's trap, she told herself. She only half listened to Zeb recount a story she'd heard many times. Oh, why had she let Reese ride away without her?

Reese rode among the hills, his gaze on the ground. After he crossed a small, dry creek bed, he picked up fresh hoofprints. He followed the tracks along the winding creek until they headed toward Fort Worth. Whoever it was, he was trying to stay out of sight.

He turned his horse toward town. Felton was waiting for just the right moment to strike, and he seemed to be a very patient man.

Saber had made her purchases and added them to Reese's account and was assured by Mr. Potter, the shopkeeper, that the supplies would be delivered the next day. She noticed that Zeb stayed right beside her, and he wasn't one to accompany a woman from shop to shop or to worry unnecessarily. Something was definitely troubling him. Where was Reese? Surely he should have rejoined her by now.

In her nervousness, she knocked a roll of silk thread off the shelf and bent to retrieve it. As luck would have it, the spool unwound across the floor. Going down on her knees, she picked it up and began rewinding it.

She heard the tinkle of the bell over the door and saw two young ladies enter. She could see them clearly, but they hadn't yet seen her. One of them giggled and ran to look out the window.

"There he goes," she said, sighing. "I'd just die if he'd ever look at me."

"Well," her companion said in a superior tone, "he spoke to me once, and I thought I would swoon away at his feet."

"Pity he's married," the first girl said. "You might know he'd marry someone beautiful like Saber Vincente. He surely didn't show any interest in any of the women around here."

Her friend giggled. "Wouldn't you like to be Saber for just one night."

Saber smiled to herself, knowing she had to stand up, and that when she did, it was going to cause the two young girls embarrassment.

Zeb was grinning from ear to ear. Apparently he'd been listening to the girls' conversation, too. He took Saber's arm and led her toward the door. Saber looked neither left nor right, but she couldn't keep from smiling. When they stepped outside, Saber broke into laughter. "It seems I broke all the young ladies' hearts when I married Reese."

"It'd 'pear so. Looks like you're going to have to get you a gun so you can keep all the women 'way from him."

Saber looked serious for a moment. "Don't think I wouldn't if I thought there was a reason."

They both laughed and went to find Reese.

Chapter Twenty-nine

Dust hung heavily in the air as Reese watched Earnest Maddingly from Casa del Sol direct his drovers to cut the bulls from the herd. The trail boss pushed his dusty hat off his forehead and turned to Reese, grinning.

"Easiest drive I ever had. Looks like they made it without losing much poundage."

Reese's gaze went over the thousand head approvingly. He'd never seen a finer breed. "They look good to me."

"You want a head count? As far as I know, we only lost two."

"Your word is good enough for me, Earnest.

If you'll come up to the house I have a bank draft for you to take to your boss."

Earnest blotted the sweat from his brow. "Can't do it, Mr. Starrett. I don't handle the money side of the business. Mr. Vincente will take care of that."

Reese had taken a mortgage on the ranch to get the money to pay Noble, so he wanted it in his brother-in-law's hands as soon as possible.

"There's food at the bunkhouse. Take the men up there and see that they're fed."

"I heard tell Zeb's been cooking," Earnest said meaningfully. "There ain't a man of us that can drink that old man's coffee."

Reese laughed. "I heard that about his coffee—that's why I've steered clear of drinking it. But I believe my wife helped him cook today."

The older man nodded in approval. "Then we'll feast. Miss Vincente—er, Mrs. Starrett's quite a cook."

Reese motioned for Jake and Gabe to drive the cattle onto the mesa, where there was more sweet grass. "Come on, Earnest, I'll ride to the house with you."

It was after sundown before Reese got a chance to look at the herd. Noble had chosen prime beef for him. He shook his head. This was a mighty fine herd, and they would yield good beef for the army.

He glanced over the valley dotted with cattle. Life was good, and with Saber beside him, it got better every day!

It was a beautiful midsummer day, the sun was shining, and a warm breeze blew from the south.

Reese had workers building a new bedroom and enlarging the parlor, as Saber had wanted. She had been stuck in the house for over a week because the men had been too busy with the large herd and unable to ride with her.

She needed fresh air, and she was tired of listening to the hammering of the builders. Reese had said he'd be riding to the west pasture that morning, and she made up a basket of food and decided to ride out and surprise him.

She thought Zeb might be in the barn, because he was never far away from her. He wouldn't mind riding out with her. There had been no word of Graham Felton, so she'd begun to relax. Word had reached them that Matthew had been transferred to serve under the command of Capt. George Armstrong Custer in the 7th Calvary, so there would be no point in Felton pursuing her any longer. Probably Mr. Felton had left Texas, because every lawman in the state was looking for him. She knew that Noble had put a large bounty on Felton's head, and most likely every bounty hunter in the country was after him, too.

But Reese was still worried about her safety, and she tried not to take any unnecessary chances.

Zeb was nowhere in sight when she reached the barn, so she saddled her horse and mounted. When she rode away from the ranch house, she still hadn't seen Zeb.

She rode to the top of the hill and glanced about her, overcome as she always was by the beauty of this land. Reese had a fine ranch here, and now with the army contract he would soon have nothing to worry about.

She nudged her horse toward the herd of cattle Reese and Noble were breeding for experimental reasons. The cattle scattered as she passed through, and she smiled when she saw several cows heavy with calf. Apparently the experiment was working. Put a bull with cattle, and you were going to get calves, she thought.

She reached down and touched her abdomen. She hadn't told Reese yet, but she was sure she was going to have a baby. Warmth flowed through her as she thought of his baby growing inside her. She hoped it would be a boy with fierce silver eyes and dark hair like his father's.

Lately Reese had been more relaxed, and she no longer felt such tension in him. She also noticed that he laughed more these days. Would he be happy about the baby? She was almost sure he would be.

She'd tell him tonight. As she rode along, she planned just what she would say to him. Laughter bubbled out of her, and she spurred her horse to a faster pace, anxious to see her husband.

Graham Felton had been watching the Starrett ranch for weeks, just looking for the chance to catch Saber Vincente alone. He never thought of her by her married name, because in his mind she still belonged to the bastard who was responsible for the death of his sister.

He'd grown a beard and let his hair grow long, and no one seemed to recognize him, not even in Dallas or Fort Worth, where he was known. Of course, he took care not to draw attention to himself when he was around people.

He had set up camp in a secluded, rocky canyon where grass wouldn't grow; Reese Starrett didn't run cattle there, and it was unlikely that any of his hands would ride that way.

He climbed up a hill from which he could see the entire valley, just as he did every day. He spotted a dust cloud, and as he watched it for a few moments he could see it was a lone rider. He lifted his field glasses and trained them on the rider. His mouth curved into a smile.

It was Saber Vincente, and she was alone!

Saber loped at an easy pace, thinking she should have seen Reese by now. When she heard a rider behind her, she reined in her horse and waited for him to approach. It wasn't Reese—the man wasn't tall enough. When he rode closer, a prickle of fear spiraled down her neck. He wasn't one of Reese's men, or Noble's, either. He was a stranger to her.

Instinct warned her to get out of there. She jabbed her horse with the heel of her boot, and the blooded animal shot forward at an all-out run. But when she glanced back, the man seemed to be gaining on her.

"God," she prayed, "help me—it must be Graham Felton!"

Reese was on his way home ahead of his men when he saw something on the ground just ahead. Puzzled, he dismounted and discovered that it was a basket with its contents scattered about as if it had been dropped. He recognized the basket as the one Saber always used when she brought him lunch.

His heart stopped beating, and he glanced about, taking in everything around him. Something had happened to her! He bent down and looked closely at the hoofprints. She had been riding fast. He walked a little farther and found the prints of a second horse; it had also been running fast.

"Oh, God, no," he cried, leaping onto his horse. With the expert eyes of a tracker he followed the trail, kicking his horse into a run. The tracks were fresh. He had to find Saber before Felton caught her!

He felt as if someone had reached inside him and ripped his heart out. That crazed fool was bent on killing Saber, and Reese had to find her fast.

Felton drew even with Saber and called out for her to stop. When she didn't obey him, he leaped off his mount, dragging her off her horse to the ground. He quickly got to his feet and pulled her up beside him.

"Didn't you hear me tell you to stop?" he yelled at her.

Saber was trying to catch her breath. At the moment all she could think about was whether the fall had harmed her unborn child. She drew in several painful breaths before she was able to stand straight.

"What do you want with me?" she asked angrily.

"Don't you know who I am?" he asked, staring

at her for a long moment. "Surely you can guess."

She looked him over carefully, finally able to put a face to the man who had caused her so much pain. His pockmarked face and pale blue eyes made him look like a wild man, but the most frightening thing about him was the crazed look in his eyes. "You're Graham Felton, and I have no reason to think well of you."

"Now that I see you, Miss Vincente, I know why that fancy major was so hot to have you."

"I am Mrs. Starrett," she corrected him, hoping she could make him see reason.

"Not to me, you're not. To me you're the reason my sister's dead."

Reese dismounted and grabbed his rifle. Silently he made his way up the cliff, taking care to stay out of sight. He could hear Saber talking to someone, and he flattened his back against the cliff, his heart drumming with fear for her.

"Mr. Felton, I don't know why you are doing this to me. I don't even know you."

"Well, I know all about you."

"Then you know I'm not married to Matthew Halloway. If you have something against him, take it up with him."

"I'm not a fool, though many people think I

am. Do you know the kind of man Major Halloway is?"

"I know he caused the death of your sister."

Reese could hear the fear in Saber's voice. Every instinct in his body cried out for him to rush to her aid, but he knew he had to be cautious or Felton might hurt her. He slowly edged closer until he could see them. Felton had Saber's arm twisted behind her, and his other arm was about her waist. He couldn't get a clear shot at Felton because Saber was between them. Somehow he had to distract the man.

Pain shot through her arm, and when she tried to move, Felton only pulled it tighter. "Mr. Felton, the reason I didn't marry Matthew was because I discovered that he wasn't the man I thought I knew."

"He's a devil! My sister was just sixteen, blue eyed and pretty. She always watched Major Halloway when he swaggered into town. He always teased her and asked her if she could like an older man."

"She was only sixteen?"

"Yeah. I didn't see what was happening before my eyes. She'd disappear from the house for hours at a time, but I was used to her riding off alone, so I didn't pay it much mind."

Saber saw tears in the man's eyes, and she felt

pity for what he must have suffered. "I'm so sorry."

He yanked on her arm, and she cried out in pain. "You're not half as sorry as you're going to be."

"I told you I had nothing to do with your sister's death."

"Maybe not. But killing you will tie a knot in Halloway's gut. He'll know what it feels like to lose someone he loves."

Saber realized that Felton's grief for his sister had driven him to the brink of insanity. There would be no reasoning with him. She only prayed that someone would miss her and come looking for her. But no one would look for her here.

"My sister killed two people that day," Felton continued. "She killed herself and the babe Halloway put in her belly."

Saber gasped in horror. "Please let me help you. I know what you must be suffering. Let's sit down and talk about it."

"You don't know how I feel." He wiped a huge hand across his eyes, blotting his tears. "You didn't have to cut her down from the barn rafter where she'd hanged herself. You didn't have to see her beautiful face distorted and red from the rope cutting into her neck. You didn't see where she'd clawed her neck, trying to undo the rope at the last moment."

Saber was sobbing now. "I had no idea. Mr. Felton, I am so very sorry. It must have been hideous for you. I wish there were something I could say to make the pain go away, but there just isn't."

Felton paused, turning her face up to his. "Are you crying 'cause you're scared, or 'cause you're sorry about my sister?"

She drew in a breath of air, wishing her body would stop quaking. "Both, I think," she admitted honestly.

He loosened his hold on her arm. "You look something like my baby sister. Her hair was about the color of yours, and you both have blue eyes." His eyes hardened. "That's probably why that bastard picked my sister to practice his fornication on. She reminded him of you."

"I'm as appalled by what Major Halloway did as you are. That's why I could not marry him."

Felton grabbed his head. "No, you're just trying to confuse me. You've got to die. I can't let him get away with this." He unholstered his gun and held it to Saber's head. "I'll give you time to make your peace with God. That's more than my sister got. They buried her in unconsecrated ground away from the Christians because they said she was unclean and unworthy."

Saber raised her head, feeling the gun barrel cold against her temple. "If you think this will make your sister rest easier and make you grieve less about her death, then go ahead and pull the trigger, Mr. Felton."

Reese waited to hear no more. He stepped forward, his eyes on the man who held Saber's life in his hands.

"Put the gun down, Mr. Felton. My wife is as innocent as your sister. She was duped by Major Halloway just as your sister was."

Felton's eyes held a desperate light, and Reese recognized a man on the edge of madness. Suddenly Felton shoved Saber away from him and aimed the gun at Reese. "You can die for Halloway. I hear you're his friend. Though I never knew friends took women away from each other."

"I'm your man," Reese told him. "Let my wife go and shoot me instead. She had nothing to do with any of this."

Felton frowned and again grabbed the side of his head with one hand, keeping the gun pointed at Reese with the other. "You're confusing me! I came to kill the woman."

"Saber, make him a promise," Reese said, thinking quickly. "Promise him that if you live, you will see that his sister is buried in consecrated ground."

She shook her head. She thought of telling Mr. Felton about her own baby, but she decided against it. Reese would only grieve twice as much if he knew she had died carrying his unborn child. "Reese, I can't let him kill you."

"Promise him, Saber! Tell him you'll see to his sister's burial in the churchyard," Reese said forcefully.

"No!" she cried, reaching for Reese. "Mr. Felton, don't listen to him! He's only doing this so you'll let me live." She turned her sad gaze on Reese. "Don't you know I wouldn't want to live in this world if you weren't in it? I love you—I have from the first."

In that moment their gazes locked, and their eyes said the many things that had gone unspoken between them from the first. Love radiated from Reese's silver eyes, and Saber's tear-bright gaze was gentle with love.

Saber was the first to see Felton cock the hammer on his gun. All she could think about was that he was going to shoot Reese, and she couldn't allow that to happen. She whirled around, her feet almost tangling in her gown, and dove at Reese. "No, not him," she cried. "Not my husband!"

Reese caught her in his arms and tried to shove her away, but the gun fired, and her body jerked as the bullet tore through her back.

377

As he cradled her to him, a tear rolled down her cheek. "I . . . couldn't let him hurt you, Reese." She licked her lips. "Don't grieve for . . . me."

Rage and unbearable grief tore at Reese's insides. He felt the hot, sticky blood beneath his hands, and Saber's head slumped over on his shoulder.

Felton seemed to be shocked into stillness by the sight of Saber's blood. But the urge to kill coiled inside Reese like a venomous snake. Gently he laid Saber down and touched her cheek. Her eyes were closed. She had sacrificed her life for his. Like her, he didn't want to live in a world without her.

"You murdering bastard," Reese cried, diving at Felton. The gun flew out of his hand, and the two men struggled on the ground. Reese, being the stronger, pinned Felton's hands above his head. "This is the day you die!" he said in a growl.

Grasping the now docile man about the waist, he rolled them both to the edge of the cliff, where there was a two-hundred-foot drop. When Reese's intentions became clear to Felton, he began struggling and clawing to get away from the edge.

"You'll kill us both!" the frightened man cried.

"That's exactly what I intend to do, you bastard."

Saber raised her head and tried to cry out, but her voice was only a whisper. Reese was going to take himself and Felton over the cliff.

She watched as they disappeared over the side, and she heard Felton's scream, than a sickening thud. All was silent.

With her waning strength, she tried to crawl to the edge of the cliff, but darkness overcame her, and she lost consciousness.

Jake and Zeb had followed Reese's tracks and witnessed the whole tragedy, but they couldn't get there soon enough to prevent it from happening. As they ran forward with guns drawn, they found that they were too late.

Zeb went down on his knees and lifted Saber, while Jake ran to the edge to see about Reese.

"Did you see what happened?" Jake asked with tears in his eyes. "I heard a story like this once. Reese and Saber gave their lives for each other."

Zeb lifted Saber in his arms. "Don't be so sure that 'bout that. She's a fighter." The old man's eyes were misty with tears. "Yes, sir, she's a fighter. And if I know Reese Starrett, he's a fighter, too. Go down and get him, boy. We'll take 'em back to the house and send riders for the doc and Rachel and Noble."

Jake started his descent into the crevice. "I don't see how anyone could survive a fall like this. But Reese is a hard man to kill!"

Chapter Thirty

The house at the Starrett ranch was a place of sadness. Everyone walked around quietly and spoke in whispers. Neighbors had stopped by to inquire about Saber and Reese, and even the governor had sent a letter stating his concern for them.

Reese had been placed on a cot in the parlor. He'd suffered broken ribs and a broken arm. The doctor had concluded that he had a serious concussion but no internal injuries that he could tell.

Saber was in the bedroom, and she was even more seriously hurt. The bullet had hit her lung. As the doctor was removing the slug, she had started hemorrhaging. That was when the doctor discovered that Saber was going to have a baby. He told Noble that his sister would probably miscarry.

Noble had not left Saber's bedside day or night. He wouldn't let go of her hand, and he talked to her and sometimes prayed that God would not take her away from the people who loved her.

On the fifth day Reese opened his eyes. Rachel was sitting beside him, and when he groaned, she took his hand.

"Try not to move, Reese. You have broken ribs and a broken arm."

He attempted to focus his eyes, but everything was a blur. He couldn't remember why he was there or what had happened. His arm was in a sling, and there were tight bandages taped around his ribs. "I'm . . . thirsty."

Rachel held a glass up to his lips and raised his head just a bit. "Take small sips. Then later you may have more."

Obediently he did as she instructed. "What . . . are you doing?" Suddenly everything came back to him in a flash, and he gripped Rachel's hand, his heart heavy with grief. "She's dead, isn't she? Oh, my God—Saber!"

Rachel forced him back against the pillow,

which wasn't hard to do because he was so weak. "Saber isn't dead, Reese."

His vision was clearing, and he looked into Rachel's eyes. "You're telling me the truth, aren't you?"

"I will not lie to you, Reese. Saber is alive, but she is gravely ill."

He wet his cracked lips. "I have to see her." He raised himself up, and now no amount of cajoling would make him lie down.

"Noble, I need you," Rachel called out, knowing Reese must not get up so soon, or he would only make himself worse.

Noble was beside her in an instant, and with their combined strength they managed to restrain Reese.

Rachel spoke to him in a soothing voice. "If you will lie still, I will tell you everything."

Reese drew in a ragged breath and accepted the inevitable. "I promise. But tell me the entire truth."

"I will, because I know Noble would want to know if it were me in Saber's place." Rachel and Noble stared at each other with tears in their eyes. Rachel tried to speak, but she knew that if she did she would start crying, and that would only upset Reese more than he already was. She saw the naked fear in Reese's eyes, and she looked at Noble.

"Noble, please tell him," she said at last.

Noble got on his knees, so he was level with Reese. "That bullet hit Saber's left lung, Reese. The doctor removed the bullet, but she's lost a lot of blood." He lowered his head in sadness and waited a moment before he could go on. "As for the baby, the doctor isn't sure he can save it. She's been hemorrhaging."

Reese closed his eyes, and tears seeped out of the corners. "Baby." There was torment in his voice. "Oh, God, she was going to have my baby, and I didn't know it." His chest heaved with the emotions that he had kept locked inside for so long. He tried to rise, but blackness overtook him, and he fell blissfully into unconsciousness.

It was dark when Reese opened his eyes again. Rachel was still sitting beside him, holding his hand.

"Don't talk if you don't want to. We'll just sit here quietly."

"I want to see Saber."

"You can't get up yet, Reese. But if you will eat a little, I'll ask the doctor if you can see her tomorrow."

"She's dead, and you aren't telling me!"

"No. I promise you she's not. In fact, the hemorrhaging has stopped, and so far she hasn't lost the baby."

A sob escaped Rachel's lips when she saw the

tears in Reese's eyes. She knew the agony he must be feeling.

"She's all I ever wanted," he said, unashamed of the tears that clouded his vision. "Did you know she jumped in front of me and took the bullet meant for me?"

"Yes, Zeb told me. He saw the whole thing, but he couldn't get there in time to help. He and Jake carried you and Saber home. Zeb also told me you went over the cliff and took Graham Felton with you."

"May he rot in hell."

"He's dead, Reese. But by the grace of God, both you and Saber survived. I have to believe you will both get well, because you deserve to be together."

"Where is the doctor? I want to ask him about Saber."

"He's bedded down in the bunkhouse. But he's been here the whole time. He won't leave until you are both out of danger."

"I'll eat," Reese said, turning his head toward the bedroom where Saber lay, "if you promise I can see Saber tomorrow."

"I promise. I'm sure just hearing your voice will help her."

His silver eyes were transparent with tears. "Did you know that Saber loves me?"

Rachel smiled. "Yes, I have known it for a very long time."

"I tried to hide my love from her because I didn't think I was good enough for someone like her."

Rachel clasped his hand. "She knew you loved her, Reese. You don't think she would have married you otherwise, do you? She had just been waiting for you to admit it to yourself and then to tell her."

He managed a grin. "She's too good for the likes of me."

Rachel returned his smile. "You just keep thinking that, but I don't think Saber would agree with you."

Jake and Noble supported Reese's weight as they helped him into the bedroom. Reese eased himself down on his knees and took Saber's limp hand in his. He touched her face, kissed her lips, and ran his fingers over her hair. "Can you hear me, Saber?"

Noble nodded for Jake to leave, and then he followed him out, closing the door behind them. Noble looked at Rachel, and she could see the tired lines beneath his eyes. Neither of them had slept since they'd received word of the tragedy.

"I don't know if she's going to make it, Rachel," Noble said, pulling his wife into his arms, needing her closeness.

"I believe she will, Noble. We just have to keep on believing."

When Jake left, Noble sat down in a chair and stared at the ceiling. "That this should happen when she is going to have a baby makes it a double tragedy."

Rachel sat in his lap and laid her head on his shoulder. "Saber's not the only one who is going to have a baby."

Noble looked at her questioningly. "Are you saying that you . . . that we—"

She thought this was the right time to tell him, because he had wanted a child so badly, and he needed to hear something good after so much tragedy. "I'm saying you're going to be a father, Noble. How will you like that?"

He smiled and held her tightly. "I like that just fine. You have made me a happy man, Rachel." His eyes filled with wonder. "A baby, Green Eyes. I like that just fine."

Their eyes went to the closed door. "It's all right if we take a little happiness, Noble. Soon we will have a little Vincente running around, and Saber will have a little Starrett who can play with our baby."

* * *

387

Reese laid his head lightly against Rachel's chest to make sure she was breathing. He heard a good, strong heartbeat, but she was so pale—and why didn't she wake up?

His hand moved to her stomach, where his baby grew; the child too, was fighting to live. "Saber, you are my life. I don't know how I lived until I met you. Since that day you came crashing into my life, I have never been the same. I love you. Please open your eyes."

He laid his head down beside her, and great sobs shook his body. "I love you so. I never told you that. I never told you that since you became my wife, I have looked forward to each new day. When I am away from you, I can't wait to get home, because you'll be here waiting for me." He placed a kiss on her hand. "Just the sound of your voice or the way you hummed when you went about your work made me happy." He laced his fingers through hers. "You have to get well, do you hear me? I need you. Our baby needs you."

He pressed his tear-wet face against her. "My heart, my love, I can't live without you."

After an hour passed, Noble and Rachel went into the bedroom, thinking Reese needed to get back in bed. They found him curled up with Saber, his arms around her, his cheek pressed against hers, fast asleep.

They quietly tiptoed out, thinking it was best for the two of them to be together.

"Besides," Rachel told Noble later, "I wouldn't want to be the one to tell Reese Starrett that he couldn't be with Saber."

Reese came fully awake, feeling that something was different. He had felt Saber move!

Raising his head, he gazed down at her and watched her eyes flutter open. For a moment she looked puzzled, and then she smiled. "Am . . . I dreaming, Reese?"

He laughed, his heart feeling as if it could take wing. "If you are dreaming, I'm in the same dream."

Suddenly her eyes widened, and her hand went to her abdomen. "Our baby! Oh, Reese, have I lost our baby?"

He covered her hand with his and bent to kiss her. "No. You haven't lost our baby. And you are going to be all right, Saber."

She touched his face and felt the stubble of a beard. "You need a shave."

He was afraid to move lest he cause her pain, so he kissed her forehead and then her lips. "I love you. Did you know that, Saber Starrett?"

Her smile held all the love she felt for him.

"Yes, I know you do. I have known it for a long time."

He tried to take her hand, and muttered because his arm was in a sling. "Starting today, I'm going to tell you how much I love you every day of our lives."

"I'll hold you to that, cowboy." She looked at his face and saw he was pale. "What are your injuries?"

"Nothing, considering the fall I took. I have broken ribs and a broken arm."

"You are really all right?"

He gently touched her cheek. "I am now." He moved forward and gently laid his head against her stomach. "To think you are having my baby." His eyes were filled with pride when he looked at her. "I hope it's a girl who looks like her mother."

"And I hope it's a boy, stubborn and hard-headed like his father. It took falling off a cliff for you to admit you love me."

Noble and Rachel heard laughter from the bedroom, and they burst in, not knowing what to expect.

"Noble," Reese said between bouts of laughter, then grabbed his aching ribs, "do you know what your sister said to me?"

Noble looked confused. "I can't guess."

Reese had another bout of laughter. "She said

my baby was going to be hardheaded like me."

All four of them laughed, although later Saber would wonder what had been so funny. It was just that life was so good.

Reese had finally admitted he loved her!

Epilogue

It was raining the day Gwen Felton was buried behind the church in a small village not far from Fort Worth. With Noble's influence and Saber's insistence, it had been possible to have her buried in consecrated ground.

The only ones in attendance at the short ceremony were Reese and Saber. She cried for the young girl who had died so needlessly, and for the baby who never had a chance at life.

When the service was over, she glanced up at her husband, whose head was bowed, and she swallowed a lump in her throat. There were sadness here today, but there was also the promise of life, the life that grew within her body.

Reese met her gaze, and his eyes were warm with love. "I want you to put this tragedy behind you, Saber. Nothing can make up for what Matthew and Graham Felton did. But at least we kept a promise. Take comfort in that."

She stood for a moment with her head bowed in prayer, then placed the flowers she clutched in her hand on the fresh grave. "I didn't do it for Felton. I did it for the girl Matthew wronged."

His arm was still in a sling, so he used his other hand to guide her away from the grave. He helped her into the buggy and climbed in beside her.

They drove out of town in silence, each lost in thought.

At last Saber said, "It will be good to get home."

His gaze took on a glow she knew and loved so well. "It will be good to get in bed with you when we get home. It's been too long."

She snuggled close to him, resting her head on his shoulder. "There will be three in our bed," she said, smiling to herself.

He drew back on the reins and stared at her. "Saber, I don't want any ghosts in our bed. What happened to the Feltons was not of your doing."

She shook her head, still smiling. "I wasn't speaking of a ghost, but a real living creature. I was speaking of our baby, silly."

He laughed, his silver eyes dancing with delight. "You have made me a happy man in every way. You made my house a home, and now we have a family." He placed his hand on her slightly rounded abdomen. He wanted her to swell with his baby so everyone could see. "I can't wait to hold this baby who came from our love, Saber."

"I do love you so, Reese."

He drew in a quick breath as contentment swelled through him like a tidal wave. His eyes softened, and he had to wait a moment before he could speak. "My baby is growing inside you." He pulled her to him and held her tightly. "Saber, I should have known that first day I saw you, looking so forlorn and frightened, that you were going to turn my whole world upside down."

"And I should have known that first day that you were the one man in the world for me. I never told you that when you touched me that day, even when I thought you were Graham Felton, I felt drawn to you."

He tilted her face up to his and rested his cheek on hers. "I love you so much, Saber. I never knew what happiness meant until you came storming into my life."

"I want to make you happy," she said, glowing under his love. "I always knew you had a great capacity to love—you just had to learn to trust."

He shoved the sling aside and gathered her close. "Saber, never stop loving me."

"Not until my last breath," she promised.

Reese closed his eyes and breathed in the essence of his wife. She had shown him how to love and trust. "What can I ever give you to repay you for all you have given me?"

"That's easy." She drew back and looked at him with a mischievous glint in her eyes. "You can give me three or four more little Starretts running around the house."

He threw back his head and laughed, then picked up the reins and headed the horse toward the ranch. "That, my dearest heart, will be my pleasure."

Saber laid her head back against his shoulder and said a prayer of thankfulness that they had lived to find such a powerful love.

Texas Proud

Constance O'Banyon

Rachel Rutledge has her gun trained on Noble Vincente. With one shot, she will have revenge on the man who killed her father. So what is stopping her from pulling the trigger? Perhaps it is the memory of Noble's teasing voice, his soft smile, or the way one glance from his dark Spanish eyes once stirred her foolish heart to longing. Yes, she loved him then . . . as much as she hates him now. One way or another, she will wound him to the heart—if not with bullets, then with her own feminine wiles. But as Rachel discovers, sometimes the line between love and hate is too thinly drawn.

___4492-7 $5.99 US/$6.99 CAN

Dorchester Publishing Co., Inc.
P.O. Box 6640
Wayne, PA 19087-8640

Please add $1.75 for shipping and handling for the first book and $.50 for each book thereafter. NY, NYC, and PA residents, please add appropriate sales tax. No cash, stamps, or C.O.D.s. All orders shipped within 6 weeks via postal service book rate. Canadian orders require $2.00 extra postage and must be paid in U.S. dollars through a U.S. banking facility.

Name_____
Address_____
City_____State_____Zip_____
I have enclosed $_____ in payment for the checked book(s).
Payment <u>must</u> accompany all orders. ❑ Please send a free catalog.
CHECK OUT OUR WEBSITE! www.dorchesterpub.com

San Antonio Rose
Constance O'Banyon

Sam Houston knows he needs all the help he can get to defeat Santa Anna's seasoned fighting men. But who is the mysterious San Antonio Rose, who emerges from the mist like a ghostly figure to offer her aid? Fluent in Spanish, Ian McCain is the one man who can ferret out the truth about the flamboyant dancer. Working under Santa Anna's very nose, he observes how the dark-haired beauty inflames her audience, how she captivates El Presidente himself. But as she disappears with a single yellow rose, he knows that despite the tangled web of loyalties that ensnare them, he will taste those tempting lips, know every secret of that alluring body. And before she proves just how effective she can be, he will pluck for himself the San Antonio Rose.

___4563-X $5.99 US/$6.99 CAN

Dorchester Publishing Co., Inc.
P.O. Box 6640
Wayne, PA 19087-8640

Please add $1.75 for shipping and handling for the first book and $.50 for each book thereafter. NY, NYC, and PA residents, please add appropriate sales tax. No cash, stamps, or C.O.D.s. All orders shipped within 6 weeks via postal service book rate. Canadian orders require $2.00 extra postage and must be paid in U.S. dollars through a U.S. banking facility.

Name_____
Address_____
City_____State_____Zip_____
I have enclosed $_____ in payment for the checked book(s).
Payment <u>must</u> accompany all orders. ❑ Please send a free catalog.
      CHECK OUT OUR WEBSITE! www.dorchesterpub.com

WISHES ON THE WIND

ELAINE BARBIERI

Born of Irish immigrant parents, Meghan O'Connor's background dictates her hatred of the affluent Lang family. When a mining accident devastates her family, she realizes her friendship with David Lang places them both in peril. But as friendship blossoms into love Meghan will have to listen to her own conscience and follow her heart. . . .

Pampered heir David Lang lives in a world of opulence and luxury. But in Meghan O'Connor he finds the one person to whom he can entrust his heart and soul. Torn between loyalty to his family and love for the wrong woman, David knows his dreams of sharing the passion of a lifetime with Meghan are more than wishes on the wind.

___52348-5 $5.50 US/$6.50 CAN

Dorchester Publishing Co., Inc.
P.O. Box 6640
Wayne, PA 19087-8640

Heartland

Rebecca Brandewyne

After her best friend India dies, leaving eight beautiful children in the care of their drunken wastrel of a father, prim Rachel Wilder knows she has to take the children in. But when notorious Slade Maverick rides onto her small farm, announcing that he is the children's guardian, Rachel is furious. Yet there is something about Slade that makes her tremble at the very thought of his handsome face and sparkling midnight-blue eyes. And when he takes her in his arms in the hayloft and his searing kiss brands her soul, Rachel knows then that the gunfighter Slade Maverick belongs to her, body and soul, just as she belongs to him.

___52327-2 $5.50 US/$6.50 CAN